Submission

Submission

CHERIE FEATHER

HEAT
New York

THE BERKLEY PUBLISHING GROUP
Published by the Penguin Group
Penguin Group (USA) Inc.
375 Hudson Street, New York, New York 10014, USA
Penguin Group (Canada), 90 Eglinton Avenue East, Suite 700, Toronto, Ontario M4P 2Y3, Canada
(a division of Pearson Penguin Canada Inc.)
Penguin Books Ltd., 80 Strand, London WC2R 0RL, England
Penguin Group Ireland, 25 St. Stephen's Green, Dublin 2, Ireland (a division of Penguin Books Ltd.)
Penguin Group (Australia), 250 Camberwell Road, Camberwell, Victoria 3124, Australia
(a division of Pearson Australia Group Pty. Ltd.)
Penguin Books India Pvt. Ltd., 11 Community Centre, Panchsheel Park, New Delhi—110 017, India
Penguin Group (NZ), 67 Apollo Drive, Rosedale, North Shore 0632, New Zealand
(a division of Pearson New Zealand Ltd.)
Penguin Books (South Africa) (Pty.) Ltd., 24 Sturdee Avenue, Rosebank, Johannesburg 2196,
South Africa

Penguin Books Ltd., Registered Offices: 80 Strand, London WC2R 0RL, England

This is an original publication of The Berkley Publishing Group.

This is a work of fiction. Names, characters, places, and incidents either are the product of the author's imagination or are used fictitiously, and any resemblance to actual persons, living or dead, business establishments, events, or locales is entirely coincidental. The publisher does not have any control over and does not assume any responsibility for author or third-party websites or their content.

First edition: February 2009

Library of Congress Cataloging-in-Publication Data

Feather, Cherie.
　　Submission / Cherie Feather.—1st ed.
　　　　p. cm.
　　ISBN 978-0-425-22368-0
1. Artists—Fiction.　2. Women art historians—Fiction.　I. Title.
　PS3623.H5798S83 2009
　813'.6—dc22

　　　　　　　　　　　　　　　　　　2008032857

PRINTED IN THE UNITED STATES OF AMERICA

10　9　8　7　6　5　4　3　2　1

Submission

Prologue

My Dearest Thinking Woman,
You are a powerful deity, and I am a mere mortal, but bestow
strength upon me, please.

I encountered the most frightening man today. Not fright-
ening in a grotesque way, but he terrified me just the same.
The very instant he roamed his dark gaze over me, my pulse
pounded in shameful places and I struggled to breathe. I tried
to inhale, to exhale, to behave as rationally as I could, but I
felt as if the ties on my corset were being pulled tighter and
tighter.

But first, I shall explain where I was when this unholy ex-
perience occurred.

Papa and I entered Curtis House, the hotel in which we'd
come to stay. Curtis House caters to artists, entertainers, and

writers, and Papa was in awe of its Southwestern grandeur. So was I. The architecture, with its colorful tiled floors and high, beamed ceilings, was part of what was now being called the New-Old Sante Fe.

I got Papa situated on a wooden settle, which was padded with a soft leather cushion, and he sat there, coughing intermittently into a handkerchief. He was terribly weary from our journey, but happy nonetheless. For him, this was a dream come true.

As I approached the front desk, a dark figure clouded my peripheral vision. The man who frightened me.

Black hair. Black eyes. A black heart?

I shudder thinking about him. Tall and impeccably attired, he carried himself with a sense of extreme wealth and lewd grace, if such a thing exists.

While I signed the register, he stood off to the side of a sun-drenched window and scandalized me, undressing me with his devil-dark eyes. After the assault, I fussed with my jacket. My ready-to-wear traveling suit had been designed for warm weather, but not for the scorching heat of an arrogant man. Even the rosette on my serviceable little hat threatened to wilt.

Try as I might to ignore him, I ended up challenging him instead, meeting his bold gaze with a haughty stare. But it was ineffective.

He had the nerve to smile, to be cockily amused. The slight tilt of his lips proved predatory. There was no warmth attached to him. Only the calculating aura of a rich rogue who took what he wanted and cast it aside when he was good and done.

And I could tell that he wanted me.

Imagine. Me. Nicole West, a willful twenty-year-old, struggling to save her father. Papa had toiled his health away in a tannery in Pittsburgh, and I couldn't bear to lose him to his illness.

Coming to Santa Fe was my idea. I intended to seek employment, any type of work I could find, while Papa recovered from his lung disease and crafted his poems. Someday my father was going to be a famous poet.

If he didn't die first.

Please, Thinking Woman, keep him alive. Give him a chance to sell his poems, especially the one he wrote about you. You are all we have right now. We so need your help, which is why I chose to confide my fears in you. With that in mind, I shall continue this letter for you to ponder.

While I obtained the keys to our room, I stole a quick glance at Papa. Although his cough had quieted, he still pressed the handkerchief to his lips. He was pale and thin, with narrow shoulders, grayish blond hair, and lavender shadows rimming faded blue eyes.

So different from . . .

The dark, dangerous man staring lustfully at me. I met his gaze once more, and he angled his regal head. He was no longer smiling.

With his perfect posture and fluid lines, he reminded me of a matador. I could almost see him waving a red cape at a bull, enjoying the fevered discipline and raw courage of the bloody sport.

He appeared to be of mixed origin. Had he been born to a

noble Spanish mother and powerful Anglo father? In my estimation, his privileged lineage ran deep.

Finally he turned away from me to gaze upon another woman who entered the hotel. Brimming with flair, with natural flirtation, she made me look like a sugar-sprinkled daisy next to a wild-grown rose. She was a highly buxom, long-limbed brunette, whereas I was a petite, honey-colored blonde.

She crossed the lobby to reach him, moving with a hip-swaying gait. She sported a flamboyant red dress, and the narrow skirt revealed far too much leg, a fashion trend that was both daring and new.

They greeted each other, embracing with familiarity, and a twinge of something—I wasn't sure what it was—knotted my stomach.

I walked away and headed over to Papa, letting him know that a bellboy was waiting to escort us to our room.

"Do you see them?" my father asked, heightening my discomfort. He was speaking of the brazen couple.

"Yes," I responded, realizing that Papa wasn't aware that the man had been eyeing me earlier. "Who are they?"

"I don't know who she is, but he's Mr. Curtis."

A pulse fluttered at my neck. I tugged at my ruffled white collar to thwart it. "As in Curtis House?"

"Indeed." Much too impressed, Papa said, "Javier Curtis. He owns this fine establishment."

Oh, goodness. Oh, gracious. I hadn't considered the possibility. Not wanting to dwell on the hotel proprietor, I reached for my father's arm. "Let's get you to bed. You need to rest."

He sighed. "I am quite tired."

"I requested a room on this level." I knew that climbing the ornately carved stairs that led to the second and third floors would be too exhausting for him.

He gave me a loving smile. "You're a good daughter."

I returned his affection. He was a good father, too. Mama died when I was but a baby, and he'd raised me by himself.

I helped Papa to his feet, and the bellboy approached. The three of us moved in the opposite direction of Mr. Curtis.

I tried to refrain from looking back at him. Truly I did. But I took a curious chance and glanced over my shoulder, expecting him to be thoroughly engaged with his lady friend.

But he wasn't. By now, they stood side by side, and both of them, yes both of them, were purposefully watching me.

One

What the hell was she doing? Kiki Dion asked herself, as she drove to a party at Curtis House.

She frowned at the bug-splattered windshield, the mountain road twisting and turning in front of her. Curtis House used to be a hotel, but it had been transformed into a sprawling residence ages ago, and the new owner was . . .

Was what?

Dark? Dangerous?

Not that Kiki knew firsthand. She'd yet to meet Ethan Tierney. Of course she'd seen pictures of him and his paintings and sculptures splashed all over the Internet.

In his photographs, Ethan looked like a pagan god, with jet black hair and hypnotic blue eyes, and to make matters worse, his artwork depicted various degrees of BDSM.

She gripped the steering wheel a little tighter. BDSM was the abbreviation for bondage and discipline, domination and submission, and sadism and masochism. It was also referred to as kinky sex, power exchange, fetish, sex magic, and the lifestyle.

She knew a lot about BDSM, but only because she'd researched the subject, via the Internet and books. Not hands-on research. She wasn't interested in being whipped, chained, or handcuffed. No one was going to put a collar around her neck, stuff a gag in her mouth, and make her behave. She wasn't about to let a man like Ethan Tierney strap her to a table and drip liquid wax all over her naked body.

When a weird kind of warmth settled between her legs, she blamed it on the hot-wax image. So maybe that *was* kind of sexy, in a purely artistic way.

After all, Kiki had a deep appreciation for art. She was the historian for the Santa Fe Women's Art Museum.

A few more moonlit turns, and she arrived at the entrance of Curtis House. Holy shit. She'd seen some mansions in her time, but this . . .

This . . .

Curtis House looked like a Southwestern castle locked behind a huge iron gate. She stopped at the security booth and a uniformed guard checked her invitation, which had been provided by a friend, and allowed her access to the property.

A long, foliage-flanked driveway led to the historic three-story structure, where sky-high statues—wildly stunning nudes, no less—made for a salacious welcome.

Clearly Ethan had added them to the mix, giving the original architecture a decadent flair. But Kiki should've expected as much. From what she knew of Ethan, he was the black-sheep heir of a billionaire family, and his obscure artwork and daring lifestyle had earned him a cult following from here to the depths of Atlantis.

She parked amid scores of other vehicles, and as soon as she exited her car, the thrusting, thrumming beat of Sid Vicious singing a Frank Sinatra song echoed from the mansion, where the party was well under way.

Kiki took to the walkway and became instantly aware of prominently positioned security cameras roving above her head. At the moment, she was the only guest in the courtyard. Everyone else was inside.

With a shaky breath, she adjusted her fringed shoulder bag, smoothed her broomstick skirt, and got a self-conscious chill.

Would there be orgies at this party? Was that why she'd ventured into Ethan Tierney's realm? So she could watch?

Lately she'd been fantasizing about watching other people have sex, and the vivid imaginings both embarrassed and excited her. But Kiki couldn't seem to stop it, no matter how hard she tried. When she was alone in her mosquito net–draped bed, she always seemed to give up the fight, slipping a hand inside her panties and getting off on the threesomes and foursomes in her mind.

So *was* that her agenda? To observe the debauchery at Curtis House? Or was it Ethan himself who intrigued her? According to rumor, he loved blondes and brunettes, but he devoured natural redheads.

And Kiki had long, wavy, authentic red hair, with a smattering of freckles across her nose to go with it.

Tugging at one of her curls, she cursed her stupidity, even as she headed for the big, double-front doors and prepared to cross the threshold and step into a world in which she didn't belong.

She went inside and the music got louder. By now, the song had changed, and the main tune from *Dirty Dancing* rattled the walls. Apparently Mr. BDSM had diverse taste in music.

Overwhelmed, she stood in the entryway, with a view of the massive living room. At one time, it had probably been the lobby of the hotel.

No one came forward to greet her, leaving her alone in a crowd. Most of the guests were twenty-somethings, decked out in a variety of exotic garb. The Ethan Tierney cult, she thought. The groupies. They drank lavishly, danced provocatively, and ate luscious-looking appetizers. But there were no orgies. Of course who knew what types of activities were going on in playrooms or dungeons or whatever?

Fighting the urge to flee, Kiki moved forward and assessed the house. The erotic artwork in every nook and cranny was expected, and the early mission furniture, leaded-glass light fixtures, and Spanish accents complemented the architecture. But the medieval artifacts, the ancient torture devices, were another matter.

A trio of busty blondes in rubber dresses sat on the edge of a stretching rack and sipped champagne, as if it was the most natural thing to do.

Kiki decided that she needed a drink, too.

She headed for the nearest portable bar and ordered an old-fashioned rum and Coke, something simple and to the point.

The bartender, a good-natured guy with a shaved head and a spiked collar around his beefy neck, caught her frowning at a metal contraption on the wall.

"It's a breast ripper," he said. "It was used to—"

She held up her hand to stop his explanation. "I know what it is." The four-prong design was crystal clear.

He didn't drop the subject. "That's how women were punished for heresy, blasphemy, adultery, erotic magic, and other supposedly immoral acts." He motioned to another displayed metal device. "And that, as I'm sure you can tell, is a chastity belt. Don't you just love the engraving?"

"It's peachy," she responded, studying the hearts-and-flowers pattern. "But there's no firm evidence that chastity belts were ever used. Some say they're a medieval myth. The first image of one appeared in a book in 1405."

"Yes, but the myth is erotic."

"Oh, sure," she quipped, trying to seem less nervous than she was. "I can just imagine rattling around in that thing, waiting for my beloved to come home."

The bartender grinned. "Is this your first time here?"

"Are you kidding? I'm one of Ethan's girls." She stuffed a few dollars in the tip glass and downed half of her rum and Coke. "I'm a prize in his harem."

"I'll bet you will be before the night is out." He waited for her to finish her drink and made her a fresh one, heavier on the rum. "He's going to go cock-raging mad for you."

Before this conversation took her any deeper, Kiki grabbed her glass, spun around, and ran straight into Amber Pontiero, the friend who'd invited her to this whacked-out shindig. Amber was also the girl who'd taught her how to do blow job shooters, a cocktail she was deliberately avoiding tonight.

"I'm so glad you made it." The leggy brunette gave her a Hollywood-type hug, rife with two pretty little air kisses. Amber was an internationally spoiled heiress: the daughter of a female fashion icon. She spoke with a glamorous accent and looked as delectable as a runway model, with a long, lean body and a vintage Vidal Sassoon haircut. "I expected you to chicken out."

"Me?" Kiki made an easy-breezy gesture, swigging her second drink and placing the empty glass on a nearby table, where a graveyard of other beverages had been laid to rest.

"Yes, you." Amber stepped back to study her. "What is this outfit you're wearing?"

"Don't pick at my clothes." Not here. Not now. She was already out of her element.

"I'm not, darling. I love your style, except . . ."

"What?"

"It's nothing that can't be fixed." Taking it upon herself to paw her way through Kiki's throng of turquoise, mother-of-pearl, and sterling silver necklaces, Amber undid the first four buttons on Kiki's blouse, then put the jewelry back in place until one of the pendants dipped into her cleavage like a hidden treasure. "There. That's better. In fact, it's perfect."

For whom? "My bra is showing."

"Yes, and it's such a sweet little garment, too."

Sweet? The blush pink demi was the sexiest lingerie Kiki owned.

Amber reached for her hand. "Come on. It's time for you to meet Ethan."

"So, where is the lord and master? Wielding his power over naked slaves in a deep, dank dungeon?" Which seemed fitting now that the Swayze-movie song had ended and Nine Inch Nails was tearing up the home entertainment system.

"No, darling. He's with the cook in his kitchen."

Somehow that seemed even creepier. Kiki knew a bit of history about the house. The original owner of the hotel had been killed when the kitchen caught fire. Javier Curtis had expired in a fiery blaze, along with his beautiful young wife, Nicole. Of course a lot of people had lived here since then. Curtis House had survived the tragedy.

While Amber tugged her along, Kiki struggled to close her blouse and popped two buttons in the process, snagging them on a chain around her neck. She cursed and gave up, leaving her bra exposed.

The Spanish-tiled kitchen was state-of-the-art, as big as a restaurant cookery and decorated with indigenous stoneware and sensual artwork, mostly cheeky pinups. But at least there weren't any medieval contraptions around.

Sure enough, the eccentric billionaire, clad in a moth-eaten Edwardian shirt, a black tuxedo jacket, and time-worn blue jeans, conversed with his chef. They leaned over the counter, inspecting a batch of pumpkin tamales, spiced with vanilla and cinnamon. The sweet aroma filled the air.

Amber nudged Kiki forward, causing Ethan to glance up. Wham! Bam! He zeroed right in on her.

Holy hell, she thought. His eyes were even bluer in person, his features more shadowed, more sharp and angular. He had killer cheekbones and a jaw like a Marvel Comics hero. His short black hair fell across his forehead in razor-blade disarray.

"Did you bring me a present?" he asked Amber, looking at Kiki as if he meant to eat her alive. Even his chef backed away.

"Only if she wants to be your toy," Amber responded.

Kiki had never been tongue-tied in her life, but she couldn't think of a damn thing to say, not one silly, smart-mouthed word.

Fe, fi, fo, fum, she thought, as he closed in on her.

"Do you?" he asked.

She shook her head. She had to look up to meet his gaze. He had the advantage of height.

"I think you do. Why else would you be here?"

"For the rum and Coke," she finally said, wishing she had another glass of liquid courage. Something to quench her thirst. Something besides him.

"You're the girl Amber has been telling me about." Ethan moved closer, so close she could see every dark eyelash. "Kitten Dijon, right?"

"Kiki Dion." She frowned at him for making a mockery of her name, but her scolding wasn't very fierce.

He flashed a scoundrel's smile, and she got the feeling he'd messed up purposely. Her heart started to pound, which wasn't like her at all. She didn't get bumpedy bump over men.

"Are you into the lifestyle, Kitten?"

"*Kiki*. And no, I'm not."

"Then what are you into?"

Eyewitness sex, she wanted to say, but she kept that naughty little thought to herself. "Nothing out of the ordinary."

He changed tactics. "Will you let me paint you?"

"Paint?" She almost gulped the word.

"In fetish gear." He glanced down at her bra, and when he lifted his gaze, they made eye contact once again.

"Why me?" she asked, hoping it wasn't a dumb question.

"Because," he whispered against her ear, "if I can't chain you to my bed and make you beg for my cock, then I want to immortalize you."

Oh, my. Oh, goodness. Like the desperate female she was, she waited for him to tempt her with the body part in question, to press his pelvis against hers. But he didn't. Still, she suspected that he had a hard-on. A nice, big one.

"I'm not a model," she said, wondering how it would feel to pose for him.

"I can make it easy for you." He kept his mouth close to her ear, his breath tickling her skin. "I can paint you from a picture."

She fought for her sanity. She would still have to pose, provocatively no doubt, for the photograph. "I couldn't. I can't."

"You can wear a mask if you're concerned about anonymity. No one would know the painting is you."

"You'd know."

"I won't tell anyone."

She glanced past him and noticed that the kitchen was

busy. The chef had resumed his job. The pumpkin tamales were going onto plates, and he was shuffling them at young, attractive servers. She looked around for Amber, but her friend was gone.

She returned her attention to Ethan. "You expect me to trust you?"

"I'm an honest guy."

"Who collects medieval torture devices."

"That doesn't mean I use them."

Nudge. Bump. There went his hard-on, right against her. She reacted. Goose bumps popped along her skin, and her nipples tightened, quite noticeably, against her bra.

"Ah, yes, that's the fiery redhead Amber told me about." Another cock nudge. Another ripple of excitement. "So what are you into? Tell me your dirty secrets."

"I . . ."

"Tell me."

Should she do it? Should she share her fantasies with this man? Kiki had been celibate for almost a year, but after her divorce, she'd been too busy with her job to bother with dating. Was it any wonder that she'd developed a naughty nighttime remedy? Images to masturbate by?

"I want to . . ." She paused, drew a breath. "Watch."

He angled his head. "Watch what?"

Good heavens. "Sex." Her voice came out in a raspy whisper. "But I want to watch people who know they're being watched, who enjoy it."

"Consensual voyeurism?"

"Yes."

"How many people do you want to watch? How many willing lovers?"

"Three." She softened her voice because he'd gentled his, making her feel as if she had every right to reveal her fantasy, to say it, to think it, to feel it. "Or four. Or five. The number changes in my mind."

"Let's start with a ménage," Ethan suggested. "So, who should be the players? Who's the perfect trio? Two boys and a girl? Two girls and a guy? Or do you want three men? Or three women?"

"I've imagined all of the above."

"Yes, but which is your favorite?"

"I'm not picky." Just insanely horny, she thought. Or crazy. Or depraved. "They all turn me on."

Her companion leaned in to inhale the scent of her skin, as if sex were oozing from her pores. Maybe it was, she thought.

"You're a bad girl, Kitten."

Funny, now she liked him calling her Kitten. "I'm trying not to be."

He took another whiff of her skin. "You smell like Stella."

She blinked at him. Then she realized that he wasn't referring to a woman he knew. He recognized her fragrance. "That's what it is."

"I like it on you."

"Thank you." She liked the way he smelled, too. Male and musky.

He pumped up the foreplay. "I can arrange for a ménage to happen tonight. I can arrange for us to watch."

Kiki's pulse jiggered. "Us?"

"I want to be there with you. That would be hot, don't you think?"

God, yes. But getting voyeuristic with him made her nervous, too, beautifully, erotically nervous. "Who would be our perfect trio?"

"Just about whoever you want. Most of the people here would perform for me if I asked them to."

"Are there any private scenes already going on?"

He shook his head. "The dungeons are locked. This isn't a black sheet party tonight, but I'll bend the rules for you."

Was that what she wanted? For him to make allowances for her? "How many dungeons do you have?"

"Counting the private playroom in my suite? There're ten."

Oh me, oh my. How wild could he be? "Maybe we shouldn't do this."

"Then what should we do?"

"I don't know. I—"

Before she could complete her mixed-up sentence, he latched on to her wrists, cuffing them with his hands and backing her against the counter.

Because it was oddly exciting to be restrained by him, because her pulse suddenly pounded in her pussy, she broke free, shoving him away.

He maintained his distance, but his blue eyes had gone glassy. She wondered if that was how he looked when he worked his bondage magic, when he teased, tortured, and fucked his shackled lovers. She considered offering him her wrists again. But instead she curled her fingers into her palms, protecting herself from him. Still, she wasn't ready to walk away completely.

"We'll watch a ménage," she said.

His eyes remained strange and shiny, and she suspected that he was imagining himself inside her, making her beg, making her slick and wet and erotically weak.

"Okay, Kitten. Let's go pick who we want."

Just like that, they left the kitchen and wandered through the party, checking out the other guests as if they were eye candy. Kiki couldn't believe that she was doing this, especially with Ethan Tierney.

It seemed so . . .

Wicked, she thought, as he motioned to the rubber-clad blondes on the stretching rack.

"How about them?" he asked.

She considered the busty trio, but declined when one of the girls gave Ethan a deliberately submissive look, as if she wanted to belong to him. Not that Kiki should care, but oddly enough, she did.

Not a good sign, she thought.

He pointed to another trio, who were huddled on a leather sofa, nibbling on appetizers from a gold-rimmed plate. "They live together."

"Really?" She admired the androgynous threesome, a boy and two girls. They almost looked like mirror images of one another, with retro clothes, dyed black hair, and kohl-lined eyes. The boy was as pretty as the girls.

"They switch."

Kiki knew what that meant. She'd read about it in her

research. Switching was the practice of exchanging power, where the parties involved took on either or both roles, becoming the dominant or submissive players at different times.

Dominant with a capitol D, Kiki thought, and submissive with a lowercase s. Right or wrong, that was how the BDSM community defined it.

"I never switch," Ethan said.

She slanted him a glance. "You're always the Dom."

"*Always.*" He turned to face her. "But I'm good at aftercare."

"Aftercare" was another term she'd read about, referring to the time after a scene in which the participants calmed down and discussed the events, sharing their emotions and coming back to reality.

She frowned. "You make it sound romantic."

"It can be, Kitten. If you play with me, I'll make your experiences hot and hard and your aftercare soft and sweet."

Butterflies erupted in her stomach. "I already told you that I wasn't into the lifestyle." She made what she hoped was a powerful expression, trying to prove that she would never submit to him or anyone else. "I read about it. I researched it. But that doesn't mean I find it appealing."

"In that case, we should forget the ménage. Whoever performs for us is going to incorporate some form of BDSM into their scene. It won't be vanilla."

"I like vanilla."

"Then go home, little girl. You're at the wrong house, with the wrong man."

"I'm not a little girl." To make her point, she stood toe to toe with him, crowding him the best she could.

He crowded her right back. He even grabbed her wrists the way he'd done before, making her nerve endings ignite. "So you want to go through with it? You want to watch my friends have kinky sex?"

If he held her any tighter, he was going to leave marks on her skin. "Yes. And if you don't let go, I'm going to—"

"What? Knee me in the balls? Sorry, but I'm not into CBT."

Cock and ball torture, another term from the BDSM glossary. "Funny guy. Now let go. People are staring."

"My house. My people."

"Fuck you, Ethan."

"Fuck you, too, Kitten."

When he leaned in to kiss her, she let him. She actually let him put his hot, spicy mouth against hers. He tasted like everything she wasn't supposed to want.

His tongue pillaged hers, and she reveled in his forbidden flavor, lacking the will to fight back. But it hardly mattered. He kept her captive until he ended the connection, leaving her as spineless as a jellyfish. If only she knew how to sting him.

"You're a jerk," she said, her voice much too breathy.

"And you're the most beautiful redhead I've ever kissed."

Oh, great. Compliments in the midst of her half-assed ire. "Is that the kind of baloney that's part of your aftercare?"

He shrugged, then smiled. "I like you, Kiki."

Oh, wow. He'd used her name. And heaven forbid, but she liked him, too. "You're quite the snake charmer."

"Are you sure I'm not the snake?"

If he was, then that would make her the charmer. "Can we just see some sex, please?"

"Kinky sex," he reiterated.

"Yes, bondage, discipline, S and M, whatever." She just wanted to watch.

"You haven't chosen the players yet."

She turned to look at the androgynous threesome. They remained huddled on the sofa, but now they were focused on her and Ethan, too. One of the girls smiled. She was Goth pale with fiery lipstick and a tattoo of a black butterfly on her shoulder. The wings were a Celtic design.

"That's Fiona," Ethan said. "She's a sales clerk at a cosmetics counter."

"And the other girl?"

"Lynn. She's a floral designer. And the guy is Brad. He's a computer analyst. They're from L.A., but I flew them in for the party. That's also where I'm from. I still have a house there. And other places, too."

According to what Kiki had read about him, he had mansions all over the globe, but apparently Santa Fe was his new playground. "Who else did you fly in for the party?"

"About half of the people here. Not all of my friends can afford to jet-set on their own."

His friends? Or his groupies? To Kiki, there was a difference. "So you provide their fun?"

"What else am I going to do with my money?"

"Oh, I don't know. Donate it to charity."

"I give plenty to worthy causes." He gestured to the live-in lovers again. "Do you want to watch them?"

Kiki studied Lynn, and the floral designer smiled in the same provocative manner as Fiona had. So did Brad. They seemed to like that Kiki was looking at them, admiring them, inquiring about them. They were too far away to hear what she and Ethan were saying, but it was obvious that they were the topic of conversation.

"Yes," Kiki said, when Lynn uncrossed her miniskirted legs and flashed a pair of black lace panties. "I want to watch them." She wanted to see them kiss and touch and lick and fuck. "I want to watch everything."

"Then let's ask them if they'll perform for us, if they'll be our perfect trio." He reached for her hand. "And make you crave the lifestyle."

Two

Kiki didn't respond. But either way, she was going to do her damnedest not to crave the lifestyle. Or better yet, not to crave Ethan. Because a man with that much power, that much raw sensuality, could get dangerously addictive. She knew he was wrong for her.

Oh, sure. Was that why she was allowing him to orchestrate this naughty little ménage? Because she was being so responsible? So cautious?

"Quit stalling," he said.

"I'm not," she shot back, even if her footsteps had slowed to a halt.

"You're scared."

Scared? She was petrified. "Of watching strangers have sex? Honestly, Dr. Freud, how scary can it be?"

"Scary enough to make you shiver, Red Riding Hood."

Was she shivering? Yes, but only because the wolf wouldn't keep his paws to himself. "Quit touching me and I'll be okay."

"All I'm doing is holding your hand."

"Feels like a vise."

His lips quirked. "That could be arranged."

Lord, he was dastardly when he smiled. "I suppose you pride yourself on that smart-ass sense of humor of yours."

"Who said I was kidding? I've got a collection of breast vises that would make your toes curl."

Her stupid sense of humor kicked in. "Or my boobs ache?"

He grinned. "That, too."

The grin faded, and he glanced at her bra. Was he envisioning her in a breast vise? Maybe a couple of nipple clamps?

She shivered again, and he brought their joined hands to his lips and brushed a gentlemanly kiss across her knuckles, making her wonder who the real Ethan Tierney was. He confused, frightened, charmed, and aroused her.

"Everything that happens here is safe, sane, and consensual," he said.

The BDSM community motto. "I hope so."

"It is. Absolutely."

She quit stalling, and he escorted her to the perfect trio on the sofa. Lynn was still flashing her panties, and Kiki got warm and wet. She couldn't help it. The ménage thing was exciting. She wondered if Lynn would play a submissive or dominant role. Kiki liked that Lynn and her lovers switched. It made them seem less hard-core.

Less like Ethan.

Of course that hand-kissing stunt made him seem less hard-core, too. She'd read about "loving" Doms. Did hot, hard experiences and sweet, soft aftercare make Ethan a loving Dom? She wasn't sure, but she wasn't prepared to become his sub in order to find out.

"This is Kiki," he said to his friends, and she realized that while she was obsessing about what kind of Dom he was, he was getting to the point. "She wants to watch the three of you in a scene."

"Really?" Brad got to his feet. With his smoky eyeliner and rangy muscles, he was even prettier up close. "Well, Kiki, I think we could do that for you." He glanced back at his lovers, and they nodded their agreement.

"Tonight," Ethan put in. "Whenever you're ready."

"I'm always ready," Brad responded, as if the indecent proposal had made him instantly hard.

Kiki sucked in her breath. Would Lynn suck him? Would Fiona? She hoped so. The butterfly girl had such yummy red lips.

The women rose from the sofa, moving like sleek, sexy cats. Kiki envisioned them purring into each other's ears. Or lapping cream between each other's legs.

"Are you Ethan's new sub?" Lynn asked.

Kiki shook her head. Ethan was still holding her hand. She tugged it away. He grabbed it back. The perfect trio smiled in unison.

"You will be," Brad said. "No one can resist him for long."

In spite of the upcoming ménage, Kiki wanted to turn tail

and run. The bartender had more or less told her the same thing, and now she was trapped within a mistake of her own making. She shouldn't have come here tonight.

"Which dungeon should we use?" Brad asked.

"The Blue Room," Ethan responded.

His playrooms had names, like the parlors at the White House? Now Kiki knew she was in the land of the bizarre. But fool that she was, she let Ethan lead her to their destination.

The Blue Room was on the first floor, at the end of a long, sconce-lit hallway. Ethan released her hand and lifted a silver chain from under his shirt. Hanging from it was a solitary key.

"It's the master to all of the dungeons," he told her. "I always keep it on me."

She didn't know how to respond, so she clamped her mouth shut. Her heart was beating triple time. She could barely think, barely breathe. Was she really going to partake in this?

Yes, apparently she was. Ethan swung open the dungeon door, and they entered the Blue Room, the perfect trio on their heels.

Mercy!

The walls were a sizzling shade of cobalt, and mosaic floors showcased cerulean, azure, and indigo tiles. Even the artwork was blue, or mostly that color. Kiki recognized some of the paintings as Ethan's. A depiction of an emotionally tortured angel caught her attention. His thick, mussed hair was as black as a moonless night, and his eyes mirrored lapis stones. Naked, with his arms extended to a storm-raged sky, his big, beautifully erect penis protruded against his stomach, but his glittery blue wings were broken and battered. She glanced at Ethan, but he didn't react. Clearly, it was a self-portrait. Was that how he saw himself? As a man who'd fallen from grace?

With her curiosity piqued, Kiki checked out the rest of the room. Embroidered drapes, velvet couches, satin pillows, and an antique dressing table provided vintage luxury, but that was where the glamour ended. The bulk of the furniture consisted of assorted cages, various racks, stands with suspension slings, chairs with chains, wood and leather spankers, padded tables with metal rings, kneeling boxes, stockades, and custom-designed devices Kiki couldn't quite name. An enormous closet and tall oak cabinets were filled with Lord only knew what.

Once everyone was inside, Ethan closed the door behind them, and the click of the lock made Kiki's pulse jump.

"Any requests?" Brad asked. He looked at Kiki. "Any specific Dom/sub order you want?"

She wasn't about to make that decision. "Whatever you normally do . . ."

"We mix it up. Sometimes we have two Doms and one sub. Sometimes one Dom and two subs. And sometimes we—"

Ethan cut in. "One Dom. Two subs." He addressed Brad. "You be the Dom."

Well, then. Kiki shifted her feet. Apparently the lord of Curtis House knew exactly what *he* wanted to see.

Brad turned to his lovers. "Is that okay with you?"

"Sure," Lynn said.

"Me, too," Fiona agreed.

"Then on your knees," he barked. "Now!"

As fast as leather-and-lace lightning, the role-play had begun, and both women hit the floor in what was called the slave position. Kneeling with their legs spread, they lowered their heads and put their hands on their thighs, palms up.

Kiki took a step back and bumped into the hard wall of Ethan's chest. Without the slightest hesitation, he tugged her onto a velvet sofa with him so they could observe the scene. He seated her between his open thighs and put his arms around her, directly under her bust. As her jewelry rattled, he pressed his fly against the curve of her rear.

Brad left the women and walked over to the closet. He rolled open the door, scanned the racks, and removed a stack of fetish gear, dumping it in a pile near the dressing table. All of it was new. Kiki noticed that the sales tags were still in place. But Ethan could afford to keep his supplies fresh.

Brad dug around in the closet again. This time he retrieved a long, slim crop with tassels at the end. He returned to his subs.

"You." He wiggled the braided implement in front of Fiona. "Go find something naughty to wear."

"Yes, sir," the butterfly girl said. But when she tried to stand up, Brad cracked the whip against the floor.

Snap! Snap!

Fiona dropped back down, returning to the slave position. Kiki flinched and gasped, and Ethan shushed her, whispering, "Relax and enjoy it, Kitten. It's just a game."

Was it? God, she hoped so.

"Did I tell you that you could stand up to find something to wear?" Brad asked Fiona.

"No, sir," she responded.

"Then do it on your knees."

"Yes, sir." Fiona crawled over to the fetish pile.

"You, too." He prodded Lynn with the whip, and she crawled, as well.

Locked in Ethan's embrace, Kiki glanced up at the emotionally tortured angel with his engorged penis and damaged wings, then shifted her gaze to the subservient women, who rifled through the goods. Kiki wondered if she was losing her mind, if Ethan Tierney had stolen it from her.

The subs stripped while on their knees, an awkward task at best. Brad allowed them to stand once they had donned their new gear.

For her main garment, Fiona had chosen a latigo cincher, which she buckled, quite snugly, around her waist. She accessorized with fur-lined wrist cuffs and thigh-high boots. With her Goth-pale skin, pert breasts and waxed pussy, she looked delicate in the heavy leather. Lynn went for a pair of crotchless panties, a lace garter belt, fishnet stockings, and stripper shoes, adding four inches to her already impressive height.

The sales tags were removed, and Kiki assumed that after the scene ended, the scantily clad women would be awarded their garments, courtesy of their billionaire host.

"Put some pretty things in your hair," Brad ordered, snapping his whip once again. "And be quick about it."

The subs dashed over to the dressing table. Fiona found little butterfly barrettes to adorn her dyed black locks, and Lynn, the floral designer, clipped silk roses to hers.

"You." Brad addressed Fiona. "Get over there and lie down."

She obeyed, climbing onto a bondage table.

"Restrain her," he told Lynn. "Strap her down."

"Yes, sir." She used leather straps on the sides of the table to keep Fiona in place, making sure the other woman's legs were spread and her vulva was exposed.

While the binding took place, Ethan kept a tight hold on Kiki, and she released the air in her lungs, waiting, watching, the pressure of his strong, hard body insanely close to hers.

Brad ordered Lynn to sit on Fiona's face, and Kiki got warm all over, particularly when Ethan nudged her with his erection. He was as big and hard as the angel in the painting.

Prodding Lynn to hurry up and do his bidding, the Dom cracked his handy-dandy whip once again. He was good, Kiki thought, damn good with that vicious thing.

As the flower girl climbed on top of the butterfly girl, Ethan whispered, "Look at her mouth."

He meant Fiona. She was wetting her ruby red lips in anticipation, waiting for Lynn to make the connection.

And she did. Oh, how she did. She straddled Fiona, seating herself fully. Brad gave another command, this time to Fiona, instructing her on how deeply to pleasure Lynn through her open-crotch panties.

Kiki nearly wept. If she were home in bed, imagining this scenario, she'd be strumming her clit until her fingers burned.

Lynn arched her body. She was naturally curvaceous, with full breasts and even fuller hips.

Brad joined in on the action. He got on the floor between Fiona's bound legs and used the whip on her, teasing her with the tasseled end. He ran it along her cleft, keeping her on the edge of arousal without fulfilling her needs.

The butterfly girl made a low, tortured moan, and while she paid oral homage to the other sub, Brad continued to deny Fiona her own pleasure. Kiki felt denied, too. She wanted somebody to come.

Lynn was close. But she didn't orgasm until she asked the Dom for permission. He granted her wish, and she rocked back and forth, shuddering in hot, slick waves.

Afterward, Lynn sighed, and Brad ordered her onto the floor to take his place with the whip. She used the tassel on Fiona, who still wasn't permitted to come.

Taking his role to the sensual limit, Brad climbed on the table and positioned himself over Fiona, copping a wide knee stance. "Are you ready for me?"

"Yes, sir. Please, sir. You're all I want."

"Me or my cock?"

"Both, sir." Fiona gazed up at him, and he reached for the top button on his pants.

Beyond aroused, Kiki gripped Ethan's thighs. In response, he tightened his hold on her. She could feel him breathing against her neck. He wanted the blow job to happen, too.

But Brad prolonged the excitement, toying with his zipper, making the metal teeth rasp. Kiki nearly groaned.

Then something went wrong. She felt a chill pass through her bones. But not a sexy chill. Suddenly she got the distinct feeling that she was being watched, that there was some *real* voyeurism going on.

She glanced up, looking for hidden cameras. Was the room

under surveillance? Was she being filmed? If she was, then it was Ethan's doing. This was his house, his domain.

Consensual voyeurism was one thing, but to film her in the midst of her fantasy? That was low-down dirty.

She stared at the fallen angel. Were the cameras part of the painting? Were his lapis eyes the lenses?

Kiki panicked and pushed away from Ethan, breaking out of his clutches.

"What's wrong?" he asked, as she lunged to her feet.

She flailed her arms, shielding her face from the angel, and the perfect trio stared at her as if she were horribly, terribly ill.

Lynn stood up, and Brad got off the table and released Fiona from her restraints.

"Do you think it's subspace?" Brad asked no one in particular. He sounded nervous, unsure of what to do.

"She wasn't a sub." This from Fiona. "But maybe she imagined that she was me and you were Ethan. Maybe she absorbed the feeling."

Kiki wanted to shout at them, to insist that she wasn't sick or spaced out or fantasizing about being Ethan's sub. But she couldn't find her voice.

"It'll be okay," Lynn told her.

No, it wouldn't. The eye in the sky was getting stronger, so strong Kiki was drowning in it. She raced to the door, nearly shaking the wood from its hinges.

Ethan approached her and put a gentle hand on her shoulder. "Let me help you. Let me make it better."

Finally, she was able to talk, to yell. "You want to help? Then give me the damned key!"

"You don't need the key. No one is keeping you prisoner."

She quit rattling the wood, understanding what he meant. All she had to do was turn the lock to break free. Less panicked, she took a moment to breathe, to get her emotional bearings, to prove that she wasn't sick or crazy or both.

"Are you all right now, Kitten?"

She nodded. But regardless, she wasn't going to discuss the hidden cameras with him. He'd only deny it in that phony aftercare way of his. Already his touch was making her weak.

"I need to get out of here." She pulled open the door and walked away, as fast as her suede boots would take her, determined never to see him again.

But he had other ideas. Although he let her out of his mansion that night, he didn't let her go completely. He got her number from Amber, then called her the next day and the day after that, leaving messages on her voice mail.

Kiki deleted each and every one.

Ethan entered the Santa Fe Women's Art Museum and approached the information desk. A sixty-something lady, probably a volunteer, with smooth gray hair and stylish glasses, greeted him.

"What can I do for you?" she asked.

Help me understand women, he thought. "The historian is expecting me, but I don't know the location of her office."

The clerk adjusted her glasses, and Ethan waited while she studied his artfully rumpled appearance. He was emotionally drawn to vintage shirts and frayed jeans. Of course, sometimes he went the designer route, too. His money could buy him just about anything he wanted. Just about, he reiterated in his mind. He'd lied about having a meeting with Kiki. She wasn't expecting him. But he couldn't stand that she hadn't returned his phone calls. He couldn't stop thinking about her.

"Ms. Dion's office is on the second floor." The lady behind the counter proceeded to give him directions. "But you'll have to check in with the curatorial division secretary." She told him where the secretary's office was, too.

He thanked her, and she gave him one last look before he walked away, but he doubted that she recognized him. He didn't run in mainstream art circles, and although he loved Santa Fe, his work wasn't exhibited here. Curtis House had brought him to New Mexico.

He headed for the stairs, his black harness boots beating a rough rhythm on terra-cotta tiled floors. He bypassed the secretary's office and went straight to Kiki's door. He wasn't about to check in, not with a phony appointment.

He didn't knock. He simply slipped inside Kiki's office and hoped she wasn't engaged in a real meeting. If she was, he figured she would handle it like a pro. She wouldn't call security and kick him out. She wouldn't draw that kind of attention to herself.

Her office was smart and simple, decorated in woodsy tones with a heap of work-related clutter. It was also empty. She was nowhere to be found. He hadn't counted on her not being there.

Ethan took a chair by her desk and waited. He also took inventory of personal items, things like a cutesy picture frame with a photo of two strawberry blond kids. A niece and nephew, he surmised. He noticed a grouping of partially burned candles, too. He picked up each one and inhaled its pleasing aroma. The mingling scents made his cock half-hard. Ethan was a hot-wax freak.

The door opened as he was sniffing a candle that smelled like fresh rain. He glanced up and saw Kiki. She got a damn good gander at him, too. They stared at each other from across the small room.

He stood up, his six-foot-one frame dwarfing the cozy interior. He still had the rain candle in his grasp. He put it down, even if he was tempted to ignite the wick. He didn't smoke, but he always kept a lighter in his pocket, just as he always kept the master dungeon key around his neck.

"Get out of here," she said, shuffling a stack of files in her hands. "Leave me alone."

"Not until you tell me what went wrong." He moved closer. He wanted Kiki Dion. He wanted her as badly as Javier had wanted Nicole. Ethan knew intimate details about the historical couple. He'd purchased Nicole's letters from a private collector. They were his latest obsession. The very reason he'd bought Curtis House.

"What went wrong, Mr. Safe, Sane, and Consensual, was you filming me while I watched the scene."

"What?" He could do little more than gape.

"Don't play the innocent. I could feel it. I was being filmed."

"You think I keep hidden cameras in the dungeons? Kitten, you're paranoid. I would never do that."

"I knew you'd deny it."

"It's the truth. I swear on my grandmother's grave that I don't spy on my guests. There are absolutely no cameras in the dungeons or bedrooms."

She gave him a suspicious look. "I'll bet your grandmother isn't even dead."

"She's in a crypt at Westwood Village Memorial Park. It's the same place where Marilyn Monroe is buried. I'll swear on Marilyn's grave, too."

"I don't know what to think of you, Ethan."

"I told you I was honest, and I am. Granny taught me not to lie, not about the things that matter." Fudging his way into Kiki's office didn't count.

"Granny was important to you?"

"My trust fund came from her." And she was the only person in his family who didn't scorn his art or his lifestyle. He missed her terribly.

Kiki hugged the files to her chest. "Why did I get the feeling that I was being watched? Why was it so strong? And don't say it was the scene that freaked me out. I was enjoying it up to that point."

So had he. Especially because she was there, tempting him into cock-pulsing desire. She tempted him now, too. Her hair was a riot of fiery waves, and her dress flowed to her ankles in Southwestern colors. He envisioned her gloriously naked and chained to the St. Andrew's cross in his private playroom.

Clearing his mind, he returned to their conversation. "Something went wrong. Something made you freak."

She frowned. "Maybe it was the angel."

Ethan frowned, too. There was an angel in all of the Curtis House dungeons. Not the same painting, but variations thereof. He called them his "Mercy of Pain" collection. He'd begun painting them the year his grandmother passed away, the same year his parents had asked him to stop celebrating religious holidays with them.

Kiki spoke again. "I imagined that his eyes were the camera lenses. But eyes are the windows to the soul, right?"

"That's what they say." Ethan had inherited his startling blue eyes from his father, a man with whom he shared little spiritual connection.

"Artistically, I thought the angel was beautiful. But emotionally . . ."

She didn't elaborate and he didn't ask her to. He knew how twisted his self-portraits were. "I still want to paint you, Kitten."

The files went closer to her chest, as if she were shielding herself with them. Paper and ink armor. "I'd be crazy to say yes."

"Just think about it, okay?"

She sighed. "Okay. And Ethan?"

"Yes?"

"I'm sorry I was rude to you. That I accused you of being deceitful. I'm not used to your world."

"I know." But knowing was only half the battle. He wasn't going to be able to get her out of his system until he dominated her.

As deeply and desperately, he thought, as Javier had dominated Nicole.

Three

My Dearest Thinking Woman,

It's me again, here to relay my latest tale, to give you the details, as well as relive them in my mind.

I so wish I could mail these letters, but where would I send them? To a Pueblo altar in the sky? All I can do is seal each envelope and keep them hidden in my luggage, as if they might reach you by some sort of ancient magic.

After I got Papa tucked into our room, I ventured to the hotel eatery, El Restaurante, for lunch. Quite simply it means "The Restaurant" in Spanish. Of course I didn't know that until the waiter told me.

I chose to dine outdoors and was given a table with a spectacular view. Curtis House sits high atop a hill, presiding over

Santa Fe with a courtly air, much like its arrogant owner. I glanced around, but I didn't see him. Relief burst low in my belly, as did a shock of disappointment.

What did that mean? I asked myself. Was I losing my innocent mind? As you well know, I pride myself on being a virtuous girl.

I ordered a sandwich with a fruit and cheese accompaniment, and although it was the least costly fare on the menu, it wasn't quite low enough.

I sat there thinking about how Papa and I couldn't afford Curtis House. But since it was the hotel he had set his heart upon, I couldn't bear to deny him. Still, in consideration of our budget, I decided that I would consume only half of my meal and bring the remainder to Papa. Between the two of us, one lunch would suffice, especially since my father's appetite often waned and he ate little these days.

While I waited for the food, an embroidered napkin on my lap, a soft, aromatic breeze blew. Sweet-smelling sage blanketed the hillside. As soon as I found a job, Papa and I would have to get a small apartment. But for now, I would give him the luxury of staying at Curtis House.

Someone approached my table, and I lifted my gaze. There stood Mr. Curtis's lady friend, bold as you please with her daring fashion sense and long, dark dresses.

"May I join you?" she asked. "Seeing as we're both alone?"

"Yes, of course." To refuse would have been rude.

She occupied the chair opposite me, and the waiter brought her a menu and silver setup.

"I'd like a glass of sweet tea," she told him. "With fresh mint." She didn't scan the food selections, as she was already familiar with them. "I'll have the chicken, and a big plate of apple fritters. I so love treats."

"Yes, miss."

She waved him away and smiled, quite playfully, at me. Her eyes were a leafy shade of green, framed with luxurious, ready-to-bat lashes. "I'm Lenore La Shay." She extended a manicured hand. "It's not my real name. But it has a fine ring, don't you think? I'm a stage and soon-to-be screen actress."

"It's a pleasure to meet you, Miss La Shay." I should have guessed that she was a performer.

"You can call me Lenore, darling girl. And who pray tell are you?"

"Nicole West." Did my name have a fine ring, too?

Within no time, the waiter returned with her tea. After he departed, she leaned in close.

"Are you aware of Javier Curtis?" she asked. "Of who he is?"

"Yes." I nearly fidgeted in my chair.

"Then I shall be frank." She lowered her voice to a secretive whisper. "He wants to fuck you. But I would caution against it."

The word she'd used didn't elude me. The men at the factory where Papa worked spewed it when they cussed, and so did some of the uncouth boys in our old tenement building. I knew it was a vulgar reference to sexual intercourse.

Reacting to Lenore's statement, I squeezed my thighs

together. I remembered, all too clearly, the way Mr. Curtis had undressed me with his eyes.

"He can be quite the rake," she said.

Thinking about the hotel proprietor made me warm and slick and sinfully wet. To be on the safe side, I squeezed a bit harder. "I'm a virgin."

"Well, of course you are. A good girl like yourself."

I nodded in agreement. Back home, I'd only had one beau, and I'd barely let him kiss me.

"Javier would chew you up and spit you out." Lenore was still whispering. "He has a taste for, shall we say . . . the unusual."

I had no idea what she meant, and I didn't want to know. My clenched thighs were beginning to ache. "Are you and he? Do you . . . ?"

"Javier and me? Ha!" She removed a slim gold cigarette case and matching holder from a beaded bag, then signaled the waiter so he could light the tobacco for her.

The waiter left, and I took the opportunity to query her further. "So, you and Mr. Curtis aren't . . ."

"Heavens, no." She blew out a dramatic puff of smoke. "I don't dally with men." Contemplating my confused expression, she added, "I fancy other women."

Unable to articulate a response, I went fear-drenched, stonewalled silent. Did she desire me, too? Was that why she was warning me about Mr. Curtis?

"It's not what you're thinking," Lenore said.

"It isn't?"

"Not in the least. You're lovely, darling girl. You remind me of Alice in the Wonderland book. But you're hardly my type."

Our lunch arrived and she put out her cigarette. We sat quietly, engaged in our food. I picked at mine, determined to save half of it for Papa.

Lenore glanced up, a fritter partway to her lips. "Bloody hell."

"What's the matter?" I glanced up, too. Mr. Curtis was headed directly for us, taking long, lean, sexually motivated strides.

A bonfire erupted beneath my skirt, and I fought to snuff the flame, but I couldn't squeeze my thighs together tight enough. Not this time.

He moved closer, and suddenly I identified with Alice and her distorted adventures. Only when I tumbled down the rabbit hole, my clothes would disappear and I would land in Mr. Curtis's outstretched arms.

"Ladies." He inclined his head. He spoke with a well-schooled American accent, but I suspected that he laced his dialogue with Spanish when it suited him. "Are you enjoying your lunch?"

I barely nodded, clutching the handle on my fork. Why did he have to be such a fine cut of a man? Why couldn't he be squat, spectacled, and bald?

Naturally, his predatory gaze was focused on me.

Lenore snared his attention. "Javier, darling?"

He lifted his brows at her. "Yes?"

"*If you so much as breathe on this sweet girl, I'll chop your testicles in two.*"

"*Will you now?*" He turned back to me with a slight bow. "*Please accept my apology. Lenore is one of my dearest friends, and I love her like a sister, but she tends to forget her manners. My* cojones *are far from proper table conversation.*"

If I hadn't been so nervous, I would've snorted. He wasn't fooling anyone with his gentlemanly act. He was amused that his cojones—I was right about him relying on Spanish when it suited him—were being discussed. It didn't take a genius to make the translation.

I managed to speak, to find a civil voice. "Lenore has been nothing but kind to me."

"How kind?" he asked. "Kind enough to inform you of how truly wicked I am?"

Lenore spoke up. "Leave her be, Javier."

"I intend to."

"Since when?" my companion asked.

"Since Candace surprised me with a visit." He gestured to a table occupied by a voluptuous young woman sporting a décolleté dress and a big, ostrich-plumed hat. She watched us with a cool eye.

"Ah, yes." Lenore wrinkled her nose at the other female. "Your latest whore."

"Do I detect a note of jealousy?"

"Over her? I'm a better actress than she is."

"She gets more work than you do."

"Because she sleeps her way to the top. You're not her only wealthy conquest, Javier."

"I'm aware of her conquests." He announced it as if he didn't care. Then he chided Lenore and said, "Have you forgotten that you've never once been charged for your accommodations?"

"That doesn't make me a whore. Just a friend in need." With thespian flair, she offered him her hand. "It was nice having this little chat with you. But, please, go away before Candace pitches a fit and comes over here. If she shows up, my stomach will sour."

"And your fritters will go to waste?" He chuckled and kissed her proffered hand. "Such snap. Such bite. You charm me, Lenore."

"Does that mean my room remains free?"

"I suppose it does." He shifted his dark gaze to me. "You, I'm afraid, will have to pay for yours. Unless you can find a way to charm me, too."

My heart hit my breastbone, rattling my corseted rib cage. He was staring at my mouth. "I won't exchange favors with you, Mr. Curtis."

"Someday you might." With that, he took his leave and joined Candace at her table.

"He's going to fuck her hard and deep tonight," Lenore said. "But regardless of how much she pants and moans, he'll be thinking about you. You'll be the woman on his mind."

I dared him a glance. Luckily his back was to me. "He can think of me all he wants, as long as he leaves my virginity intact."

"If he manages to take it, you'll be his first. As far as I know, he's never deflowered an innocent. Tarts like Candace are more his style."

"Then I'm safe." *Because I would never succumb to being his tart or his whore or anything even remotely close.*

Kiki hoped she didn't regret what she was about to do. Ethan had sent a limo to her apartment to pick her up, and she rode in the back of the elegant vehicle, fidgeting like an errant schoolgirl on her way to the principal's office.

She should've driven her own car, but she'd accepted the limo ride as a leap of faith, proving that she trusted Ethan enough to rely on him.

Shaky trust, at best. What if he tried to foist a pair of crotchless panties on her, like the naughty pair Lynn had worn? No way was Kiki going to model for him with her lower half exposed. Or topless for that matter. She intended to keep a modicum of decency.

So why was she doing this?

"Because I'm crazy," she said out loud.

And because he was hot, handsome, and talented, and she wanted to be immortalized by him. But at least she wouldn't be posing live. He was going to paint her from a photograph. Of course that meant he would be snapping fetish-clad pictures of her today.

The limo arrived at the mansion and parked in the driveway. The chauffeur opened Kiki's door and offered her a hand. She stepped outside, glanced up, and saw Ethan waiting on the front steps.

The chauffeur returned to the car, and she studied Ethan. Sunlight skittered across his shoulders and fell in shadows across his face. He wore a plain white T-shirt, a battered belt with a sterling buckle, and a pair of old jeans, heavily frayed around the fly. On his feet, he sported Harley Davidson boots. He looked wild and sexually free, like the BDSM artist he was.

He sent her a whips-and-chains smile, and Kiki imagined dropping to her knees and sucking his cock.

Oh, God, she thought. There it was. The fantasy she'd been suppressing. The *real* reason she'd agreed to do this. As ridiculously submissive as it sounded, she wanted to play with Ethan Tierney, to experiment with his lifestyle.

And that, ladies and gentlemen, scared the living hell out of her.

"Hey, Red Riding Hood," he said. "Are you ready to have some fun?"

Was she? She forced herself to walk toward him, her heart pounding with every step. "Yes, but I'm sticking to the mask thing. I don't want my face to be seen."

"That's not a problem. Come in and we'll get started."

They entered the mansion and she asked, "So, who else is here?"

"No one. It's just us. I figured it'd be easier to maintain your anonymity that way."

She was completely alone with him? "What happened to your chef, your housekeeper, your personal assistant, your entourage, or whoever?"

"I sent everyone away." He gestured in the direction of the kitchen. "Can I get you anything? How about some champagne?"

"It's ten in the morning. That's a little early to start partying."

"I'm not suggesting that you get drunk. But a little buzz wouldn't hurt. A lot of inexperienced pinup models drink champagne during the creation of their centerfolds or whatever. It takes the edge off."

"Who said I was edgy?"

"I just assumed . . ."

"I'm okay, Ethan." They stood in the middle of his massive living room, where the stretching rack and antique torture devices were. "I'm perfectly fine."

"Then let's go to my studio."

She hesitated. So much for being perfectly fine. "Where is it?"

"Upstairs, along with my suite and private playroom. The entire third floor is mine. No one creates sex, art, or havoc there except me."

"Maybe just a little champagne," she decided. If other models did it, then why not her, too?

"We'll bring the bubbly upstairs. Dom, Cristal, Bollinger, or Krug?"

"You choose." She didn't know one from the other.

She expected him to pick Dom, mostly because of the name, but he went for Krug, Clos du Mesnil, 1995. When she asked him why, he told her it was his favorite vintage for special occasions.

Kiki assumed that meant it was rare and expensive. But she wasn't about to argue. She figured the billionaire knew best.

Off they went to the third floor, with an ice bucket, the champagne, and two flutes.

His studio was bold and bright, with a stunning skylight and square footage most artists could only dream about. Of course there were easels, tables, and shelves crammed with supplies, along with an array of BDSM furniture/props, but he'd also incorporated a spacious bathroom, two luxurious dressing rooms, and a huge fetish-fashion closet into the layout.

"You've got everything you need," she said.

"All of my studios are designed this way." He put the champagne on a table, allowing it to chill in the ice bucket a bit longer. "Why don't you look through the closet and see what strikes you."

"You're going to let me choose my own outfit?"

"It depends on what you pick. Mostly I was thinking we could decide together. But either way, I'd like to get a feel for what you're drawn to."

She considered her options. "How about something that covers me up? Like one of those full-body latex suits?"

Ethan shook his head. "Not a chance."

"But that's bondage gear, isn't it?"

"Yes, but a girl like you needs to show some skin."

"Says the boy who wants to see her naked."

"I'm not a boy."

No, he was a man, who was looking at her with primal heat in his eyes.

She glanced at the champagne. "I think I'd like my drink now."

"It's not cold enough." He motioned to the closet. "Go take a look."

Kiki walked across the studio floor, her tennis shoes squeaking. She'd tossed on simple clothes this morning, but her wardrobe would soon be sizzling.

She hardly knew where to begin. The closet was packed with every sexy, slinky, naughty garment imaginable. Everything was brand-new, like the clothes in the Blue Room.

She noticed a faux fur bikini top and rubbed her fingers along the tiger print. "I like this."

He came up behind her. "So do I."

"Does it have matching bottoms?"

"It might. But even if it does, that's too predictable. You need something decadent to go with it." He dug around and produced a leather thingamajig. "How about this?"

She made a face. "What is it?"

"A chastity device." He maneuvered the garment, explaining how it was supposed to fit. "After it's in place, you add some little padlocks, and you're all set."

"I don't know . . ."

"Just try it on and see how it looks. If you hate it, we'll come up with something else."

Upon closer inspection, she agreed that the device might work, but only because her crotch would be swathed and locked, and that seemed strangely sensible. As for her butt, her cheeks would hang out, but at least there was a heart-shaped patch of leather designed to cover the hole.

"Can I gag you, Kitten?"

Oh, Lord. Her heart started pounding again. "With what?"

He looked lustfully at her lips. "I could do it with my belt. I could tie it off in back."

Because his suggestion sounded a little too dominant, she shook her head. "No gags."

"Then I want you to wear some extra-shiny lip gloss."

"That's fine." She heaved a shaky sigh of relief. It was bad enough that she wanted to suck him. Being gagged would only make it worse.

"How about gauntlet gloves and stiletto boots?" he asked.

She agreed, and he chose the accessories. The boots were exceptionally wicked, with buckles all the way up the sides.

"Is the champagne cold enough yet?" she asked, praying she could pull this off.

He nodded, and she followed him to the ice bucket, where he proceeded to remove the cork. She waited for the customary pop, bracing herself for the shotgun effect, but a gentle sound emerged.

"What happened?" she asked.

"Nothing. I opened the bottle that way purposely. *Le soupir amoureux*. It means 'the sigh of love.' "

Oh, great. Now he was going to make her melt.

He handed her a flute and lifted his in a toast. "To my favorite redhead."

"Lucille Ball?" she asked, shattering the romance and making him chuckle.

"I really should gag you, Kitten."

"Yes, but then I'd moan and groan behind it, and you'd go crazy listening to me."

"I'm already going half nuts. I can't wait to see how you're going to look."

She sipped the champagne, allowing the remarkable vintage

to work its voodoo and help her relax. "What kind of mask am I going to wear?"

"We'll find something that complements your costume. I've got plenty of masks to choose from. But you should get dressed before we decide."

"Okay, but I'd like another glass of bubbly first." More Krug courage, she thought.

He refilled her flute. "Your portrait is going to go in my private playroom."

An erotic shiver raced up her spine. "Is that where you keep your favorite redheads?"

He nodded. "It's the Red Room."

"Yes, of course. I should have guessed." She sipped the heavenly champagne, grateful for its effect.

He watched as her mouth touched the rim of the glass. "I could paint you with my dick. I swear, I could."

She burst into a silly laugh. "Now there's a sexy image if I ever imagined one."

He laughed, too.

After a moment of silence, she gathered the fetish garments and headed toward a dressing room.

Then Ethan called her name. "Kiki?"

She turned around.

"You need the padlocks."

"Oh, yes." She waited while he rummaged through a cabinet. What good would a chastity device be without the locks?

When he gave them to her, their hands connected during the exchange, making her skin tingle.

"What about the keys?" she asked.

He tucked them into his front jeans pocket. "I'll keep them on me. They'll be safe here." He patted the denim.

Oh, sure, right next to his cock. If she slid to her knees, would he unzip his pants? Would he tug at her hair? Would he order her to suck him hard and deep?

Much too aroused, Kiki backed away, and once she got into the dressing room, she removed her clothes and stood in front of the three-way mirror. Then, to relieve the pressure, she touched herself, rubbing a shaky finger over and around her clit.

In her mind's eye, she was Ethan's sub, his sweet little blow-job slave, enjoying every face-fucking thrust of his hot, hard, semen-spilling power.

Before she went too far, Kiki dropped her hand. She couldn't stand here and fantasize while he was out there. What if he heard her making breathy sounds? Or what if he analyzed the orgasmic flush on her face?

Determined to behave, she climbed into the leather device, clamping down on the locks, making her throbbing clit unavailable, even to herself.

She finished getting ready and emerged in the wild outfit. She knew how sexy she looked. She'd inspected her appearance in the mirror, stunned that the fire-haired, chastity-belted, tiger-printed, stiletto-booted nymphomaniac was her.

"Damn," Ethan said, walking in a wide circle, checking her out from all angles. Finally he took deliberate strides toward her, stopping when they were only inches apart.

"Come here," he ordered, his voice a harsh whisper.

She moved forward, and he kissed her, deep and rough, pulling her tight against him. Her pussy nearly wept beneath the locked-up leather.

Just as Kiki considered sliding to her knees to fulfill her fantasy, he swatted her bare butt—a little too hard—and said, "Let's find you a mask."

She rubbed her stinging cheek, the left one, and scowled behind his back. He'd already walked away.

"You're a dirty Dom," she called after him.

"Why?" He turned to face her. "Because I left you wanting more? That's part of the game."

"I don't like it."

"You will," he responded, too damned confidently.

She glanced at his fly. He had a big, healthy bulge, but that didn't seem to matter to him, which only made things worse for her. Sooner or later, he was going to own her—lock, stock, and blow-job barrel.

"I was going to get on my knees for you," she snapped.

"Oh, yeah?" he challenged.

"Yeah," she snapped again. "I was going to let you fuck my mouth."

"Listen to you. Talking dirty. Bad girls get punished around here, Kitten."

"Shut up, Ethan."

He laughed, pissing her off even more. Then he ignored her and opened a drawer. He looked through it and came up with a glossy-black feline mask made completely of feathers.

Intrigued, she moved closer. "Let me see that."

"Only if you're going to play nice."

What could be nicer than offering a man a blow job? Still peeved, she snatched the mask out of his hand.

She put it on and fluffed her hair out around it. She loved it, absolutely, positively loved it. When she looked in the mirror, she felt soft and sweet and dangerously pretty. She added the lip gloss Ethan had requested earlier, creating a shimmering effect.

How could he not want her mouth? She should just forget about him and pleasure herself, like she'd almost done earlier.

"It's perfect," he said. "Now get over there so I can chain you to the wall."

There went her heart, pounding all over again. She glanced at the wall in question, where an iron grid was mounted. "You never said anything about restraints."

"I didn't say anything about you licking my boots or begging to be blindfolded or riding on the bondage wheel in my private playroom, either, but eventually all of that is going to happen, too."

"I'm not spit-shining your boots." No way. No how.

He grinned. "I just threw that in to scare you."

"Well, it wasn't funny." But she was tempted to laugh anyway. Ethan had a way about him.

She smacked his arm, wishing she didn't like him so damn much, and he scooped her up, tossing her over his shoulder. While she wiggled and squirmed, he carried her over to the grid.

Preparing her for the sensation of being a sub.

Four

Ethan chose a pair of steel manacles to cuff Kiki's gloved wrists. He rarely used this type of hardware during play. It was harsh and uncomfortable for long-term activity, but for the sake of his art, he wanted her bound this way.

He posed her standing against the wall, facing forward so he could see her elegantly masked face. He lifted her arms above her head, shackling her in what he considered a highly erotic position.

When he knelt down with a spreader bar, she flinched.

"You don't need to use that thing."

"I want to make sure your legs stay open."

"I can do that on my own. See?" She widened her stance.

"It isn't the same." He looked up at her, and their gazes

locked. She was so fucking hot, she kept him in a constant state of arousal.

"I can't believe I'm letting you do this to me."

"Don't worry, Kitten. Once I get some good shots, it'll be over." He preferred to paint live, but live sittings, especially with him, were too taxing for an amateur. He forced his models to exert themselves with the poses he chose.

"I know you promised the photos would be quick, but . . ." She exhaled a heavy breath.

"What?" he prodded, urging her to explain. He was still looking up at her, and she was still gazing down at him. "Are you having second thoughts?"

"No, but it feels weird being restrained."

It felt incredible to him. All he could think about was all the dominant things he longed to do to her. "So you're okay to keep going?"

She nodded.

"Then I'm going to use the spreader bar now. So stay just as you are. Nice and wide."

She nodded again, and Ethan adjusted the bar to the desired length and wrapped the attached leather cuffs around her booted ankles.

When he had secured the locks and dropped the key into his pocket with the rest of them, his cock strained. Would his hard-on go away once he started snapping pictures? He honestly didn't know. He'd never gotten an erection during an art-related project. Work was work, and play was play. But with Kiki, he was all mixed up.

He got to his feet and smoothed the feathers around her eyes and brought her hair more forward. "Ready?"

"Just tell me what to do." She rattled her chains and laughed a little. "What little there is I can do."

He stepped back and picked up his camera. Her laughter was nervous, sensual. Could he be any more turned on? "Lift your chin and look right at me."

She followed his direction.

Snap. Snap. Snap.

His hard-on wasn't going away. "Rattle your chains again, Kitten, but do it harder. Fight your bonds."

Once again, she obeyed.

He took another set of pictures. He was using a digital camera and was able to see the images on the display screen. She was passionately photogenic. Painting her was going to leave him breathless.

"Let's do some without the top." He was eager to capture more of her.

"What?" She blinked at him behind the mask.

"You heard me."

"But I wasn't going to pose topless."

"And now you are." He put down the camera and walked toward her. "I'm taking off your top." He waited a beat, giving her a chance to say a resounding no, to stop him.

But she didn't refuse. She just chewed her bottom lip, which made her look even sexier.

Ethan moved closer, excited that he was making her nervous. Her fear was sweetly erotic. He stood in front of her and reached up to play with the string tie around her neck, to make the moment last. When he touched her, he could feel her pulse beating sensuously beneath her skin.

"Do you still want to give me a blow job, Kitten?"

Her pulse beat faster. "Yes."

He undid her top and the tiger fur dropped. "Are you skilled with your mouth?"

Another quickened beat. "I try to be."

Ethan circled her nipples, tracing each peak with callused fingertips. Her tits were soft and full and beautifully sloped. Natural breasts, perfect for his artist's eye. He loved women in their true form. He wasn't attracted to cosmetically enhanced bodies.

He retrieved his camera and captured her wild-haired innocence, her sweet seduction, feeding off the chemistry between them. She arched her back, creating fluid lines. Her nipples remained aroused. He suspected that her pussy was wet beneath the padlocked device.

Lust and leather, he thought. Cold, hard steel and slick, glossy feathers. He couldn't wait to paint her. He took more pictures.

After he got an image of her wetting her lips, he asked, "Are you thirsty? Do you want some water?"

"I think I'd like another glass of champagne."

Damn, he thought. This girl knew how to drive a man crazy. He poured the sparkling liquid and brought the flute to her lips, holding it while she drank.

"Enough?" he asked.

"A little more."

He tipped the flute, his hard-on getting harder, if that were even possible. He felt as if he were going to explode. He wanted her mouth on him in the worst way.

She drained the glass. "That was good, Ethan. We didn't spill a drop."

What was good was the wild and wanton way she was looking at him. He took one more picture, then freed her. He released the spreader bar and unlocked the manacles.

She removed her gloves, then shed her mask. Her cheeks were delicately flushed. The freckles dusting her nose highlighted her skin.

When she dropped to her knees, he thought he might die. For a long, drawn-out moment, he just stood there, staring down at her, while she gazed submissively up at him.

Loving his role as the dominant male, as the leader of the sexual pack, he peeled off his T-shirt and discarded it. Next he got rid of his belt. When he opened the snap on his jeans, she let out a ragged breath.

But before he proceeded, he made sure, damn sure, that she knew what she was getting herself into. "Once we do this, Kitten, there's no turning back. I'm going to want more and more from you."

She continued to gaze up at him. "I know."

"I'm not going to be gentle."

"I'm not expecting you to coddle me. I meant what I said about you fucking my mouth."

Christ, he thought, could she be any sweeter? Any nastier? Any more nervous? In spite of her brave words, she was scared.

He cupped his bulge, showing her how big and hard he was

beneath his jeans. "I'm going to tell you exactly how I like it, and I expect you to do everything I say."

Kiki nodded her agreement, watching every aggressive move he made. Next time he would insist that she call him sir; next time he would take her further. For now, it was enough that she was on her knees.

Eager for her mouth, Ethan unzipped his jeans and shoved them past his hips. His fully erect cock sprang free.

Kiki's oh-so-pretty face was just a heartbeat away. He tugged on her long wavy hair and brought her closer. She seemed to like that he was using her flowing locks as reins. Good, he thought. Because he liked it, too. He tugged a little harder, giving them both an extra thrill.

"Lick the head," he told her. "All around, in a nice wet circle."

She didn't hesitate. She brought his straining cock to her lips and laved him like a lollipop, making girl-sweet sounds.

He watched her. His kitten. His new playmate. "Lick the hole, too." By now he was leaking with pre-cum.

She obeyed, paying special attention to the opening. Her tongue was as soft as butterfly wings. He tightened his hands in her hair as she tasted the pearly drops.

"Now suck a little. But just the head." He wasn't ready to push all the way in. He was getting off on the foreplay.

Giving him the buildup he craved, she nursed the tip and met his gaze for approval. He traced the outline of her bowed lips, aroused by her obedience.

So aroused, he couldn't control his hunger anymore. He steadied his stance, retangled his hands in her hair, and thrust deep.

She moaned excitedly, and he moved in and out with hard, slick strokes. He wasn't just fucking her mouth; he was fucking her entire face, rocking back and forth, making good on his promise to be rough. She accepted every copulating inch, sucking him all the way to the back of her throat.

"That's right," he praised, his voice rasping with male-driven heat. "Take as much as you can."

She cupped his ass, squeezing his glutes. He looked down at her, watching her cheeks hollow.

He was almost there, almost ready to come. To make it more exciting, he withdrew, fighting his orgasm.

"Lie down," he told her.

"Where?"

"Right there. Right where you are."

She got on the floor, and he climbed on top of her and straddled the pretty face he'd been fucking, anxious to play some more. While in this position, he reached for the manacles.

She shifted beneath him. "Are you going to chain me up again?"

"Unless you try to stop me." He tested her, seeing how far she would let him go this very first time. She'd offered to blow him, but she hadn't offered to do it under lock and key.

Several beats of anxious silence passed between them.

He remained poised above her, waiting for her decision. His big, blasting cock and tightly drawn balls were just inches from heaven.

Finally, she heaved a beautifully aroused breath and stretched her arms back, giving him permission.

Ethan's body surged. He chained her wrists to the bottom of the grid. Just one quick restraint, he thought, with the most brutal hardware he owned.

It was perfect. *She* was perfect. Within no time, she would be his sub in every way.

He leveled his hips and pushed his aching cock back into her mouth. She nursed him desperately, taking him to new heights.

At that thrill-seeking moment, he wanted to collar her, and Ethan never collared his subs. To him, that was too much of a commitment.

Steeped in her sensuality, in her hot, sweet suckling, he came hard and fast, his semen flowing like milk.

She swallowed what he gave her, pleasuring him to the very end.

When it was completely over, when he stopped shuddering, when he could focus on something other than collaring her for the rest of his life, he removed the manacles and held her as close as he could.

～

Kiki snuggled in Ethan's arms. She was aware, of course, that they were half-naked on his studio floor, but it felt so good she didn't care.

He kissed the tip of her nose. "You give great head, Kitten. I could've come a thousand times."

She couldn't help but laugh. "Now, there's a romantic line."

He laughed, too. Then he made a face. "You're nudging me in the nuts."

She glanced down. One of the padlocks on her chastity device was pressed against him. She moved her hips away from his. "Sorry. I'm not used to cuddling in hardware."

"It's okay." He pulled up his pants and closed the zipper. "I put you in that sexy thing, and I'm keeping you in it for the rest of the day."

"Please tell me you're kidding."

"Would I kid about something like that? I like keeping you locked up."

She got practical. "What if I have to pee?" She had drunk three glasses of champagne. Soon, her bladder would be feeling it.

"I'll give you the keys for that, but you'll have to give them back after you're done."

"You're key obsessed." She glanced at the master dungeon key around his neck.

"And you're my prisoner."

She thought about how wild her affair with him was going to be. "You meant what you said about wanting more from me."

"You're damn right I did." He stood up and offered her a hand. "But we need to talk about it. I need to know what your limits are, how far you're willing to go."

Her skin turned warm, then taut, then tingly. Being chained to the floor, with him kneeling over her, pumping into her mouth, had been the most erotic experience of her life.

And the most dangerous, too.

"Can I at least put a top on?" she asked.

He picked up his T-shirt off the floor. "You can wear this."

Kiki dragged it over her head, enjoying the simple way it caressed her body. The fabric felt like him. It smelled like his cologne, too.

"Are you hungry? The chef left some food in the fridge." He ran a finger across her lips. "Not that you didn't just have some protein."

Lord, he was lusty. She knew he was talking about his cum. "Some real food would be nice." She leaned forward to whisper in his ear. "But I like what you gave me, too."

"Careful," he whispered back. "You're making me hard again." They separated, and he guided her toward the closet mirror. "Look how hot you are, Kitten." He stood behind her and rubbed her already-erect nipples through the T-shirt. "You're a Dom's dream."

She studied her image. Her hair was a tangled mess and her mouth was swollen from sucking him.

Ethan lowered his hands and toyed with the padlocks on the chastity device. "I can't wait to get you naked, to take possession of my prize." He pressed his fly against her rear. "I think I'll leave you in the boots. You look like a vixen in them."

Her nerves skittered. He overwhelmed her. "If my ex-husband could see me now."

"You were married?" He kept her in front of the mirror. "What kind of idiot would let you go?"

"The corporate kind. He wanted me to cut my hair and wear stylish suits. To stop being so . . . artsy."

Ethan flashed a painter's grin. "Maybe we should invite him over to see your portrait when it's done."

"You and your sense of humor." She turned to face him. "Have you ever been married?"

"Me? I don't do commitment. I don't even collar my subs."

"You don't? I thought collaring could be committed or casual."

"It can. But it feels committed to me."

"So I won't be receiving a pretty little leather choker from you?" she said to tease him.

"I considered it when you were going down on me." He paused, frowned. "But I was caught up in the moment."

Kiki didn't know what to say, so she changed the subject. His hypnotic blue eyes were much too intense. "Can we have lunch now? I think I need some nourishment."

His expression remained the same, just as focused, just as determined. For a man who didn't commit, he looked downright possessive.

"We can discuss your limits while we eat," he said.

"That's fine." She glanced at herself one last time in the mirror. "But I don't know if I can sit at your dining table in this outfit."

"Why not?"

Because she was wearing a bare-assed chastity device and his body-warmed T-shirt. "I'd just feel more balanced in a robe."

"I already told you that the house was empty."

"I know, but . . ."

"You're getting shy on me now?"

"Please, just one itty bitty robe." Was she actually begging him for a garment? Yes, she was, and the independent woman inside her cringed.

He opened the closet and came up with a retro-style dressing gown. Before he handed it to her, he removed the tag. Like all of the play clothes he provided, it was new.

Kiki slipped it on. The black silk clung luxuriously to her skin. "This is nice. I like it."

"Me, too." He scanned the length of her. "The sash is going to make a nice blindfold."

When he reached for her arm to escort her downstairs, she shivered from his touch. "Is everything Dom/sub to you?"

"What do you expect me to feel when I'm with you? You're my new muse."

And he was the fetish artist who was single-handedly changing her life.

Before they went downstairs, she got the chastity keys from him and used the bathroom. Afterward, she locked herself back up again and returned the keys, just as he'd requested.

They headed to the kitchen and decided to eat in the breakfast nook, a much cozier area than the formal dining room. The chef had prepared picnic-type foods, so they munched on Southwest-style lettuce wraps and a variety of tasty salads.

"You're spoiled," Kiki said.

"And now I'm spoiling you." He leaned over to kiss her cheek. They sat side by side in a wooden booth, with a votive candle burning as the centerpiece. From the window, she could see a magnificent gazebo and a portion of the Curtis House garden.

Instinctively, she behaved like his lover and offered him a bite of pasta salad from her fork. In turn, he gave her a nibble of a stuffed tomato from his plate.

"So is breast bondage okay?" he asked. "Are you going to let me do that to you?"

He got right down to business, didn't he? Kiki swallowed the food in her mouth and took a sip of lemon-garnished water.

"Yes," she responded.

"Tit torture, genitorture, and spankings?"

She hurt just thinking about it. But, already steeped in his wild brand of magic, she agreed to give him free rein.

He tugged on the silk sash around her robe, then kissed her cheek again. "What about blindfolds?"

Did he have to be so sweet, so loving during this conversation? A cozy "Yes" came out of her mouth.

"Dildos and vibrators?"

She nodded.

"Gags and muzzles?"

Earlier she'd told him no. This time, she said, "Okay," wondering if he'd cast an aftercare spell on her.

"How about gun play and knife play?" he asked.

Kiki almost teetered in her seat. She'd read about both types of play, and the idea of toying with weapons went beyond the realm of kink, at least to her. "You're into that?"

He shook his head, and she narrowed her eyes. "Another of your jokes, Mr. Tierney?"

He laughed. "Sorry. The look on your face was worth it." He sobered up. "But if you want to try it, I'm game. I'll do anything with you."

"Really?" She decided to push his buttons, too. "Then I want to switch."

His response was quick, serious, definite. "Anything but that."

"Spoilsport." She went back to her lunch and wondered what dominating him would be like.

In the BDSM community, it was said that power flowed from the bottom up, from the sub to the Dom, because the Dom couldn't do anything without the sub's permission. But at the moment, she felt as though she was at Ethan's mercy.

Was that her power? Or her weakness?

"We haven't talked about wax play," he said.

Kiki studied the candle on the table. She wanted him to drip colored wax all over her. She'd imagined that from the beginning.

"That's a definite yes," she told him.

He slipped his arm around her. "Leather restraints and hot wax. That's my favorite type of play."

She leaned against his shoulder, wondering how something so bizarre could sound so romantic. "I think it's going to be mine, too."

Side by side, they admired the flame on the candle.

But not for long.

Suddenly, as if someone had blown a deliberate breath across the wick, it went out.

"That was weird," Ethan said.

Yes, weird, Kiki thought, as goose bumps peppered her skin, as the overwhelming feeling from the Blue Room came back, the déjà vu of being watched.

An eye in the sky.

A desperate observer.

The feeling intensified, and she turned to Ethan and stared at him. He was preparing to relight the candle, using a silver and black lighter he'd removed from his pocket.

"It wasn't my imagination," she said.

He gave her a confused look. "What wasn't?"

"The voyeur."

His expression soured. "You think I'm filming you again? I already told you, I would never do that."

She glanced around, her heart flip-flopping in her chest. She could sense the emotional presence of another person, yet the house was empty. "It isn't a camera. It's . . ."

He went back to being confused. "It's what, Kitten?"

"I don't know." She was confused, too. But even so, the feeling got stronger, with a deep, dark, painful ambience attached. "It isn't only me," she said. "It's both of us the voyeur wants to see."

The two of them together.

My Dearest Thinking Woman,

I saw them together in town today, kissing on a public street, and I stood out in the open and watched, heat curling low in my belly. Other people grumbled or giggled or pretended not to notice, but none of them watched the entire kiss.

Except for me.

Why was I in that predicament? Because I'd left Papa at the hotel and gone into town to seek employment, and lo and behold, there was Mr. Curtis and the woman named Candace, embracing outside of a dressmaker's shop.

Their bodies were pressed close, and he had one of his hands on the swell of her back. When he slid it up and down her spine, I got feverish.

Had he bedded her last night and fantasized about me? At that moment, I sincerely hoped that he had. I wanted to be the woman who consumed his mind.

As I stood on the street and watched them, I imagined that it was my lips he was kissing, my back he was caressing. Yet I'd vowed that I would never become his whore.

They separated, and Candace blotted her mouth with a lace-edged handkerchief and turned to enter the dressmaker's shop.

He glanced up and saw me, and I feared I might faint, especially when he walked toward me in that matador way of his. As always, he brimmed with strength and masculine grace. He wore his thick, dark hair slicked straight back, and his suit fit him dashingly well.

"Miss West," he said, by way of a greeting. "Did you enjoy the show?"

"Was that what it was?" I asked, clearing the frog from my throat.

"It's always a show with Candace." He reached into his breast pocket and removed a silver case. Upon opening it, he offered me a cigarette.

I wanted to accept the offering, to feel more grown-up, but my effort would probably backfire and I would cough my fool head off.

"No, thank you," I said.

He lighted a cigarette for himself and studied me with pitch black eyes. "I could arrange for you to watch more than a kiss." He blew a lazy stream of smoke. "If that would please you."

Clearly, he was talking about sex. My face went hot, and the fear of fainting returned. We stood beneath a portal where we were shaded from the sun, but I could have been a cactus in dire need of water.

"You offend me, sir," I managed.

"And you tempt me. I think you're a she-devil in disguise." He leaned in close. "I wasn't offering to let you watch Candace and me. I was referring to Candace with another man. Or possibly two other men, if that would be more to your liking."

Two men and one woman? Like in a Greek orgy? I'd heard about paintings and sculptures of this nature, with body parts exposed, with the participants engaging in lewd acts. But what he was suggesting wasn't art.

"Are you trying to shock me?"

"No. Just please you, as I said before. Candace enjoys multiple partners, and she is an actress, after all. Why not ask her to perform for us? We could watch together."

I wished I had a fan in my bag so I could cool myself. "I should slap you for that."

He shrugged, the cigarette burning between his fingers, gathering a long, gray column of ashes at the tip. "It wouldn't be the first time a lady cracked her delicate hand across my cheek."

"Nor the last, I suspect." But even so, I kept my slap to myself. I wouldn't dare touch him. His forbidden proposal was spinning in my mind. Somewhere in the pit of my condemned soul, I was wondering what watching an orgy with him would be like.

"You told Lenore that you would leave me be," I said.

"Then I suppose I lied." He glanced toward the dressmaker's shop. "Women like Candace are becoming tiresome." He shifted his lethal gaze back to me. "I'd rather corrupt a sweet little puritan like you."

"I'm not a puritan."

He angled his regal head. "Truly? You're not?"

I lifted my chin, defying his mocking manner. "No."

"Then prove it." He dropped his cigarette and crushed it beneath his shiny black shoe. "Come closer and kiss me. Put your tongue in my mouth."

Oh, Dearest Thinking Woman, I wanted to. How I wanted to. My heart was bumping and jarring like the train Papa and I had taken to get to Santa Fe.

But I said in my haughtiest tone, "Go to hell, Mr. Curtis."

He was unfazed. His casual response was "Only if you'll come with me."

Just then, the door to the dressmaker's shop opened and Candace emerged, carrying several packages. She looked at Mr. Curtis, then pointedly at me, then back at him.

"Javier?" she queried. "What are you doing?"

He didn't turn toward her. His dark gaze remained fixed on me.

"I'm just having some fun," he said.

"At whose expense?" she wanted to know. "Mine or hers?"

He didn't specify, snaring both of us in his dastardly web. Candace clutched her packages and tapped her foot, making her annoyance known. She was a curvy brunette with pale skin, rouge-tinted cheeks, and long, lovely eyelashes. I could see where she and Lenore vied for the same roles.

"Screw you," she said to her lover.

"Go buy another dress," he responded.

He was still looking at me. Fool that I was, I was now looking at him, too. But even so, I caught sight of Candace from the corner of my eye.

"I will, you prick," she said, glowering behind his back. "The most expensive gown they have. And you're going to pay for it."

"Don't I always?" he retorted without malice.

He smiled roguishly at me, and she returned to the shop to spend his money, flouncing off in a theatrical huff.

For some crazy reason, I wanted to laugh. So did Mr. Curtis. His smile turned to a chuckle.

"Maybe we should find another woman to watch," he said. "That one is too temperamental."

I covered my mouth to stifle a horribly amused giggle. He was the most deplorable man I'd ever met. But at that spellbound moment, I liked him.

I liked him very much.

Five

"I think it's a ghost," Kiki said.

Ethan paused in the midst of preparing to relight the candle. "You're reaching, Kitten." As far as he was concerned, she was overreacting to something in her head.

"The original owners died here." She gestured toward the kitchen. "They burned to death. That could leave some restless spirits."

"I've lived here for three months. I would know if my house was haunted."

"Three months isn't very long."

"It's long enough to know if things are going bump in the night."

"A lot of old houses have ghosts." She snared his gaze. "And I'm feeling something. Something I've never felt before."

"So you chalk it up to a ghost?" He flicked the lighter and held it over the wick, but the damned candle wouldn't accept the flame. It wouldn't light.

"See?" Her voice jumped. "See? Something isn't right. Something . . ." She glanced toward the kitchen again. "Fire probably makes it nervous."

"I've been burning candles every day since I moved in." He fought with the lighter, trying to ignite the wick. "There. See for yourself, smarty." The flame was burning bright.

A second later, it went out, and Kiki shot him a smug look. He scowled back at her. "Okay, Kitten, since you're the all-knowing medium, who's our ghost?" He considered the couple who had died. "Javier or Nicole?"

She went silent, crossing her arms, as if she'd gone cold, as if the silk robe wasn't keeping her warm. Then she said, "I think it's her. It feels too soft, too sad, too emotional to be a man."

"I still think you're reaching."

She angled her head, her wild red hair framing her face. "You don't believe in ghosts?"

"Of course I do. I'm an artist. I believe in just about everything. But I have Nicole's letters, and if she was going to make herself known to someone, it would be me." And he didn't feel a damn thing.

Kiki's eyes went wide. "What letters?"

Oh shit, he thought. He'd just unleashed the historian in her. "She wrote letters to a Pueblo deity, a character in one of her father's poems. I think it was her way of keeping a diary, of putting her feelings on paper. She started writing them the day she met Javier and kept writing them up until the day they died."

"Oh, my God. Where did you get them?"

"I bought them from a private collector. Erotic literature is one of my passions, so I'm always looking for interesting buys."

"Erotic literature? The things Nicole wrote were sexual?"

He nodded. "Javier was into what I'm into. Only in those days, it wasn't a community the way it is now. It was highly secretive. Much more forbidden." He put his lighter away, wishing he felt what she was feeling. But there was nothing in the air, nothing he could detect, other than a moody candle that wouldn't stay lit. "After I acquired the letters, I wanted to own Curtis House, too. So I found a way to buy it, to make it one of my homes."

"Oh, Ethan. You have to let me read Nicole's letters. I need to know who she was and what was happening in her life."

He made a wide open gesture. "Why don't you just ask her?"

"That's not funny. Besides, I don't feel anything anymore."

"How convenient."

She rounded on him. "You're just jealous because she's my ghost and not yours. You can't stand not being in control. You want everything to belong to you."

Okay, so she had a point. But that didn't mean he was going to concede, not without a foolhardy fight. "If you want to read the letters, you can beg for the privilege."

She gaped at him. "You can't be serious."

"Try me, sub girl."

"Piss off, Dom boy."

"I already told you that I wasn't a boy." He ran a finger along her ribs. "Do it. Beg for what you want."

She looked at him as if he'd gone mad.

"Fine," he said to taunt her. She *was* driving him mad. "Then forget about the letters."

Frustrated, she shoved at his chest, and he caught her wrists, holding her while she tried to fight him off.

Then, like the explosive new lovers they were, they ended up kissing, pawing each other at the table.

"Please," she whispered. *"Please."*

Her heartfelt plea made him gentle his hold. She was begging to read the letters, but she was begging to play, too. She wanted him to take her upstairs and do away with the chastity device so she could come beneath his dominant touch. He heard it in her voice. He saw it in her eyes.

"Don't defy me like that again," he said.

"I won't," she promised, even though they both knew that she would. She was too rebellious not to misbehave.

He wondered if she was some sort of beguiling witch, if she was capable of stealing his already-condemned soul. Once again, he considered collaring her. With diamonds and rubies, he thought. With a collar that was as beautiful and fiery as she was.

"Let's go." He wanted to own her, to torture her, to make her scream in orgasmic bliss, for however long their affair lasted.

They returned to the third floor and entered his suite, where his private playroom was attached.

She looked around, and he examined his quarters through her eyes. His enormous suite was decorated in mission furniture to complement the house. The four-poster bed was rife with restraints. Even his bathroom was equipped with stainless steel chains, anchored to the walls in a custom-built shower stall and whirlpool tub. The tub sat upon a tiled platform, with a shelf of waterproof sex toys nearby.

Kiki glanced his way, and he shrugged. He was what he was, a man who shackled his lovers in any capacity he could.

His playroom, the Red Room, was just as impressive. Or as lavishly demented, he thought, depending on your perspective. The dungeon furniture had been constructed to his specifications, using fine woods and polished metals. The fabrics he'd chosen were rich red velvets and burgundy brocades.

When the atmosphere turned uncomfortably hushed, he turned to see Kiki staring at the broken-winged angel on the wall. In this depiction, he was standing amid a sea of naked redheads who lay at his feet. Blood flowed from his outstretched arms and dripped onto the women, melding into their hair.

The painting wasn't subtle. Ethan's pain was evident. The women had lash marks all over their bodies, yet it was the angel who was bleeding.

Most of Ethan's subs reacted the first time they saw it, as it was the size of a mural. But Kiki's emotional expression affected him low and deep, where the pain came from.

She searched his troubled gaze, and they behaved awkwardly, reminding him that they were borderline strangers.

He geared the conversation to their upcoming scene. "We need a safeword."

She nodded. Apparently she knew that when a sub uttered a safeword, all BDSM activity stopped. He hoped that didn't happen, that she didn't panic in the middle of their play, but his style of sex was new to her. Anything was possible, and it was his responsibility to make her feel safe, to give her an out if she needed it.

"How about Nicole?" He suggested Javier's wife's name, the supposed ghost, as their safeword.

Kiki glanced up at the ceiling, as if she were expecting the female entity to make a sudden appearance. From there she looked at the damaged angel, then at Ethan.

"Do you think it would be okay with Nicole?" she asked.

"To be your protector? I think she would appreciate it. Javier didn't use safewords. He just did what he wanted to do."

"Did that scare her?"

"Sometimes. But it aroused her, too. He seduced her into his lifestyle."

"The way you're seducing me into yours."

Ethan didn't take control, not yet. "Do you want to know everything that's going to happen this time? Everything that I'm going to do to you? Or would you rather be surprised?"

She exhaled a big, voracious breath. "You can surprise me."

He liked that she'd given him free rein. That she was trying to work past her nervousness. He stepped in front of her and untied the sash on her robe, preparing for the eroticism to begin.

This was it, Kiki thought. The moment of truth, of becoming Ethan's sub. *Her.* A woman who clung to her independence, who didn't like being told what to do, who'd fought with her ex-husband because he'd tried to control her.

But that control hadn't been sexual, she reminded herself. This was different. This was for pleasure.

Still, she was afraid—oddly, emotionally, sensuously afraid, the way Nicole had probably feared Javier.

Nicole. Her safeword. Her ghost.

Although Ethan wasn't convinced that Nicole was a ghost, Kiki knew that the other woman was haunting the house. How could she be sure? The feeling was too strong, too significant, too real, to chalk up to her imagination. To Kiki, it was a sixth sense that couldn't be ignored.

Ethan removed her robe and let it slide to the floor. She wondered if he was going to pick up the sash and blindfold her with it, but he didn't. Her vision wasn't obstructed. Her eyes were wide open, able to see her sexually chilling fate.

"When we're in a scene, you're going to refer to me as sir," he said.

The way Lynn and Fiona had addressed Brad, she thought.

"Do you understand?" he asked.

"Yes. S-sir," she added, the word tripping uncomfortably off of her tongue.

He frowned, his dark brows slashing above his brilliant blue eyes. "Say it again."

Kiki stalled.

"Don't fuck with me, Kitten."

"I'm not. I'm just . . ."

"Scared?"

She nodded. "Yes, sir." This time she said it softly.

"I understand that you're afraid." He touched her cheek, as if he were collecting her freckles with the pads of his fingers. "But I'm still going to teach you how to submit. Totally. Completely. With or without fear."

She got dangerously aroused, wondering what her first lesson was going to be. He was dominant, but he was gentle, too.

His put his mouth against hers, and they kissed, making her sigh.

A moment later, he tugged off the T-shirt she was wearing and tossed it aside, leaving her in the chastity device and stiletto boots.

Next, he led her to a wooden structure called a St. Andrew's cross. According to legend, Saint Andrew had been martyred on this type of X-shaped cross because he considered himself unworthy to be crucified like Christ.

To Kiki, it seemed fitting for Ethan, the fallen angel, to gravitate toward religious symbols. Of course, this wasn't something he'd cooked up. St. Andrew's crosses were common in BDSM dungeons, as they were practical and easy to construct.

He attached her to the cross, standing upright, with her arms raised above her head and her legs open, aligning her body with the X pattern.

"I'm going to make you hurt," he said.

"Good pain?" she asked, using a term that meant pain that had been mutually agreed upon.

He didn't respond. He walked away, and Kiki's heart thumped in her own ears.

She watched him open a cabinet, the safeword spinning in

her head. He returned with tweezer-type nipple clamps connected by a fancy chain.

When he glanced at her breasts, she tried not to rattle her restraints. She was scared out of her submissive wits, but she was excited, too.

"Let's see how sensitive you are." He lowered his head and licked her nipples, teasing each one, switching back and forth. They tingled under his touch, rising to stimulated peaks. She moaned her pleasure, wishing she could run her hands through his hair.

She nearly forgot about the clamps until he used them, igniting her like a set of jumper cables.

Her breath caught hard and quick, and he smiled like the handsome sadist he was, tightening them a little more.

They pinched, almost to the point of numbing her. But damn if she didn't like it. Good pain. Good, good pain.

Did that make her a masochist?

"It hurts," she said.

"I know, Kitten."

How could he possibly know? He'd never been a sub. He was speaking from a Dom's point of view.

"The sensation is going to get stronger when I release them," he told her. "When the blood rushes back to your nipples."

"Are you going to release them now?"

"No, I'm not." He stepped back to look at her. "You're going to wear them a bit longer."

"Yes, sir," she responded, drawing strength from the pain. She knew it was crazy, but she felt sexy in the clamps, like a goddess, a temptress. She loved that he was fixated on her image, lusting after her, wanting her.

She waited for his next move, and he reached into his pocket and produced the keys to her chastity.

Oh, sweet heaven. He was finally going to set her pussy free.

When it happened, when the chastity was gone and she was exposed, he got down on his knees and kissed her.

At that wildly tender moment, she tried to press closer to his mouth. She wanted him to worship her with his tongue, to eat her soft and slow, to make her creamy and wet.

"You're pretty down here." He praised her with romantic words, with a flutter of breath, with another warm kiss.

Kiki shivered. She got regular bikini waxes, but she wasn't completely bare. She had a small patch of pubic hair and the color was a deep, dark auburn.

"I belong in the Red Room."

"Yes, you do." He stood up, making her ache for more. More of him. More of his luscious mouth. But he had a different game in mind.

He returned to the cabinet and came back with another chain and clamp. This one made Kiki's pulse pound. She knew what it was. She'd come across references to it in her research.

Ethan studied her nervous expression. "Apparently you know what I'm going to do with this."

"You're going to attach it to the center of the nipple chain and then you're going to clamp it to my clit." The soft, sweet part of her he'd just kissed.

"That's right, and both chains are going to make a nice

little Y design. From here to here." To punctuate his point, he traced the pattern with his finger.

Fear tightened every muscle in her body. "May I see it up close?"

He obliged, dangling the clit clamp in front of her face, and she looked at the tiny, rubber-coated device.

"Are you ready for me to use it?"

She wanted to say no, but it wouldn't do any good. To end the nipple-numbing, pussy-clenching madness, she would have to say "Nicole."

"Are you?" he asked again.

Kiki nodded, praying that she could tolerate the added pain. The delicate little device looked like it packed a punch.

Ethan drew out the process, making her anticipation worse. Slowly, he attached the chains, letting the clit clamp sway between her trembling legs.

"This is your last chance to stop me."

"I'm ready," she lied.

He dropped to his knees, but he didn't use the clamp. Instead, he spread her labia so her clit popped out like a gummy bear.

He was milking this for all it was worth, making her his sweet, little treat. And that, she realized, was what identified him as a Dom and her as a sub. The way he was teasing her felt so good, so annoyingly exciting, she wanted to scream.

Finally, finally, he got on with it and clamped her good and tight.

This time, she did scream, out of pain, out of pleasure, out of a kinky craving she never knew she had.

The sensation was insanely erotic, and she thrived on the intimate pressure, especially when he licked her, giving her oral sex while she was all clamped up.

Her rosy pink nipples. Her gummy bear clit.

"Don't come," he whispered against her mound. "Don't you dare come."

Now he was being unfair, now he was being a *true* sadist. All Kiki wanted to do was come.

"Please," she implored. "Please, sir," she added, hoping her obedience would help.

But it didn't.

"No way," he taunted. "No fucking way." He licked her again, swirling his tongue, making her juices flow. "You haven't suffered nearly enough."

Orgasm denial was a significant part of BDSM play, and Kiki didn't know if she could handle it. If she hadn't been chained to a cross, she would've pitched forward and spread herself across Ethan's gorgeous face, moaning her desperation.

Already she was on the verge of a warm, wet spasm.

He drew back, stopping right in the middle of what was sure to be the creamiest climax of her life.

At this point, she couldn't think beyond what she needed, what she wanted. "Let me come."

"I said no." For effect, he tightened the clit clamp another notch, making the sensation stronger.

Caught between hating him and worshiping him, she made ragged sounds. He was so hot, so wicked, so damned evil. She wanted to pull his hair out.

"I'm going to fuck you instead," he said.

Oh, thank God. Soon she would have his big, beautiful cock inside her.

"With a dildo," he clarified, making her curse beneath her breath.

"Keep it up, Kitten, and I'll end this now."

He wouldn't take away her pleasure! Would he? "I'll be good."

"You better be."

Ethan moved closer, kissing her on the mouth, making her warm and slick and eager for his touch. And while their tongues darted and danced, he removed the clit clamp, then the nipple clamps.

Kiki gasped into his mouth. The devices being removed hit her hard and strong. In the midst of the heat, she accidentally bit his lip, but he didn't punish her. He seemed to like it. He intensified the kiss with even more force.

Did that make him a masochist, too?

"Are you ready for me to take you off of the cross?" he asked.

"Yes, sir." She was ready for whatever he had in mind. She could feel his heart beating against hers.

"I'm just going to chain you up somewhere else," he warned, his blue eyes glowing.

"You can do whatever you want with me." As long as he remained close, as long as his heart kept tagging hers.

He released her from the cross. Neither of them said anything. Silent, they stood like statues, surrounded by the power of the Red Room, and gazed at each other.

The bleeding angel was right above their heads.

An emotional chill grazed her spine. And that made her want to use the safeword, to get out while she still had a chance. But she couldn't bring herself to say it.

One more beat of silence passed before he asked, "Are you okay, Kitten?"

Was he aware that "Nicole" had crossed her mind? Had he seen it on her face?

"I'm fine."

He smoothed a strand of her hair, tucking it behind her ear. "Are you sure?"

"Yes." She was determined to keep going. "I want to play some more."

He gestured to a padded table. "Then lie down and spread your legs. Show me what I want to see."

Kiki didn't hesitate. She got into position.

He restrained her wrists and ankles, keeping her legs wide open and her knees bent. Next, he walked over to his handy-dandy cabinet to get a dildo.

The curved silicone phallus he selected was a bright cherry color. More red. More fire.

"It warms to the body," he said. "It should feel good going in."

"It's big," she responded, commenting on the impressive size.

He flashed a wolfish grin. "Is that your Red Riding Hood impersonation? 'My, what a big dildo you have . . . ' "

She laughed a little, the sound raw and anxious. Being strapped to a table, waiting for her lover to insert an oversize sex toy into her vagina wasn't an experience she'd ever imagined.

He covered the dildo with a condom and applied a water-based lubricant. He dabbed some of the lube inside her, too.

Then it happened. He inserted the dildo, inch by erotic inch. The toy was exceptionally warm, and so was the lubricant, providing sinfully slick contact.

The curved shape of the device conformed to her body, finding her G-spot and stimulating her clit with its special design.

Heaven on earth, she thought. Ethan knew just what she needed. She closed her eyes as he worked his experienced magic.

"You can't come without my permission."

Her eyes flew open. He couldn't possibly expect her to control her orgasm, not with him rubbing her G-spot *and* her clit.

"I don't know if I can be that good."

"You can, and you will." Upping the ante, he pumped the dildo a bit faster, a bit harder.

Kiki wanted to explode right then and there. He controlled her with every thrust.

She lifted her bottom off the table, but tightening her ass didn't help. It only made her more aware of the pressure.

When Ethan climbed on top of her, she feared she would lose it for sure. He kept fucking her with the toy, but now he was kissing her, too.

She nipped brutally at his lips, wishing she could claw his back. Being restrained was driving her crazy. She wanted her freedom. She wanted to attack her lover in every mindless way she could.

Pump, pump, pump went the dildo. Bang, bang, bang went

her heart. Ethan Tierney was a perilous man. Kiki wanted him to free his cock, to fuck her in the flesh, but he kept using the handheld toy.

She moaned; she gasped; she writhed on the table, battling his body weight and fighting her restraints.

"You're a hellcat, aren't you, Kitten?"

She almost lost herself in his eyes. So blue. So glittery. So oddly mystical. "Let me come."

"You need more pain. Good pain," he whispered against her lips. "Good, sexy pain."

Yes, she thought, trying to angle herself toward the dildo, imagining that the body-warming phallus was him. "When are you going to fuck me for real?"

"This *is* for real."

"I want your cock."

"You already had it in your mouth."

"I want it inside of me."

"Then you can keep begging for it."

Damn him. Damn him all to hell. She fought her restraints again, but he pinned her down, reminding her that she was his sub.

Kiki strained for relief. Her clit was on fire, and her G-spot burned like a bitch. The torture went on and on, dragging her under.

She wanted to rage, to scream, to tell him that she was *never, ever* going to let him put her through this kind of agony again. But that would've been a lie.

She kept pushing against him. His body was big and heavy and brutally strong. "I need . . ."

"Not yet."

"Please . . ." If he wanted her to beg, then she would beg. "If you won't give me your cock, then at least let it be over."

Ethan remained on top of her, thrusting the dildo between her legs. He watched her intently, examining the achy-breaky expression on her face.

She looked painfully back up at him.

Then he put his mouth to her ear and, in a deep, hot voice, said, "Okay, Kitten, you can come now. You can do it for me."

As soon as his words washed over her orgasm-deprived body, she let go, convulsing feverishly.

Just for him.

Six

Kiki wasn't quite sure when the climax ended. All she knew was that the dildo was gone and Ethan was on his feet, undoing her ankle restraints and removing her boots.

After he discarded the stilettos, he unshackled her wrists. She blinked at him, her brain still fogged.

"Turn over, Kitten."

She obeyed his softly spoken command. She had no desire to defy him. At this point, she was one dreamy girl.

Within seconds, he was rubbing massage oil onto her back and kneading her muscles. Oh, wow. He was giving her a massage.

And was he ever skilled.

Strong, deft hands. An artist's touch. Kiki felt as if she were being sculpted from clay.

"Whatever you're using smells heavenly." She detected notes of almond, nutmeg, sandalwood, and lavender.

She stretched like a cat, and he caressed her back, buttocks, legs, and feet. She'd never been to a spa or had a deep-tissue massage, and she realized what she'd been missing.

"You're amazing." She sighed into the padding on the table. "Not that I didn't curse you a few times."

"Yeah, I know. Now roll over and I'll do your front."

No way was she going to refuse. She flipped herself like a lazy flapjack, offering him the rest of her naked body.

He started with her arms, paying special attention to her wrists, taking away the tightness of having been shackled. He even rotated her hands with his, using what seemed like a professional technique.

"I'm not done with you today," he said. "We're going to play again later."

She looked up at him. "Are you going to fuck me?"

"I might."

"You'd better."

He massaged her breasts, taking away the ache there, too. "Don't get bossy. Or I'll chain you up again."

She decided to behave. She didn't want to spoil his stress-relieving touch.

He slid his hands lower. He rubbed the top of her mound, caressing her pubic bone, but he didn't put his fingers inside her. His massage was sensual without being sexual. Kiki was duly impressed. She sighed with pleasure and closed her eyes.

After it was over, after he'd relaxed every part of her, he

kissed her softly on the lips. Her eyes drifted open, and she imagined how Sleeping Beauty must have felt when the prince made his sweet foray.

He brought her a fresh robe, a plush terry-cloth wrap with a Curtis House monogram. She stood up, and he held it open while she slipped it on.

"Nice touch, Ethan. I like the logo."

"I had them made for my guests. In some ways, this house is still being run like a hotel."

She thought about Nicole. "A haunted hotel."

He guided her toward the bedroom portion of his suite. "I still think you could have imagined her."

She ignored his skepticism. "Are you going let me read her letters?"

"Yes."

Her pulse jumped. "Right now?"

"Yes, but you can't read all of them."

"Why not?"

"Because I'm going to use them as rewards. Every time you do something that pleases me, you can read one."

So much for him being a prince. She wanted to knock him off of his superior pedestal and end their affair right here and now. Baiting her with the letters was unfair. "You're an ass."

"And you're a spitfire."

"My temper goes with my hair. Now give me one of those dang letters."

"I'll give you three, one for the hot blow job, one for wearing the Y-clamps, and another for letting me tease you with that big, cherry dildo."

She shook her head, and in the next instant they both sputtered into laughter. Could their relationship get any weirder?

He gestured to a recliner in the sitting area across from his four-poster bed. "Have a seat, and I'll get the letters."

Suddenly the historian in her felt downright giddy. In fact, when he turned over her rewards, she sniffed each piece of yellowed paper, inhaling their old, musty scent. He'd actually given her the originals. She'd expected copies.

He lifted his eyebrows in a half-amused, half–almighty Dom expression. "I scored some points."

"Yes, you did." She examined the faded, but still legible ink. "Look at her handwriting."

"Yeah. Nicole had a great penmanship." He angled his head. "You're really into this, aren't you?"

"I could come in my panties."

"You're not wearing any," he reminded her. A moment later, he fell silent, allowing her to sink into the letters.

She devoured each word, and when she completed the third letter, with Nicole and Javier standing in front of a dressmaker's shop, she looked up at Ethan. "You have to give me another one. I have to know what happened the next time she saw him."

He sat on the edge of his bed. "Okay."

Just like that? He was going to give her what she wanted? "No begging, no pleading, no erotic favors?"

"Don't jump the gun. You're going to owe me."

"By doing what?"

"I'll let you know."

"So that's it? I'm supposed to agree without being aware of the consequences?"

"You are if you want to read Nicole's next letter. Otherwise, you'll have to wait until I decide when you should read it."

"That's blackmail."

"Take it or leave it, Kitten."

Kiki weighed her options. He couldn't ask her to do anything that wasn't consensual, so she figured she was safe. Or she hoped she was. Playing with Ethan was like playing with sex-fueled fire.

"I'll take it."

"Good girl. Now kiss me to seal the deal."

With trepidation, she approached him, and he stood up and took her in his arms. When she touched her lips to his, he held her reverently, confusing her all the more.

Now that he'd gotten what he wanted, he went into after-care mode, behaving like Sleeping Beauty's prince again.

When it ended, he rewarded her with another letter, another glimpse into Nicole's life.

My Dearest Thinking Woman,

Since the day Mr. Curtis proposed that I watch an orgy with him, my heart has been spiraling out of control.

Candace clings to her lover like a sap-filled vine, and every time he looks my way, she fights harder for his attention. He seems to enjoy being the object of two women's fretful fancy. He smiles charmingly at me from behind her back, baiting me to steal him away from her. He behaves like the cad of cads, the worst of the worst, yet I flutter inside whenever he is near.

Am I a fool to have gentle feelings for him? Lenore says

that it isn't my fault that I've been swayed by him. She claims that he is a natural-born womanizer, and many a female has been left in his emotional wake. Of course none of his conquests have been innocents like me.

Regardless, Lenore suggested that I use my girlish wiles and appeal to his most gallant quality. According to her, that would be his giving nature.

Why do I need his generosity? Because I cannot find employment and Papa and I are almost out of money. I worry that Papa's health is failing, too. Although he puts on a brave front, he seems wearier with each passing day, coughing more roughly, sleeping more fitfully.

So I took Lenore's advice and approached Mr. Curtis, hoping, praying to soften his roguish heart.

I located him in his office at the hotel, sitting behind an extraordinary desk.

He got to his feet, the way a gentleman should when a lady enters a room, but he did so in a slow, sensual manner, scanning the entire length of me.

A trail of smoke drifted between us. He'd left a cigarette burning in an ashtray beside him. As always, he was impeccably groomed. I'd done my best to look proper and pretty, donning my best daytime dress.

"To what do I owe the pleasure?" he asked.

I held his gaze, fighting my nervousness. "I'd like to apply for a job."

"Here? At Curtis House?" He seemed intrigued. He gestured for me to sit. "In what capacity?"

I perched on the edge of a chair. I didn't have any specific skills, but I tried to sell my willingness to work, to do whatever it took to earn a respectful living. "I could learn to run the front desk. Or I could serve food or wash dishes at the restaurant. Or I could clean rooms." I was prepared to be a maid.

"None of those positions are available."

"What is available?" I asked, hoping he wouldn't mock me for having limited knowledge of the hotel business. I'd mentioned the only jobs I could think of.

He stamped out his cigarette and sat back in his chair, looking much too lordly in his elegant vest and perfectly knotted tie. "You could apply as my new mistress."

I was prepared for a sexual advance. Lenore and I had discussed what his initial offer might be, but his words made me panic just the same. Or maybe it was the heat in his eyes that was making my pulse jump. "I won't be your whore, Mr. Curtis."

"Then I have no other work for you."

"Please," I implored him. "I need a legitimate job." Lenore had told me to beg if necessary, to shame him into helping me. "My father is ill, and we're running short of funds. Soon we'll have to leave the hotel and—"

"Live on the streets?"

I nodded, and he had the gall to say, "Then I suggest you swallow your pride and fuck me."

I went ramrod stiff, hating him, as well as myself, for being at his mercy, especially since I still had feelings for him. "I'd rather die."

He lifted both eyebrows. "As opposed to what? Allowing your father to die?"

I banked my tears, refusing to let him see me cry. I'd brought Papa to Santa Fe, and the journey had worsened his health.

Mr. Curtis softened his voice. "Become my mistress, Nicole. Let me take care of you and your father."

He'd never used my given name before, and it sounded oddly romantic coming from his lips. But that didn't change the facts. He was still prodding me to be a whore.

"I can't," I responded.

"My mother was my father's mistress."

"She was?" His admission stunned me. I'd assumed his birth had been nothing short of noble. "You're a bastard?"

"In more ways than one." He said this without humor, without warmth. The softness in his voice had vanished.

"Were you born and raised in America?" I asked.

He nodded. "Papa had been part of what has become known as the Santa Fe ring. Corrupt businessmen, ranchers, and politicians who once controlled every aspect of this town."

"You speak of him in past tense. Is he gone now?"

"Yes, dead and buried. Mama, too."

"So that is your legacy? A corrupt man and his mistress?"

"Papa left me his fortune. Bastard or not, I am his only heir."

"And now you wield your money over women like me?"

"I wield it over women like Candace. You turned me down."

"Do you have any bastard children?" For some stomach-churning reason, I needed to know if he and his father were alike.

"No, I don't. Nor do I intend to."

"Then you plan to marry someday?"

That made him laugh. "Only if Satan wants to share one of his brides with me."

I furrowed my brow. "Is the devil married?"

He laughed again. "You're as sweet and juicy as a peach, Nicole. Are you sure you don't want to fuck me?" His laughter faded, and he said quietly, "I'll be gentle your first time."

An unbearable ache traveled from my breasts to my thighs, making me smooth my dress over my undergarments. "I doubt you would know how to be gentle, Mr. Curtis."

"I could try. But just that one time, of course. After that, I'd be horribly wicked, using you for the lewdest of pleasures."

Needing to flee, I stood up to leave. "Thank you for your time, but I'll find a way to survive without your help."

He remained in his chair. "Say what you will. But you'll be back, purring like a homeless kitten at my feet."

"Never," I retorted.

Holding my head high, I left his office, and as soon as I closed the heavy wooden door, as soon as I knew he couldn't hear me, I let myself go.

And broke into tears.

"Javier was a jerk," Kiki said.

Ethan took the letters she'd just read and locked them in a safe where he kept the rest of Nicole's Thinking Woman correspondence. "What makes you say that?"

"Are you kidding? Look at the way he treated her."

There was something, maybe the mutual darkness in their souls, that made him defend the other man. "He wasn't that bad."

"How do you figure?"

"He married her, didn't he?"

"Oh, yeah." Kiki made a perplexed face. "They were husband and wife when they died." She made the same expression, only with a bit more intensity. "How did that come about?"

"The wedding? You'll have to read more letters to find out."

"Then let me have them now." She batted her lashes, looking sexy and submissive and everything in between. She was still wrapped in the Curtis House robe. "All of them."

"Nice try, Kitten. But you still owe me on the last letter."

He walked over to the bar on the other side of his suite and poured two ginger ales with lots of ice. He crossed the room and handed her one.

She took a sip. "So, what do I owe? What's my penance or punishment or whatever?"

He more or less guzzled his soda, wishing he'd added a few shots of whiskey. He could've used a Jack and Ginger about now. "I want you to move in with me."

Kiki looked at him as if he'd just sprouted two dicks and a tail.

"Not indefinitely," he clarified. "Just for a couple weeks."

"Why?" was all she could seem to say.

"Because I want you to be here when I'm in the mood to

play. Day and night. I don't want to wait around for you to show up."

"I have a job, Ethan."

"Then you'll have to take a vacation, won't you?"

She gave him another of those incredulous looks. "Just like that? I'm supposed to arrange for time off so I can be your beck-and-call sub?"

"If it's a money issue, I'll pay—"

"Like hell you will." She got instantly offended, much in the way Nicole had been over Javier flaunting his wealth.

"I wasn't offering to pay you to fuck. I was offering to cover your wages."

"Just so you know, I get paid vacations."

"Then what's the problem? Take a few weeks off and hang out with me."

"Everything can't be your way."

"Sure it can. Besides, what's so bad about lounging around, eating gourmet foods, and swimming in a resort-size pool while your new lover paints a beautiful picture of you?"

"Okay, so you have a point."

"Of course I do." Ethan's lot in life was getting what he wanted, by whatever means he could. "And just think, if Nicole's ghost is real, you'll have plenty of time to get close to her, to make a connection while she's blowing out candles or whatever."

"Another good point."

"Then you'll stay with me?"

She didn't jump at the chance. Instead, she rebelted her robe, burrowing deeper into the fabric. "I'd feel more comfortable if I had some time to think about it."

Her reluctance frustrated him. He wasn't asking her to give birth to the next Rosemary's baby. He was talking about a few sexually magic weeks. "What's there to think about?"

"It seems kind of intimate."

"What does? Sharing an enormous house with me? Come on, Kitten. That's a lame excuse."

She took another sip of ginger ale and the ice clinked in her glass, the sound echoing between them. "I'm not used to things going this fast."

"It's just sex."

"I know, but sometimes you kiss me like a prince."

That gave Ethan pause; he tried not to frown. Because he didn't know what to say or how to feel, he made a joke. "You'd prefer that I kiss you like a frog?"

She laughed and put down her drink. The glass was sweating in her hand. "No, I suppose not."

"Then there you go. You've got your own dominant prince." He was tempted to give her one of his disturbing kisses, but he figured this wasn't the best time to lock lips. "Let's play, Kitten. Let's do something naughty."

"Like what?"

"Like put you in a cage."

Her eyes went blinkingly wide. When they'd discussed her limits, she hadn't agreed to be kenneled. But she seemed oddly, nervously intrigued. "For how long?"

"For as long as it takes."

"For as long as what takes?"

"To get yourself off. I want to watch you."

Her voice all but vibrated. "In a cold, steel cage?"

103

"I'll make it warm and cozy. I'll give you a cushy rug and some fluffy pillows. I'll dress you up pretty, too. Like a harem girl, with a gemstone in your navel."

A beat of sensual silence skittered between them, and Ethan waited, his heart picking up speed. Was she envisioning herself as his bejeweled slave, touching herself for him?

He searched her gaze. By now his heart was thudding in his jeans, giving his erection a pulse. "Will you do it?"

"Yes." She sounded wildly aroused, too.

Unable to suppress the urge to kiss her, he lunged forward and covered her mouth with his. In the midst of tangling with her tongue, he opened her robe and pushed it from her shoulders, leaving her bare. He smoothed his hands along her spine. Her skin was soft and warm, slick from the oil massage.

"Stay with me," he said, refusing to drop the vacation issue.

She leaned into his touch, finally giving into his persistence. "Okay." Her voice was breathy.

Damn. He clutched her ass, dragging her front against his fly. If being naked in his embrace was the deciding factor, he was going to keep her naked all the time.

"I'll have to talk to my boss at the museum." Kiki pressed closer, looping her arms around his neck. "But she already knows about you, so hopefully she'll understand and let me have the time off."

"What do you mean, she already knows about me?"

"She knows Amber has been trying to set us up."

"Amber was a good matchmaker."

"So it seems." She rubbed against him. "What size cage are you going to put me in?"

"One that's big enough for you to sit in front of the bars with your legs spread."

She shuddered in his arms. "I must be crazy."

Beautiful crazy, he thought. He was going to fuck her hard and deep. But first she was going to perform for him, feeding his harem-girl fantasy.

Ethan scoured three different wardrobe closets until he found the perfect outfit, which consisted of body glitter, no top, and a pair of genie pants that billowed on the sides and were slit provocatively in front.

He added a navel jewel, wide bracelets, and a jangling belt. He didn't put her in a veil, because he wanted to see her expression when she made herself come.

He did, however, instruct her to enhance her eyes with smoky shadows and Cleopatra-style liner. For her hair, he wanted it half-down and half-up, the curls falling haphazardly.

When his living, breathing masterpiece was complete, he admired her exotic beauty. She was everything he'd imagined.

He took her to the Red Room and made her wait while he draped the interior of the cage in flowing fabrics and soft pillows.

"Are you ready?" he asked, opening the cage door.

She nodded shyly, keeping her sultry eyes downcast and playing her part to perfection. Or maybe she really was feeling shy. Maybe the enormity of what she was about to do was weighing on her modesty.

She entered the metal confinement and got on her knees, assuming the slave position.

His kitten was learning fast.

He closed and bolted the door, and when she finally lifted her gaze, she looked at him as if he really were some sort of prince.

And that made him want to keep her locked up forever.

Seven

As silence sizzled between them, as Kiki gazed at her lover, she wondered how being imprisoned by him could seem so romantic. Yet oddly enough, it did.

She waited for him to speak, but he remained quiet. He simply looked at her while she looked at him.

A pin could've dropped.

Finally, he dimmed the lights and lit some incense, creating an even softer ambience. Then he got a chair and placed it in front of her cage.

Excitement bundled beneath her skin. But so did her nerves.

After he sat down, he undid the snap on his jeans, apparently making more room for his hard-on. She couldn't help but notice his distended fly. In fact, she studied all of him: his smooth, muscular chest, his rippled abs, his denim-clad legs, the heavy leather motorcycle boots on his feet.

As she lifted her gaze to his face, to those stunning blue eyes, he said, "I'm ready to watch the show."

Her breath whooshed out. Why on earth had she agreed to do this? What was it about him that lured her into the forbidden?

"What are you waiting for?" he asked.

"Nothing." Fighting her emotions, she propped a pillow behind her back and opened her legs, exposing herself through her crotchless genie pants.

"That's nice," he told her. "Very pretty."

She actually felt pretty. But she felt vulnerable, too.

"How many girls are in your harem?" she asked.

"Is that question part of this fantasy? Of the characters we're pretending to be? Or do you want to know for real?"

"For real." A harem in the BDSM glossary was a group of subs who served one or more Doms. In this case, she was asking about women who served him exclusively.

Typical of his gender, he got evasive. "Why does it matter?"

She glanced at the angel on the wall. There were at least twenty redheads at his feet. "It just does."

"I don't keep count."

Instinctively she clamped her legs shut. "I don't want you being with anyone else while you're with me."

"Since when does a sub give orders to a Dom?"

"I can't share you. I don't do that sort of thing."

"But you'll climb into a cage and tell me what *I* can and

can't do? You've got moxie, Kitten. I could walk away and leave you in there. I could make you stew in your own juices."

"I'm not wet," she challenged.

"The hell you aren't."

Okay, so maybe she was. Maybe dressing up like a slave aroused her, but she was still keeping her thighs together.

He shot her a frustrated look. "If you want out, use the safeword."

"I don't want out." She glanced at his fly. He was still raging hard. "And I don't think you want to let me out."

"If you weren't such a newbie, I'd paddle your ass."

"I didn't agree to be spanked."

"Yes, you did."

Did she? At this point, she couldn't remember half the stuff she'd said yes to. "What's so wrong about not wanting to share you with your harem?"

"And what makes you think that I want to be with anyone else while we're together?"

Was he making a commitment? Was he agreeing that while they were lovers, she would be his only sub, his only harem girl?

To show her appreciation, she opened her legs again.

He scooted forward in his chair. "I really should paddle your ass."

She didn't respond. She was trying to be a good sub.

"Don't just sit there. Touch yourself."

Reacting to his order, she dipped a finger into her pussy and spread the moisture around. She wanted to please him. She wanted to please herself, too.

"Good. Now lick it off."

She tasted her finger.

"Do it again."

She repeated the process. But this time she pinched her clit while she was down there, reminding him of their rough play, of the clamp he'd made her wear.

He watched her, hunger deep and raw in his eyes.

She could only imagine how she looked, her navel jewel shining, her skin shimmering with body glitter.

Arousal hit her hard and quick, and she moaned and stroked herself softly, soothing the self-inflicted pain.

"Do you like doing this for me?" he asked.

"Yes." She liked showing him how pink and moist she was. She liked massaging her aching clit.

"Move closer to the bars."

She got as close as she could.

"What are you thinking about, Kitten?"

"Getting nasty." She envisioned rubbing herself all over the cage door.

"How nasty?" he wanted to know.

She told him, and he wet his lips.

"Try it," he coaxed.

Kiki did her best. She stood up, even though there was barely any head room. From there, she pressed provocatively against the metal.

Ethan's breath rushed out. "I swear you're one of the hottest girls I've ever been with."

"I don't know where it comes from." And if she thought too deeply about it, she would be embarrassed about being so bold.

"You make me want to collar you. Damn it, why do you

keep doing that to me?" He sounded pissed. But he sounded desperately aroused, too.

Unsure of what to say, she fell quiet. But she kept sliding along the metal, making herself feel good and letting him watch. As she moved, her jangling belt chimed.

"You should have been an exotic dancer." He angled his head, enthralled with the show. "I'm going to buy a stripper pole and install it in my bedroom just for you."

Feeling sleek and beautiful and oh so crazy, she nodded her approval. If he wanted her to dance for him, she would. But for now, she was being his harem girl.

She reclined on the pillows again, rocking her hips and touching herself, spreading her legs dangerously wide.

"Look at you." He praised her. "Look at my Kitten."

"I can't help it." She was getting close to a climax, and she needed to show him how glorious she felt with the lights turned low and incense sweetening her arousal.

His voice turned hot, rough, powerful. "I should do it, too. Right on you."

She knew instantly what he meant. He was threatening to stand up, to move closer to the cage, to stroke his big, erect cock and shoot his semen through the bars, creaming her with a warm, sticky mess.

But he didn't. He only said it to plant the image in her mind, to make her feel more like a sub.

And it worked. Torn between fear and excitement, she almost begged him to do it. Then her imagination took a shaky turn, and she pictured him in a cage, performing for her and spilling all over himself.

Caught in the throes of an erotic battle, she lifted her ass in the air and rubbed her clit even harder.

Coming in a state of lust and confusion.

⌒

After Kiki's breathing returned to normal and she sat upright, gazing at Ethan through post-orgasmic eyes, he opened the cage door.

She exited her confinement and walked straight into his arms, where she shivered against him. He stroked a hand down her hair, wondering if the cage had been too much for her.

"Come on. You need to relax." He took her hand and led her to the bathroom.

While she waited in her costume, he filled the tub with warm water. He opened a cabinet, looked though the products he kept on hand for his lovers, and chose a citrus-and-strawberry body wash.

Kiki removed her skimpy clothes and got in the tub. Ethan turned on the jets.

"This feels nice." She sank into the scented bubbles. "Are you going to join me?"

He shook his head, then said, "I'm sorry if I've been pushing you too hard." He had to keep reminding himself that this was only their first play date.

"It's okay. I like it. But maybe if we switched once in a while it would be easier for me to—"

"Don't start in about that." He sat on the edge of the tub. No one was going to make a sub out of him, least of all her. "I should have just spanked you and gotten it over with."

She made a face, and he wished she wasn't so damned appealing. He watched her wash the glitter off her body. She opened her legs and soaped her pussy, too. His cock tightened in his pants.

"Am I a SAM?" she asked.

A smart-ass masochist, he thought. A sub who challenged her Dom, who enticed him to punish her. "Sometimes it seems like you are. But I don't think you're doing it on purpose." He lifted his eyebrows. "Are you?"

"No, but I've always had a stubborn streak."

"Did you get in trouble a lot when you were a kid?"

"All the time." She sighed. "In high school, Kaylee Dion was forever in detention. I was a regular Breakfast Clubber."

"Kaylee?" He picked up a washcloth and motioned for her to turn around so he could wash her back. "Is that your real name?"

"Yes, but I nicknamed myself Kiki when I was a toddler, because I couldn't say Kaylee."

He sponged soap and water over her skin and dampened the loose tendrils of her scarlet hair. "Kiki suits you."

"So does Kitten. I like hearing you say it."

He nuzzled her shoulder. She tasted as fresh as spring, as sweet as summer. No damn wonder he wanted to collar her.

Frustrated, he pulled back.

She turned back around, and their gazes locked. "What's wrong?"

"Nothing."

As time elapsed, he gave in to his frustration and leaned over to kiss her. He wasn't sure why. Other than that he needed to restore their connection.

Her eyelids fluttered, but before she got too dreamy, he flicked water at her, encouraging her to finish her bath.

When was she done, she stood up, and so did he, reaching for a towel to dry her off. He supplied another monogrammed robe, too. They'd left the other one on the floor in the playroom.

Once she was bundled up, he hugged her.

"Sweet aftercare," she said.

"I told you I was good at it." Rough play and warm embraces. He wasn't sure what kind of man that made him.

"Was Javier ever gentle with Nicole?" she asked, still snuggled against him.

"He didn't practice aftercare if that's what you mean. But I think he tried to treat her right."

Kiki stepped back and crossed her arms, as if she'd gotten a sudden chill. "Did she love him?"

"Yes." That much was clear from Nicole's writings. That much Ethan knew.

"Did he love her?"

"She wanted to believe that he did, but . . ."

"You're not convinced?"

"No, I'm not." The love thing was a major issue for Nicole. Too major, he thought. As far as Ethan was concerned, it had destroyed her and her husband.

"Can I read her next letter?"

He raised his eyebrows. He'd been doing that a lot lately. "You think you deserve a reward?"

"I was good in the cage. Or sort of good. Or—" She stopped, flustered and glancing around. "Oh, God."

"What's wrong?"

"I think she's here. In this room with us. I've got that being-watched vibe again."

Ethan checked out their surroundings, too. But he didn't feel anything.

"I think she's upset," Kiki told him. "I don't think she liked what you said about Javier not loving her."

Great. Now he had a temperamental ghost on his hands. "I can't change the past for her, and neither can you. Javier was what he was."

Kiki expelled a heavy breath. "She's fading."

"What?"

"I can hardly feel her anymore."

"That was fast."

"Maybe her energy isn't that strong. Maybe she's struggling to be near us."

"And maybe you're imagining her."

"Stop doubting me, Ethan."

"Fine. Whatever. Just get your ass in bed so I can give you the letter."

She hesitated, but only for a moment. When they exited the bathroom and reentered his suite, she followed his instruction.

At this point, he couldn't tell if she was being genuinely good or if she was only doing it to get her reward.

Either way, he still wanted to dominate her.

Was it a lost cause? Would he ever control her completely? Or was he delusional, thinking he could make a loyal sub out of a woman as headstrong as Kaylee Dion?

Regardless, he collected the letter and dropped it onto her lap, where it fluttered before it settled.

Creating a soft, paper wedge between them.

My Dearest Thinking Woman,

Lenore devised a daring plan and convinced me this was my only recourse, my only chance of survival. As you know, Papa's health continues to deteriorate and we have but a few cents to our name.

Lenore arranged a private meeting with Mr. Curtis, and she and I joined him in the hotel parlor—a grand room decorated with craftsman furniture, exquisite paintings, and elegant sculptures.

He ordered coffee, tea, and sweets to be served, and we sat across from him, sipping hot drinks and eating frosted cakes and fruit cobblers.

Mostly I moved the sugared delicacies around on my plate. I was far too nervous to fill my stomach. Lenore quite enjoyed herself, taking second helpings.

Mr. Curtis occupied a willow armchair made of basket-style weaving and cushioned in velvet. He drank black coffee flavored with a spot of whiskey.

"Are you here to purr at my feet?" he asked me.

Lenore jumped in and responded, "She most certainly is not."

Mr. Curtis eyed his friend, then turned his dark gaze on me. Steam rose ominously from his clear glass cup. "You can't speak for yourself?"

"Of course I can." Was my voice vibrating? Scraping along my windpipe? I cleared my throat, then sipped my tea, hoping the honey I'd added would help. "I'm not here to beg."

"Then what's this about?" As always, he watched every move I made, making me terribly self-conscious.

I glanced at Lenore, and she gave me a reassuring nod. My hands were beginning to tremble. I put my teacup and saucer on a side table to keep from rattling the china. Struggling to stay calm, I lowered my hands to my lap and locked my fingers.

"Well?" he asked.

I glanced at Lenore again. She was scooping the last of a meringue-topped torte into her ruby red mouth. She looked as madly voluptuous as ever, with her brazen dress and passionately styled hair.

"Tell him, dear girl," she said.

Could I do this? I asked myself. Could I go through with it? Air rushed from my lungs. Mr. Curtis swept his sensual gaze over me, making me feel naked. I rubbed the bare portions of my arms, wishing I'd worn a full-sleeved blouse.

"Oh, for heaven's sakes." This from Lenore, who took the lead. "Nicole is prepared to offer herself to you, Javier." Before he turned smug, she added, "As your wife."

"My w-wife?" He stammered over the last word, losing a bit of his polish.

"You want to bed her, don't you?"

"Yes, but—"

Lenore cut him off. "Nicole is a good girl who should be

honored with a marital vow. If you want her, you'll have to take her as your bride."

"Fuck that," he said.

"Fine." She brushed a crumb from her napkin-draped lap. "We'll find another wealthy suitor to consider our offer."

That was a lie, of course, a ploy to get Mr. Curtis's attention. Lenore and I had discussed it ahead of time.

His scowl turned lethal. He looked as though he wanted to send both of us flying across the room. "Who?"

She responded, "I know plenty of men who need wives."

"Old fat farts who'll slobber all over her."

I wanted to cringe, but I didn't dare react in a negative way. There were no other prospects, old or young, robust or trim. Mr. Curtis was my only hope.

Lenore then said, "Her father is ill, and she needs a husband. She'll do what's necessary to survive."

"Last week all she needed was a job." He turned his glare on me. "And now she's gunning for a husband?"

I felt queasy, listening to them argue over me. I summoned the courage to speak, to back out of the deal. "I'll still take the job."

"The hell you will." Lenore refused to let Mr. Curtis off the hook. "Javier is going to put a ring on your finger. If not him, then someone else," she said to chide him.

He set his jaw. "It's not going to be me."

"Too bad. Considering how beautiful she is. How sweet and pure. Can you imagine the wicked things you could teach her? As your spouse, she would be beholden to you."

He shifted in his chair. "Stop trying to swindle me."

"Why? Because our proposal is making your cock hard?" The actress snared a bite of peach cobbler, breaking off a piece with her thumb and forefinger and popping the treat into her mouth. "I mean, truly, what could be more delicious than dominating your own innocent wife?"

With the darkest of scowls, he rose to pour himself a belt of whiskey, without the coffee.

While his back was turned, she patted my hand. I wondered what she'd meant by him "dominating" me. I leaned over to whisper, to ask her, but she shook her head, shushing me.

I had mixed emotions about marrying Mr. Curtis, and now I was even more nervous. When I'd first arrived at the hotel, Lenore had warned me not sleep with him. She'd told me that he would chew me up and spit me out, but she felt differently now. She claimed that, as his wife, I could eventually bring him to his knees. She'd come to see what she believed was genuine strength in me.

He spun around. "This is bullshit." He downed the whiskey. He actually looked tempted to get drunk, to swig the entire bottle.

"Call it what you will." Lenore was obviously pleased by his frustration. She even planted a pretty smile on her lips. "But hurry and make your decision. We have other fish to fry."

"You're a conniving little bitch," he said to me.

I didn't take kindly to his insult. My hackles were raised. If I'd been a dragon, I would've blown fire in his handsome face. "I am no such thing. I'm a decent girl trying to save her father. Papa needs a home, medical attention."

"Does he know you're negotiating a marriage deal?"

"No. I haven't discussed it with him."

"If I married you, I'd only want you for sex. Dirty sex," he punctuated.

"As will her other prospects," Lenore chimed in. "My goodness, Javier, who wouldn't want to train her to be naughty? If I were a man—"

"Shut up!" He snapped at his friend. "Just shut the hell up."

Unaffected by his ire, she shrugged and picked at the cobbler again.

He stared me down, and I wondered if I could truly bring him to his knees. A man so hard, so cold, so calculating?

"You'd have to obey me in bed," he said. "No matter what I want, no matter what I desire, you'd have to see to my needs."

"Are you speaking hypothetically?" I tried to appear more composed than I was, to keep from fidgeting. I could've used a shot of Mr. Curtis's whiskey, and I'd never consumed alcohol before. "Or are you agreeing to marry me?"

My question caused Lenore to sit upright, to quit popping crumbling bits of cobbler into her mouth. "Are you, Javier?"

He made a bitter sound. "I suppose I am. But if she doesn't hold up her end of the bargain, I'm keeping mistresses on the side. I won't be trapped in a sexless marriage."

"Honestly." Lenore rolled her long-lashed eyes. "Once you get a taste of her, you won't want anyone else."

He had better not, I thought. Or I would skin him alive. No husband of mine was making love with other women.

"You're sending Candace back to wherever she came

from," I said, *making my first wifely demand.* "*You're putting her on a train. Today.*"

He seemed suddenly amused. His lips tilted a fraction. "*May I at least fuck her one last time?*"

"*You may not!*" *I wanted to throw the remainder of my tea at him. His devilish grin made him look much too charming.*

"*Then you should make up for Candace's absence,*" *he said.* "*You should take her place tonight.*"

Caught in his rogue-about-town smile, I stalled, and Lenore gave an unladylike snort, protecting the only asset I possessed. "*You won't take her virginity,*" *she informed him.* "*Not until you're legally wed.*"

"*I won't deflower her.*" *He downplayed the importance of my maidenhead.* "*She can use her mouth on me instead.*"

My cheeks flamed in what I knew must be crimson colors. Embarrassed by his suggestion, by my own imagination, I envisioned kneeling between his legs while he opened his trousers and brought my face to his—

Lenore's voice interrupted my thoughts. "*She's going to remain pure. On all counts.*"

He cursed, then surprised us with "*I want a church wedding.*"

"*You do?*" *I gaped at him.*

"*I'm a devout man.*"

"*You are?*" *Now Lenore was gaping.* "*Since when?*"

"*Since always.*" *He appeared quite serious.* "*I was an altar boy at the cathedral.*"

"*Who knew?*" *She shifted her gaze to me.* "*Are you Catholic?*"

I shook my head.

"Then I suspect you'll have to convert to marry Javier in the church."

"She will." Mr. Curtis angled his head at Lenore. "Would you like to be my best man?"

"That isn't funny." But regardless, she laughed. Then she popped up to kiss his cheek. "I'm so proud of you."

"For wanting to fuck a virgin badly enough to marry her?" He slanted me a midnight glance. "She better be worth the trouble."

"The best always are," she reassured him.

I prayed that I could live up to her claims. At the moment, I just wanted to run and hide. What did I know of pleasing a man, of succumbing to his every desire?

He addressed me in a gruff tone. "I want you to wear silk and lace and all the trimmings. I want you to look like a virgin bride."

"And I want you to tell my father that you love me," I responded.

He stepped away from Lenore and moved in my direction. "You expect a lot out of me."

"Please. I can't bear for Papa to know the truth."

"That you're sacrificing yourself to me?"

"Papa admires you. It would make him happy to think that you loved me."

"I'll pay for his medical expenses and help him get strong enough to walk you down the aisle, but I won't spin a lie. I won't pretend to love you."

"Then I'll pretend enough for both of us."

"*Do as you wish.*" *He ran his knuckles across my cheek.* "*As long as you give me everything I need.*"

Everything sexual, I thought, his touch making me weak.

We stared at each other, until he removed his pocket watch and checked the time. "*If I'm going to send Candace home, then I should tell her the news.*"

"*Of your upcoming nuptials?*" *Lenore seemed gleeful.* "*Wouldn't I love to be a fly on the wall during that conversation!*"

He turned to leave, then glanced back at me. "*When I send you into town to have your wedding gown made, order some pretty lingerie, too.*"

I nodded, fear washing over me.

As soon as he was gone, I got Lenore's attention. "*What sorts of dominating things is he going to do?*" *She'd mentioned once before that he had unusual sexual habits, and now I was trying to make sense of it.*

"*Oh, dear, girl. It's best if we don't discuss that.*"

"*Why?*"

"*Because you'll fret over it, and you have enough on your mind.*"

She was right. So I didn't ask her again. I simply waited to become his bride.

And accepted my fate.

Eight

Kiki wanted to read more. She wanted to absorb every word Nicole had written about her life with Javier.

Silent, she studied Ethan. He was next to her in bed. He'd removed his boots, but he was still wearing his jeans.

"Do you have any pictures of them?" she asked.

"Actually, I do. After I bought the letters, I tracked down their wedding photo."

"Oh, my goodness. Really? I want to see it." Prior to meeting Ethan, she'd Googled Curtis House and uncovered a few articles that had mentioned Javier and Nicole, but there were no pictures. At the time, it hadn't mattered. Now it did.

Ethan didn't respond. Was he contemplating the importance of the photograph? Was he debating if he should hold back and use it as one of her future rewards, the way he wielded the letters over her?

God, she hoped not. His control was driving her crazy.

"I want to see it," she said again. She couldn't help but identify with Nicole, especially with the gentle haunting of her ghost, with the loneliness Kiki felt whenever Javier's troubled young wife was near.

"It's in the parlor."

"The same parlor where the marriage negotiation took place?"

"Yes. But it's off-limits to my guests. I keep that room locked."

She studied him again, thinking how intense he looked with his black hair and angular features. The Santa Fe sun was seeping through the windows, highlighting the darkness that seemed to shroud him. "Why?"

"Because that's where I keep family photos. Pictures of myself when I was a kid and all that."

Ethan Tierney was getting more complicated by the minute. "And you don't want anyone to see them?"

"They're personal. They don't have anything to do with my lifestyle, with what goes on here."

"Your self-portraits are personal, too. And you let other people see those."

"That's different. That's my art."

"Painful art," she commented.

"That's how I express myself."

Unable to stop herself, she reached out to smooth a strand of his razor-sharp hair.

His reaction to her comfort was a frown, so she drew her hand back. Kiki had never dealt with a man like Ethan. Her ex-husband hadn't shielded himself from her. He'd been an open book. Tough and critical, but open.

"You're a mystery," she said, thinking out loud. "And he's an authorized biography."

Ethan squinted. "What?"

"You and my ex. You're nothing alike."

"Is that good or bad?"

"Good.". And a bit bad, she thought. At least with her ex she knew where she stood.

"I'm not that much of a mystery," he said. "I'm just a little fucked up. But lots of people are."

The urge to be affectionate returned, but she refrained from touching him. He was good at giving aftercare, but he wasn't good at receiving it.

"What's your ex's name?" he asked.

"Wyatt Palmer. He's an education administrator. We met at a Phoenix museum where we both worked. But that didn't make him an artsy guy. He was into the corporate end of it."

"So, you're originally from Arizona?"

Kiki nodded. "I moved here after the divorce." She leaned on one elbow. "How did this conversation turn into a free-for-all about me?"

"A few tidbits isn't a free-for-all."

"It is compared to what you're willing to share." She flashed what she hoped was an engaging smile. "Will you take me to the parlor? I'd like to see your family photos. I'd like to know more about you."

"Not right now. I need a little more time before I open old wounds."

And bleed all over her? The way the Red Room angel was bleeding all over his subs? "Can I at least see Javier and Nicole's picture?"

"Sure. I'll get it and bring it in here."

She stayed under the covers and watched him walk away. Within the span of a day, she'd posed for erotic pictures, played a wild array of BDSM games, gotten hooked on historical letters, and felt the presence of a sad and lonely ghost.

Her life had never been this eventful, not until Ethan had seduced her into his world.

He returned with the photograph, sat on the edge of the bed, and handed it to her, glass side down.

"You framed it," she said, before turning it over.

He shrugged. "It seemed like the thing to do."

She flipped the picture right side up, her heart instantly bumping in her chest. The image depicted an elegant, vintage couple, posing properly for the camera. Nicole, a petite blonde with ethereal features, stood beside her tall, dark, and dashing husband, clutching a cascading bouquet of assorted flowers. Her softly beaded gown featured a high-neck collar, gathered sleeves, a fitted waist, and a flowing skirt with a cathedral train. It was everything Javier had requested. She embodied a virgin bride, right down to the delicately laced veil.

"They look amazing together."

Ethan agreed. "Because they're so different from each other."

"He looks exactly the way she described him." Kiki traced

Javier's image through the glass. "Like a matador." His crisp, finely cut suit was as traditional as her gown, and his thick, ebony hair was combed straight back. "Did she document their wedding night?"

"Every caress, every kiss." Ethan grinned. "Every knot in the rope he used to tie her to the bed."

Kiki's jaw went slack. "He didn't do that to her their very first time." She scrunched her face, trying to imagine being a young, nervous bride. "Did he?"

The grin widened. "He might've. Or not. Only the great and powerful bondage artist knows for sure."

Lord, he was gorgeous when he smiled. Of course he was handsome when he was brooding, too. She nudged his ribs, using the corner of the frame. "You're as bad as he was."

"I am, aren't I? I think Javier would have liked me. We would've been friends." He took the picture away from her and set it on the nightstand. "I was an altar boy, too."

"You were not."

"Yes, I was."

He seemed sincere, so she assumed that he'd been raised in a religious home, maybe even gone to a parochial school. "For how long?"

"For a long time." He managed to continue their conversation while opening her thick white robe, stripping her bare, and climbing on top of her. "I was a good kid until I got obsessed with girls."

Her heart pounded provocatively in her chest. "How old were you when that happened?"

"The typical age, I guess."

He lowered his head to kiss her, and she pressed against him, mesmerized by the strength of his body, the warmth of his touch, the dizzying taste of his lips.

Snap. Lock.

While their mouths were hotly fused, he cuffed her wrists, using the built-in restraints on the bed and making her his prisoner. She got nervously aroused, and he deepened the already carnal kiss.

Finally, when he came up for air, they gazed into each other's eyes. His were getting glassy, but that was what happened when he morphed into Dom mode. He all but hypnotized her.

"I'm going to leave your legs free," he said.

"So I can wrap them around you when you're inside me?" She could tell that he was more than ready to fuck. He'd been waiting all day.

He answered her question with a quick nod, then produced the black silk sash that had come from her original robe, which, as far as she knew, had been left on the studio floor. Somehow, he'd managed to set it aside for future use. Not only was he was a hypnotist, he was a magician, too.

"You're going to blindfold me?"

"Unless you'd prefer that I didn't, unless you want me to save it for another time."

As a child, she'd been afraid of the dark. Of course she'd outgrown that fear a long time ago. She hadn't even thought about it until now.

"I can handle it."

"You won't be able to see the things I'm going to do to you."

"I know." But as long as he didn't do anything they hadn't already agreed upon, she would be okay.

Wouldn't she?

Sensing her apprehension, he gave her a reassuring kiss, and it worked wonders. She melted into his embrace.

Without thinking, she tried to put her arms around him, only to encounter her roughly restrained wrists.

Damn.

"I should be used to this by now," she whispered against his kissing bandit mouth.

"Being chained up? It's still new."

"There's more to come," she commented.

"A lot more. I can't wait for you to stay with me, so we can do this every night. We'll fly to L.A. for a few days, too. To go to my favorite sex club."

Kiki hadn't considered traveling or going to public places with him. She could only imagine how decadent his favorite club was. "You're going to keep me busy."

"You're my only sub right now."

Meaning what? That she had a lot of spiked shoes to fill? She didn't want to think about the other women in Ethan's harem. She totally understood how Nicole felt, insisting that Javier send Candace packing.

"Are you ready?" he asked.

She wasn't sure. Regardless, she said, "Yes."

He used the blindfold, tying it around her eyes, and as everything went dark, she caught her breath.

"You look beautiful like this, Kitten."

"I wouldn't know."

"Trust me, you do."

Trusting him was a significant part of their relationship.

"Do you want another kiss?" he asked.

"Yes. Please." A princely kiss, she thought, from a fallen angel.

He settled his lips against hers, and her senses heightened. His heartbeat seemed stronger, and his cologne smelled spicier. Even his jeans seemed scratchier. Everything about him magnified.

He kissed his way down her body, sending delicious shivers along her skin. Grateful that he hadn't restrained her ankles, she opened her legs, hoping, praying that he would find his way there. With his mouth, she thought. She wanted him to use his tongue.

He stopped to nibble her stomach, and she smiled in breathy anticipation.

"That tickles."

"I could make it hurt."

A chill ran through her.

"Good pain." To prove his point, his nibble turned to a full-fledged, teeth-sinking bite.

Shit.

She arched and moaned. The newly born masochist in her loved it, but the other side of her, the rebellious girl she'd always been, wanted to torture him right back.

"I'm going to get you for this," she said.

"Like hell you will."

How could he be so loving one minute and so rough the next? He moved lower, spreading her labia with his fingers.

She wished that she could see him, that she could watch. She cursed her blindfold, then she cursed him.

Until he lapped at her pussy.

Suddenly she praised the ground he walked on.

"One of these times, I'm going to pierce you," he said. "Right here." For effect, he licked her clit.

Kiki rocked against his tongue. He was referring to needle play, temporary piercings with sterile needles of various gauges.

"Maybe I should get the real deal," she ground out, fighting pain and pleasure. Just like that, he was using his teeth again. "I know a guy who has his cock pierced."

"A guy you fucked?" He sounded jealous.

"No. He's my boss's boyfriend."

"Then how do you know intimate details about him?"

"She told me."

"Women talk too much."

"It's our nature."

"Are you going to tell her about the things I've been doing to you?"

"Yes. And I'm going to tell her how big and beautiful your cock is, too."

"Oh, yeah?" He went down on her in earnest, rubbing her cream all over his face. She could hear the honey-slick swish of her own juices, and it was a hot, nasty sound.

Being blindfolded was scary, but it was sexy, too. She liked listening to him pleasure her; she liked being chained to his bed like a human sacrifice.

She liked it so much, she teetered on the edge of sanity, whimpering and writhing.

"I need to come." She panted, praying that he would give her permission.

He didn't respond, leaving her in the dark in more ways than one.

"Please," she implored him.

After a few more begs, he allowed it to happen, so she let herself go, shaking and shivering in hedonistic heat.

"Beautiful Kiki," he said.

She all but purred. He was back to being loving. He kissed her weeping sex, then rose up, shifting the covers.

"Now I'm going to make you do it," he told her.

"Do what?"

"Kiss me down there."

When his zipper rasped, she knew he was removing his jeans. She waited in the dark, listening to him get undressed.

His weight dipped into the bed, and she felt him crawl across her body and kneel over her face. Or she assumed that was the position he was in. She couldn't be absolutely sure. He hadn't made contact.

He was being so still, so quiet, making her even more aware of being blindfolded.

Finally, he moved lower and the tip of his cock touched her lips.

"Do it," he said.

"Yes, sir." It was oddly arousing to kiss his penis without seeing it. The blow job she'd given him earlier was rough and erotic. This seemed softly sensual.

"Keep doing it."

Kiki got sweetly stimulated. She knew it was crazy, but

granting his request made her feel warm and dreamy, especially when she heard his breath hitch.

"I love dominating you," he said.

"I love it, too." Even if her curiosity about switching was getting troublesome. To quell those thoughts, she showered him with more sub love, inhaling his musky scent.

He turned around on her face and nestled his balls against her lips. It was an extremely Dom thing to do, and she enjoyed being subject to his sexual whims. But she secretly envied his power, too.

Gauging his expectations, she kissed his entire genitals, revering his balls and his cock.

He lowered his head, going sixty-nine, and she moaned her silk-wrapped excitement. He licked her while she used her mouth on him. She lapped lusciously at his hardened length. She nursed the bulging tip, too, sucking and swirling, intent on pleasing him.

He rocked back and forth, and Kiki wondered where he'd learned to maintain an erection. He could stay hard for what seemed like forever.

Not that he wasn't leaking pre-cum. She sipped the salty drops. But that was nothing compared to the way he dived into her, working her vulva and teasing her clit.

Ethan was a master at oral sex. No doubt he kept his harem happy. Kiki couldn't control herself. She bucked against his mouth, desperate for another orgasm.

This time she didn't ask for permission. She just came. He didn't reprimand her, and she breathed a sigh of shivery relief.

He didn't come, but she assumed he was saving it for their joining. He removed his body from hers and said, "You made the sheet damp."

"I know. I can feel it."

"You're even more beautiful now than before."

"Will you kiss me again?"

"Not yet. Not until I'm fucking you."

Her pussy contracted just thinking about it. "It's finally going to happen."

"Yes, it is." He sounded wildly aroused. She heard him tear into what she assumed was a condom.

In anticipation, she opened her thighs as wide as she could, going spread eagle for him.

"Is that your way of inviting me inside?" he asked.

"Yes." Deep inside, she thought.

"This is how missionary should be."

"With the woman restrained and blindfolded?" It certainly put a spin on the conventional position.

"Absolutely." He slid between her legs and cupped her ass, lifting her off the bed a smidgen. A gust of air escaped her lungs.

He didn't go slowly. He entered her hard and rough, plunging straight in. Kiki would've clawed his back if her hands had been free.

"Mercy," she moaned.

He fucked her full tilt, his big, blasting penis sliding all the way in, then nearly all the way out. She tried to envision the expression on his face. Were his eyes closed? Were his features taut? Were lines bracketing his mouth?

His mouth . . . .

"Kiss me. Please."

Although he swooped down and granted her pleading request, it was more of an attack than a kiss. Their tongues wrestled, their teeth clashed, their lips bumped in bruise-marring lust.

Sex had *never, ever* been like this.

With each thrust, the attack got more and more brutal. She was being pillaged by her lover, and she thrived on his bondage-driven hunger.

"Damn you," he rasped against her ear.

"Damn me why?" She wrapped her legs around him, squeezing tight. He all but hammered her into the bed.

"This makes me want to collar you."

"Then do it." At this crazed point, she was willing to be any kind of slave he desired, as long as he kept fucking her hard and fast.

"I can't."

"Then don't." What she was supposed to say? She could barely think straight, let alone help him come to a rational decision.

"You're driving me crazy."

Likewise. "Maybe we should collar each other. Maybe we should make it mutual."

"Stop talking about switching." He pinched one of her nipples, using his thumb and forefinger like metal vise grips.

"Ouch!"

He tweaked her other nipple. "You need to learn to behave."

She rattled her restraints. The tit torture felt incredible, but it hurt like a mother, too. "Maybe I'm sick of being in chains." Of giving him all the sexual power.

"Shut up, Kitten. Or use the safeword."

Not on her life. She was grateful that he was still thrusting inside her. Because she was losing her mind to this man.

She swallowed her pride and apologized. "I'll try harder. Okay?"

"You keep saying that."

Without warning, he pulled off her blindfold, and she found herself staring into his sizzling blue eyes.

Ethan looked so strong, so passionate, so annoyingly captivated by her, she could barely breathe. He reached between their bodies and stroked her clit.

He was going to make her come while they were staring at each other, and he was going to come, too. She could feel the pressure building in his loins.

One, two, three . . .

She counted the heart-thundering seconds.

. . . four, five, six . . .

He pushed deeper.

. . . seven, eight . . .

He rubbed her clit harder.

. . . nine, ten . . .

She gasped.

. . . eleven, twelve . . .

He removed her restraints.

. . . thirteen, fourteen . . .

She put her arms around him.

. . . fifteen, sixteen . . .

They both started to shake.

. . . seventeen, eighteen . . .

They climaxed in unison, lust exploding through their joined bodies, making everything disappear except the harshly tender closeness of being together.

Nine

The following evening, Kiki had dinner with her closest friends: Mandy Cooper and Amber Pontiero. Mandy was Kiki's boss and the director of the Santa Fe Women's Art Museum, and Amber, of course, was the rich and beautiful heiress who'd served as Kiki and Ethan's matchmaker.

The women dined at a late-night café a block off the plaza. Amber had chosen it. She gravitated to small, hip eateries, and this one stayed open until three a.m., a rarity in Santa Fe.

Enjoying one another's company, they shared a wobbly table that overlooked Water Street, ate hamburgers, and sipped imported beer.

Mandy had agreed to give Kiki the vacation time she'd requested, which would officially start next week. Until then, she would be completing her current workweek. But Kiki didn't mind. She thrived on her job. Being a historian was her passion.

Mandy reached for a second napkin. At thirty-eight, she was the least trendy of the three women, with her soft, mink brown hair and ladylike manners. But that hadn't stopped her from having a heated affair with Jared Cabrillo, a party boy ten years younger than she was. She'd fallen desperately in love with him, his tribal tattoos, and his penis piercing. He loved her, too. They were blissfully happy and living together at his ranch.

"You seem a little nervous about staying with Ethan," Mandy said.

"I am," Kiki admitted. "He overwhelms me."

"I would imagine bondage and domination does that to a girl." Amber pursed her glossy pink lips. As always, she looked sixties mod and contemporary chic. "I'd never let a guy tie me to the bedpost."

Kiki would've gaped if she hadn't had a hunk of hamburger in her mouth. She swallowed the food and swished it down with pale lager. "Then why did you set me up with him?"

"Because you're you, and I'm me." The fashionable brunette picked delicately at her high-caloric meal. "And I pegged you for the kinky type."

"This from Ms. Ménage? You're the queen of threesomes, Amber."

"That's a different kind of kink. And don't act as if you're not interested in group sex."

Kiki got defensive. "So I like to watch. That isn't the same as doing it."

"Maybe not, but it still puts you two kinks ahead of me."

"So I'm more perverted than you are?"

"I didn't say that." Amber smiled and lifted her beer. "We're both naughty, darling."

"Not me." This from Mandy.

"Oh, right. You and Jared are saints."

"Compared to you and Ethan, we are." She turned toward Amber. "And you and Jay and Luke."

The heiress lined up three fries on her plate. "That was a one-time thing."

"Only because Jay and Luke went back to California." Kiki watched her friend move the fries closer together, twisting and turning them into a potato ménage. Jay and Luke were L.A. actors Amber had seduced at a Santa Fe party. "You could go see them."

"I could, I suppose. But what's the point?"

"Oh, I don't know. Some fun in the sun. It's not as if you don't have a California residence, too. Your family has houses all over the globe."

Amber shrugged, and Kiki realized that the devil-may-care brunette had gotten uncomfortably attached to Jay and Luke, or as attached as someone like her could get.

"Ethan is going to take me to L.A." Kiki shifted the topic back to her lover, giving Amber a reprieve. By now, the three fries were tangled in a tight ball. "To go to his favorite sex club."

"So you can watch other people?" Mandy asked, rejoining the conversation.

"I guess so." Kiki laughed a little. "I hadn't really thought about what we were going to do there." She leaned forward, addressing both of her friends. "Can I tell you something that's troubling me?"

"Of course you can." Amber spoke up, seemingly grateful that she wasn't the only troubled female at the table. "You can tell us anything."

"I've been fantasizing about dominating Ethan, and I'm afraid that the more I'm around him, the more I'm going to obsess about it."

"Why does that matter?" Mandy's BDSM knowledge was limited.

"Because he would never switch," Amber explained. "That's one of his hard limits. Totally nonnegotiable."

"Exactly." Kiki sipped her beer. "I need to get it out of my head." But that was easier said than done. She kept picturing herself dressed like a dominatrix and wielding a whip. Not that she knew how to use one, but she could learn.

Mistress Kitten.

Like that was gonna happen. She frowned at her food, then glanced at Amber. "How did you meet Ethan?"

"An old acquaintance of mine used to be one of his subs. She was a natural redhead, too. But she wasn't as sweet as you are. Or as feisty."

The compliment made Kiki happy. The other redhead didn't. "Do you know him very well?"

"Aside from his art, his money, and his BDSM habits?" Amber laughed. "Is there more to him than that?"

"I think there's a lot more."

"Don't get in too deep, darling. I only introduced you to him so you'd have an erotic playmate." The fashion heiress turned away from Kiki to give Mandy a pointed look. "Sex isn't supposed to lead to love."

The museum director grinned, unfazed by the scolding. "Sorry I erred."

"You're forgiven. But you," Amber warned Kiki, "better not make the same mistake."

"Who, me?" The independent divorcee? The girl itching to switch? "Not a chance."

"You've already got a lovelorn ghost hanging around."

"That doesn't mean I'm like her." Earlier, she'd confided in her friends about Nicole, and unlike Ethan, they absolutely, positively believed that she was real.

"Just be careful, darling," came the final warning. "Of him and that poor ghost."

Early Friday evening, Ethan wandered through his house, thinking about Kiki, thinking about Nicole, about Javier, about himself. His mind was moving in what seemed like a hundred different directions.

Kiki was scheduled to arrive soon, and he was preparing for her visit. He was searching for Nicole, too, going from room to room, attempting to feel her presence. But she was nowhere to be found.

Was she even real?

"What about you?" he said out loud, talking to Javier. "Are you here? Can you prove Kiki's ghost theory?"

Nothing. *Nada.*

Ethan shook his head. What was he trying to do, conjure

the other man's spirit so they could do some male bonding? So they could communicate about how fucked up they were?

Flustered, he entered the Gold Room and glanced around. This was one of his favorite playrooms. It was a bit garish, he supposed, with its ornate gold-leaf décor, but he liked the shimmering effect.

He moved forward and gazed at the angel. In this depiction, he was dipped in gold paint, from head to toe, much like the Bond girl in *Goldfinger*. He looked like a statue, except for his feathery wings, which, as always, were horribly tattered.

Ethan suspected that Kiki was going to stare at it when she saw it, especially since this was the room he'd readied for their next scene.

He'd already draped a luxurious sheet across a bondage table and arranged hot wax supplies.

"You did this to Nicole before it was fashionable," he said to Javier. "You did everything to her."

Naturally, there was no response, no ghostly reaction, nothing that identified Curtis House as being haunted.

Ethan was met with eerie silence.

"Did you love her?" he asked.

Once again. Silence.

"You didn't, did you? But then, how could you? Men like us don't fall in love." Because falling in love was a form of submission. The most brutal form, he thought. What could be more submissive than entrusting your heart to someone else?

Ethan's cell phone rang, jarring him from his emotional thoughts. He checked the display screen. It was the security guard at his gate.

He answered the call. "Yes?"

"Miss Dion just arrived."

"Thanks." No one got onto the property without being signed in at the gate, including his lovers. "Tell her I'll meet her out front."

"Will do."

He ended the call and took one last look at the hot-wax setup. Javier had used tapered candles, which were reflective of his era, but Ethan preferred a variety of multicolored votives.

Anxious to see his new sub, he headed in her direction. By the time he got outside, she'd already parked her car and was climbing out from behind the wheel.

She looked as gypsy as ever in a rose-print dress with a fringed neckline and hemline. The cotton trim fluttered as she moved.

He approached her, and they took a quiet moment to lock gazes. They hadn't seen each other in almost a week.

"Hi," she finally said.

"Hi," he responded, and touched the fringe at her neckline. "Did you know that my family is in the textile business?"

"Really?" She seemed intrigued by his sudden admission. "Is that how they made their fortune?"

"Some of it."

He had no idea why he'd been compelled to mention his family. Was it because he knew Kiki was interested in that side of him? In the family photos he kept in the parlor? None of his other subs had ever asked to see pictures of him when he was a kid. None of his other subs had been especially curious about his roots.

Ethan cleared his mind. "Where are your bags?"

"In the trunk." She used an electronic key to open it. "I brought a lot of stuff with me, for here and for our trip to L.A."

"No problem." He walked around to the back of the car. "I'll get them."

"Did you dismiss your staff again?"

"Not completely. My chef and his crew are on call. I figured we could cook for ourselves, unless we're craving something fancy." He removed her luggage and placed it on the ground. "I arranged for my housekeepers to come by twice a week." He paused, realizing he should have given her a choice. "But if you want hotel-type service, I can bring everyone back."

"So I can order cocktails by the pool? Or have a maid draw my bath?" She flashed a sweet smile. "I'd rather be alone with you."

"So I can deliver cocktails and draw your bath?" He leaned in to give her a quick kiss. "The only time you'll get treatment like that from me is during aftercare."

"You already did the bath thing." She nudged him for another kiss.

He obliged, then said, "Next time I'll chain you to the tub."

She gave a little shiver. "That's not aftercare."

"No, it isn't." But he wouldn't be filling the tub for her or washing her back. When the time came, he would be doing much rougher things. Caught up in the roughness, he reached around to manhandle her ass, pulling her tight against him. "I'm glad you're here, Kitten."

Her breath hitched. "Me, too."

"Let's go inside and get you settled."

"Okay." She clung to him for a moment longer.

They entered the house, and he carried her bags to his suite. While she unpacked, he sat on the edge of the bed and watched her.

She glanced at the nightstand. "You left Nicole and Javier's picture in here."

"It's a nice picture." And he was hoping it would bring him closer to Nicole's supposed ghost, but it hadn't.

She continued to gaze at the wedding couple. "I could stare at them for hours."

"Because they look so good together?" He sent her a Dom's smile. "So do we. When you're all tied up and I'm fucking you."

Kiki tossed at him what was in her hand—a neatly folded blouse—and it unraveled in front of him. "You haven't tied me up yet. Not literally. Not with rope."

"I was speaking metaphorically. And I'll get around to using rope." He picked up the blouse and inspected it. The fabric was soft and silky, like her skin. "The twisted kind that leaves marks."

Her eyes went wide. "Permanent marks?"

"It's temporary. But it lasts for hours." A sexy reminder of adult play. He stood up and extended his hand. "Come with me. I want to show you something."

"Is it my painting? Did you finish it?"

"No. Not yet." He was still working on the portrait of her. He was pouring his heart into it. "I want to show you the Gold Room."

"That sounds pretty. For a dungeon," she added.

He led her to the playroom in question.

"Oh, wow. It's beyond gold. The angel, too." As expected, she stared unblinkingly at his self-portrait. "He's as beautiful and tortured as the rest of them." She turned to face him, empathy in her eyes. "Do you want to talk about it?"

"I didn't bring you in here for a therapy session." He didn't want to start the first day of her live-with-him vacation stripping away the layers of his soul. "I brought you here so you could see what I have in store for you."

Curiosity piqued, she looked around and spotted the hot-wax setup. She inched closer to the sheet-draped table, the multicolored candles.

He could tell from her expression that she was excited, but a little scared, too.

She picked up a votive and tipped it sideways, much in the way Ethan was going to when he dripped the melting wax onto her.

"I wonder if Nicole will let it happen," she said. "If she'll let the wicks stay lit."

Well, hell, he thought. "If she doesn't, I'll burn those damn letters of hers."

"You wouldn't dare." Kiki put down the candle. "Promise me you won't."

He didn't respond, hoping to call Nicole's bluff, if she was lurking nearby in an invisible haze, if she was eavesdropping.

"Ethan, please. Promise me."

"I'm not promising a thing." He would never set the letters on fire, but he wasn't admitting it out loud.

"If you do I'll never forgive you."

"Then your ghost better behave when I'm lighting the candles."

"Maybe if you were nicer to her, she would be *our* ghost."

How was he supposed to make nice with an entity that wouldn't appear to him, that wouldn't let him feel her presence? "I put her wedding picture on my nightstand. That should count for something."

"It does." Kiki softened her tone. "I can only imagine how nervous she was that day."

He couldn't help but notice the girly emotion in Kiki's eyes. "Do you want to read the next letter?"

"Oh, yes. Please." She latched on to his offer like a lifeline, letting him know how important Nicole and Javier had become to her.

Ethan completely understood. He'd bought Curtis House because of them. The other couple mattered to him, too.

My Dearest Thinking Woman,
As I stood in the bridal room of the church, Lenore came up behind me and smoothed my veil. I could see our reflections in the mirror. I looked more beautiful than I'd ever been, but I looked lost, too. Vulnerable in a way that only a woman selling herself into matrimony could.

As you know, preparations for the ceremony had moved at a spinning pace. A team of seamstresses worked endlessly on my dress, and I studied Mr. Curtis's faith, becoming a newly baptized Catholic convert.

With each day that passed, Papa marveled at Mr. Curtis's wealth, power, and prestige. When my future husband said, "frog," the entire town of Santa Fe hopped to its feet. There was nothing he didn't demand; nothing he didn't get.

A wedding of this magnitude would normally take months, maybe even a year to plan. Mr. Curtis finalized it within weeks.

And during that time, our relationship remained distant. I'd yet to call him by his given name, and he hadn't kissed me or courted me in any way.

"Maybe I should tell you about Javier's sexual habits," Lenore said.

"Now?" In less than twenty minutes I was scheduled to walk down the aisle. *"I thought you decided it was best not to tell me."*

"I know, but . . ." She released my veil and adjusted the bodice of her dress. She was my maid of honor, and she looked stunning in pink silk. *"I'm concerned that if I don't tell you, you'll be even more frightened when he does the types of things he does."*

I released a pent-up breath. *"Then say what you feel must be said."*

"He likes to use ropes, Nicole."

"Ropes?" I didn't understand.

"To tie up his lovers."

"That's madness." Beneath my exquisitely beaded gown, my knees nearly buckled.

"Maybe so. But it arouses him. He also favors blindfolds. And hot wax—" She stopped talking as my face went pale.

"He's going to tie me up, blindfold me, and burn me?"

"I don't think it burns. But I've heard that he does naughty things with unlit candles, too."

"Please, don't tell me any more."

"From what I understand, his lovers enjoy having these things done to them."

"I won't."

"Maybe you will."

"I won't," I insisted. How could I? If I did, I would be just as depraved as the man I was about to marry. It was bad enough that I'd allowed him to tease me that day in town, to make me wonder what watching an orgy would be like.

"I'm so sorry, dear girl." Lenore took my hand and held it. "But I still think you'll be able to bring him to his knees."

"And melt his cold heart?" I didn't see how that was possible.

"Maybe his heart isn't as cold as it seems. Look what he's done for your father already."

"Yes, of course." By now, Papa had a private nurse, and the medical care he was receiving was worth my sacrifice. "I'll just have to pretend that Mr. Curtis's deviations excite me."

"That's the spirit." Lenore managed a light laugh. "Wives are often the most accomplished of actresses. They commonly feign passion."

"So I won't be any different than most?"

"Not in the least."

I didn't want to be like all of the other miserably married women out there. I craved warmth and tenderness. Lovemaking so sweet and sugary, it crystallized.

"Maybe you should allow him to have mistresses," Lenore said when she caught sight of my expression. "Maybe—"

"*No!*" *In spite of Mr. Curtis's bone-chilling perversions, I refused to share him. Once we exchanged vows, he would be mine. He would belong to me.*

A devil. A rake. A rope-wielding rogue.

She studied my washed-out appearance. My color hadn't returned. "Let me rouge your cheeks. Let me put a little life back into you."

Lenore worked her theatrical magic and my reflection glowed. Although I was beautiful once again, I was still frightened inside.

A knock sounded at the door, and I flinched.

"It's all right, dear girl. It's probably your father."

I nodded. The time drew near for him to walk me down the aisle. I put on a brave front, and Lenore answered the summons. Sure enough, it was Papa.

I could tell that he was tired from being up and around all day, but he still looked dapper in his dark suit and white tie.

Pride shined in his eyes. I'd lied and told him that Mr. Curtis loved me and that I loved him. Papa was thrilled.

If he knew the truth, he would've died to save me from my peril. But keeping him alive was my objective, so I smiled like a joyous bride.

Lenore handed me my bouquet and arranged the train on my dress so it would glide accordingly.

"I have to join the processional," she said. She would be preceding me down the aisle and taking her place with the rest of the wedding party.

I thanked her, and we exchanged a secret look. My heart was beating so fast, I could feel it in my throat.

"You look like a princess," Papa told me when we were alone. "I wish your mother was here to see you."

"I wish I remembered her."

"We loved each other so." He reached for my arm. "And now it's your turn to marry the one you love."

There went my heart again. Thumping madly. Would I have fooled Mama the way I was fooling Papa? Or would she have seen through my ruse?

He escorted me around the building and toward the entrance of the church, where we waited in silence.

As a sacred song that had been chosen for our walk down the aisle began to play, I put one foot in front of the other.

I held firmly to Papa's arm. Even as frail as he was, he seemed stronger than I was. I was grateful to have him to lean on.

Mr. Curtis stood at the altar, watching me with a solemn expression. I tried to avoid his pitch-black eyes, but our gazes locked. Candles illuminated the church, reminding me of the wicked things Lenore had said.

The things Mr. Curtis was sure to do to me.

Papa whispered that we were almost there, as if I were eager to reach my bridegroom.

Then it happened.

Papa handed me over to Mr. Curtis, and in a mind-blurring ceremony and Nuptial Mass, I became his wife.

Ten

Ethan and Kiki sat on the balcony attached to his suite. Dusk had long since fallen, and the sky shimmered in soft, silken hues. Ethan couldn't have painted a prettier picture, particularly with city lights spinning pinwheels into the night.

"Now I'm even more fascinated," Kiki said.

"With Nicole and Javier?" He could tell the other couple was firmly rooted in her mind. But they were rooted in his, too.

"All I can think about is their wedding night and what it must have been like. Do you know how badly you're torturing me, making me wait to read the next letter?"

Yeah, he thought. Power was a beautiful thing. "A Dom's gotta do what a Dom's gotta do."

She made a pissy expression. She was so cute, so sweet

and feisty, he tapped the tip of her nose just to watch it wrinkle.

"What happened to everyone?" she asked, throwing him off-kilter.

He dropped his hand. "Everyone who?"

"Nicole's father, Lenore, Candace. What happened to all of them after Javier and Nicole died?"

"Why do you care about what happened to Candace?"

"Why wouldn't I care? She was part of the past, and that makes her seem like part of what's happening now."

He knew she meant the haunting, the ghost, the Curtis House legacy that hadn't existed until Kiki had showed up to claim it.

Not that he didn't identify with her interest in the past. He'd made a point of knowing everything there was to know about the people who were once connected to his house.

"Candace made a few of those old swashbuckling films," he said. "But her biggest claim to fame was being the mistress of a studio head from Famous Players-Lasky Corporation."

She frowned her confusion. "Famous Players who?"

"That was Paramount before it became Paramount. Of course after the studio head replaced her with a younger mistress, she was out on her ear. She did some vaudeville stints to survive, but vaudeville was starting to die out, so that didn't last long. After that, the Depression hit and she went through some hard times, washed-up and penniless."

"Now I feel sorry for her."

"She came out of it all right. Lenore befriended her."

Kiki's eyes went wide. "Lenore?"

"Apparently there was this love-hate thing between them. No matter how much they bickered, there was always something drawing them together."

"I guess that makes sense, considering that they looked somewhat alike. That they vied for the same roles." Kiki's hair blew across her cheek, and she did her best to tame the curls, batting them gently away. "Did Lenore ever make any movies?"

Fascinated by his lover, Ethan studied her. She was perched on the edge of her chair, immersed in their conversation. "She had a few film irons in the fire, but they never panned out. It didn't matter, though, because she gave up her career to help Nicole's father run the hotel."

"Oh, wow. He inherited Curtis House?"

"Javier didn't have any family left, and since his wife died with him, it went to her next of kin."

"Tell me more about him. What was his name?"

"Theodore West. Mostly he went by Ted. After his daughter died, Ted asked Lenore to remain at Curtis House with him. He recovered fully from his tuberculosis, and he and Lenore made it through the Great War and the Roaring Twenties. But the Depression wiped them out, and they lost the hotel. Ted got sick again, this time with pneumonia, and died in 1931."

"Is that when Lenore reached out to Candace?"

Ethan nodded. "By then they were both in their forties, old and poor and fighting stereotypes."

Kiki, the historian, agreed. "Forty wasn't the new thirty back then."

"Especially for former beauties, who, according to the day's standards, had lost their looks. But they banded together and made a life for themselves. In their golden years, they opened a string of movie theaters and retired in wealth and grace."

"Oh, that's nice." A heavy breeze stirred the fringe on Kiki's dress. "That makes me happy for them." The same breeze played havoc with her hair, rioting curls around her face. Rather than temper them like she'd done before, she turned away from the wind, leaning more fully into Ethan.

Christ, she was beautiful. He almost picked her up and carried her to the Gold Room, until she asked, "Did Ted ever publish any poems?"

"No."

"Not even the one he wrote about Thinking Woman?"

Ethan shook his head. "He was so distraught after Nicole died, he destroyed all of his poems. He probably would have destroyed her letters, too, if he'd known they existed."

"Then who preserved them? How did they survive?"

"Lenore found them in Nicole's belongings and held on to them. She was ninety years old when she died in 1978, and the letters were auctioned off during her estate sale. From there they made their way to private collectors."

"And then they reached you."

"And you," he said, including her in the mix.

That made her smile. "Now I want to read them even more."

"And you will. Little by little." Moment by moment, he thought. Needing to touch her, to arouse her, to dominate her, he focused on the Gold Room again. He got to his feet. "Come with me, Kitten."

"To burn some candles?" she asked softly.

He nodded, and she stood up and offered him her hand. Giving him permission to play.

⌒

Naked, with her hair wrapped in a towel, Kiki reclined on a sheet-draped table and watched Ethan check the supplies.

When he placed a knife next to the votives, she tensed.

A *knife?*

She distinctly remembered saying no weapons play. "Why do you need that?"

"It's nothing to be afraid of. It's for removing the wax afterward."

"Oh, okay." Funny, but she hadn't considered the cleanup. Still, it was a bit scary to think of him chipping dried wax off her body with a knife. "It looks sharp."

"Relax, Kitten. I've done this hundreds of times." He tucked her hair a little more fully under the towel, putting stray tendrils to rest.

That was so her hair didn't get accidentally singed. He'd taken all the necessary safety precautions, including keeping a fire extinguisher nearby. He'd even shaved her pussy, sparing her the discomfort of wax adhering to the small strip of hair that used to be there.

"I'm going to strap you down," he said.

She tried for a little humor. "When don't you?"

He chuckled and snapped her into a set of wrist cuffs,

which were already attached to the table. "In this case, the restraints are for your own protection."

"So I don't flinch and knock a lit candle out of your hand?"

"Exactly." He moved around to the end of the table and clamped her ankles.

"I feel like an experiment. Like I'm in Dr. Frankenstein's laboratory."

He chuckled again. Clearly, he was enjoying himself, thriving in his element, preparing for his favorite type of play. "Do you want me to spike my hair and put on a lab coat?"

His short, black hair was already a little spiked, but not in a mad-scientist way. "No, smarty. But a kiss wouldn't hurt."

"Listen to the sub. Trying to give orders. If I decide to kiss you, it'll be after you're covered in wax."

"The ghost might not let you."

"The ghost better."

"Did she like it when Javier did this to her?"

"She was scared out of her wits."

"So she *didn't* like it?"

"I didn't say that. I just said that she was scared."

"Did she—"

"Shhh," he scolded. "Stop talking about her."

"I didn't say her name." Because it was still the safeword. Because saying Nicole's name would mean that Kiki wanted to end the activity, and she didn't. "I didn't say anything that would—"

Ethan interrupted. "If you keep talking about her, she might show up."

Minding her Dom, she stayed quiet, and he removed a lighter from his pocket and flicked it. In the silence, he brought the flame to the first votive. The candle burned exceptionally bright.

"No ghost," he said with relief.

By the time he lit all of the candles, the Gold Room sparkled even more than usual.

Kiki inhaled a melee of sweetened aromas. Each votive was scented with a different fragrance. "I'll bet she's leaving us alone purposely."

He stepped back, allowing the wax to heat and pool. "And why is that, Kitten?"

"Because she wants us to have these kinds of moments to ourselves. She doesn't want to intrude."

"Really?" He didn't sound convinced. Nor did he follow his own rule about not discussing Nicole. "She's not above voyeurism. She and Javier used to watch other people have sex. And what about the night of the party? She was there during the threesome. You thought it was a camera, but it was her."

"None of that is the same as watching you and me. What she feels for us is more . . . romantic. Or that's how it feels to me." Deep inside, where Kiki's heart fluttered.

Which wasn't good, she thought.

Ethan didn't respond, and in the awkward lull, the flickering candles created shadows on the walls.

When he turned to walk away, her pulse jumped. "Where are you going?"

"To forget about this crazy conversation and get some ice." He pointed to a metallic freezer. "Right over there."

Ice? She craned her neck to watch him, and he returned with a gold bucket, filled to the brim.

"I hadn't counted on something cold," she said.

"It'll serve its purpose."

She fought a nervous shiver. "I thought it was just going to be hot wax."

"Mostly it is." He dimmed the lights, not enough to obstruct his view, but enough to bathe the Gold Room in a soft glow.

He picked up a votive, and she waited anxiously, wondering what part of her body would be decorated first: her arms, breasts, stomach, legs—

"I'm going to test the temperature of the wax on the back of your hand," he said. "To see how sensitive you are."

Kiki's breath rushed out. That was a possibility she hadn't considered.

He tipped the glass container. Wax dripped out and dropped onto her hand, sparking instant heat.

"Does that feel okay?"

"Yes." It sizzled straight to her bones, but it was a good kind of hot, a good kind of pain. "I like it."

"Then I'll do it some more. I'll do it everywhere."

He used the same candle to garnish her stomach, and her navel jumped, her muscles quavering. She was his lover, his model, his canvas. The wax wasn't falling in sporadic drops. He controlled the way it fell, creating artwork with each and every drop.

Soon a pink rose emerged. He added shadows and highlights, using lighter and darker shades of the same color. Each candle had a purpose, a place in the garden he was composing on her body.

He used sculpting tools to texture his work, to shape the melting wax, to spread it like ambrosia over her skin.

For fine-tuning, he chilled the application with ice and continued his artistic foray, cooling the fire, only to fan the flames once again.

Hot, cold, thick, syrupy.

Slowly, methodically, he elicited carnal sensations.

Yellow daisies dotted her legs, and ivy twined itself possessively around her arms. Two red poppies bloomed on her breasts, where the wax affected her at a feverish pitch.

She gasped, and he reacted by rubbing ice around her nipples and making them achingly hard.

She looked into his eyes. As always, they were glowing, pulling her into their dangerous depths.

"Paint something blue," she panted.

"I will, after I kiss you." He leaned over to claim her lips, to make the moment even more special, more erotic.

His tongue swept her mouth, and the garden on her body tingled. She would have spread her legs if her ankles hadn't been strapped down. Instead, she sighed her sensual pleasure.

"You're being a loyal sub tonight, Kitten."

And he was being a romantic Dom. "Wax play suits us, sir."

"Yes, it does." He kissed her again, then righted his posture and reached for a burning candle. "What kind of blue flower do you want?"

She was still reeling from his touch. "I don't know." All she wanted was for him to brand her in that color.

"How about a bluebonnet?"

She agreed, and he began to craft the official Texas state flower on her thigh, in between the daises.

"We need a toy," he said, stopping abruptly.

"A toy?"

"And I know exactly what it should be."

He crossed the room, his booted footsteps echoing.

He came back with a hands-free, remote-controlled vibrator in the shape of a delicate little bouquet. Attached to it was a long, gold ribbon.

"More flowers?" she asked.

"The sweetest of blooms." He held it up to the candlelight. "Have you ever used anything like this before?"

She shook her head. "I'm not even sure how it works."

"It fits between your legs, and this part," he indicated one of the virgin white petals, "stimulates your clit."

Anxious, her bare-naked pussy clenched.

Ethan didn't undo her ankle restraints to fit her with the vibrator. He simply tied it in place. She lifted her hips to help him accomplish the fitting, and once it was done, she glanced down. The vibrator made her look like a naughty bride.

Not that Ethan was her groom.

She struggled to clear her mind. Now wasn't the time to think about wedding nights. That was Nicole and Javier's territory.

"When are you going to turn it on?" she asked.

"When you're hot and begging for it."

"Sexy hot or wax hot?"

"Both."

Kiki's heart pounded up a storm. She was already excited, and apparently so was he. She glanced at his fly and noticed his hard-on. But when wasn't he aroused? Ethan Tierney was a deeply sexual man.

He resumed playing with the blue candle, dripping it onto her skin, detailing the bluebonnet.

But it wasn't enough. She wanted him to turn on the vibrator. The wax seemed to be getting hotter, the ice cubes colder. Everything was shocking her flesh.

"You okay, Kitten?"

Was he kidding? The blue candle smelled like fresh berries smothered in cream. She squirmed on the table. "I want to come."

"Oh, yeah?" He hovered over her. "How badly?"

She wet her lips. "Badly enough to beg."

He gave her an ice chip to suck on, then finished the bluebonnet, leaving her moaning for more.

Finally, *finally*, he ignited the vibrator, and the device purred gloriously between her legs, rubbing its sweet, white petals against her clit.

Kiki couldn't help it. The bridal sensation came back. She felt like a mixed-up virgin, steeped in a wild deflowering.

A moment later, Ethan Frenched her hard and deep, thrusting his tongue in and out of her mouth. The lovemaking motion pushed her to the edge of bridal hell and straight into clitoral heaven.

Kiki climaxed while he was kissing her, wicked sensations

spiraling through her core. She bucked on the table, thrashing beneath her restraints.

In the dizzying aftermath, she felt as if she'd just taken a big, juicy bite out of Eve's forbidden apple. Only the apple had been dipped in caramel.

No, wait. It was wax.

Ethan was drizzling two caramel-scented candles over her bondage-bound body, sweetening the garden he'd created, making the flowers warm and gooey.

The vibrator kept buzzing, heightening his game. She took a swift breath, knowing it wasn't over. He was going to make her come again and again.

Then, and only then, would he pick up the knife and pry the wax from her skin.

And give her a reward after he was done.

My Dearest Thinking Woman,
There were elegant, white candles everywhere. They shimmered in crystal holders, in wrought-iron candelabras, in Spanish chandeliers that had been made especially for this day.

The reception was being held in the ballroom at the hotel, and Mr. Curtis had chosen the décor. He'd also decided upon the china, the silverware, the table linens, the dinner menu, the music, the three-tiered cake embellished with a cascade of sugared flowers that matched my bouquet.

After the exquisite meal had ended and jovial toasts had been made, it was time for the first waltz.

Mr. Curtis reached for my arm and escorted me onto the

dance floor. Waltzing with him seemed dangerously intimate. Up until this point, we'd done little in the way of
touch. He'd kissed me during the "You may kiss the bride"
portion of the marriage ceremony, but it had been proper
and chaste, and I'd survived it with my breath held deep in
my lungs.

In this bewitching moment, he brought my body close to
his and swept me into a graceful motion. Earlier, the train had
been removed from my dress, but my gown still flowed across
the floor.

"Do you tango?" he asked.

"No," I responded. I'd heard it was a wildly passionate
dance.

"Then I'll have to request a tango and teach you."

"Please don't." It was all I could do to stay on my feet,
much less strut about the floor and pivot like a nervous gringo
in her Spanish husband's arms.

"Relax," he said.

Easy for him to say. He wasn't a virgin on the chopping
block. All eyes were upon us, hundreds of guests, most of
whom I didn't even know. I felt like a tiny glass figure in a
curio cabinet. One false move and I would shatter.

"Maybe I need another sip of champagne." I'd had my first
taste of alcohol during the toasts, and the bubbles had tickled
my nose.

His lips thinned. "And saddle me with a drunken bride on
my wedding night? You shall remain sober."

"Then so shall you." I had no desire to be ravished by a
drunken groom. Not that it mattered, I supposed. A man who

tied his blindfolded lovers to the bedpost and tortured them with burning wax was worse than a drunk.

As Mr. Curtis led me into a dizzying turn, the glittering candles flashed and flamed before my eyes. I prayed for this reception, and especially the upcoming wedding night, to end.

Within the span of another waltz, he gestured for the guests to join us, and the space became crowded with other people.

Several more songs went by, and the father of the bride was encouraged to dance with his daughter. Mr. Curtis bowed to me, leaving me alone with Papa.

My father told me, for at least the tenth time that day, how radiant I looked. But surely he was only seeing what he wanted to see. Our dance was slow and cautious, as he was barely strong enough to lead me. Soon his nurse would insist that he retire to his room to get some rest.

When the cake-cutting time arrived, I stood beside my husband, my heart beating in a sporadic rhythm.

In the Roman Empire, loaves of bread were broken over a bride's head, normally by the groom, and guests were encouraged to eat the crumbs off the floor. In the Middle Ages, tiny sweet cakes were piled high, and the bride and groom were supposed to kiss over them. But mostly the little cakes ended up on the floor.

Times and traditions have changed. Now the bride and groom feed the first piece of cake to each other.

Could I do that? Could I behave playfully with the rogue I'd just married? With a man whose dark gaze penetrated me like the ribbon-wrapped knife in our joined hands?

"Ready?" he asked in his sleek, masculine timbre.

I nodded. His hand was much too possessive against mine.

Together, we cut into the bottom tier and put our shared slice on a plate. The cake was white and the filling was banana cream.

He took the lead, breaking off a small piece and holding it up to me. The groom was supposed to feed the bride first.

I attempted to eat the cake without making contact with him. But it was impossible. He nudged the dessert gently into my mouth, along with the very tips of his fingers.

I wanted to shove him away. With the taste of banana cream on my lips, with the texture of his fingers against my tongue, liquid heat streamed through my body.

When he undressed me that night, would he have to peel my undergarments from my molten flesh? They seemed to be sticking to my skin.

"It's your turn," he said.

I blinked at him. My turn to do what? I couldn't get my bearings. I couldn't recall what was expected of me.

"The cake, Nicole."

Oh, of course. The guests were waiting for me to feed him. My heart wouldn't quit pounding, but I did the best I could, slipping into character and conducting myself like a focused bride. Chipper voices buzzed throughout the ballroom.

I broke off a small piece and offered it to Mr. Curtis. He took the cake readily. He even licked the frothy icing from my fingers, making the crowd clap and cheer.

On the outside I forced a smile. On the inside, I was shaking *desperately.* Mr. Curtis had a wicked glint in his eye. He was the king of his Santa Fe castle, teasing the virgin he'd married, letting her, and everyone else, know that he intended to invoke his husbandly rights and make good use of the marriage bed.

We cleaned our hands and blotted our mouths on damp cloths that had been provided, and a hotel employee cut the cake for our guests.

Coffee, tea, and another round of champagne were served. I tried to steal a drink, but my husband stopped me, reminding me that alcohol wasn't permitted.

"No, Nicole," he whispered. "You mustn't dull your senses."

I spoke just as quietly. "So I'll feel every painful thing you're going to do to me?"

"I promised I would be gentle your first time."

My pulse jumped. "You did?"

He nodded. "When I asked you to be my mistress."

"Yes, but I'm your wife, Mr. Curtis."

"Oh, that's right. My mistake. My promise no longer applies." He leaned in to nip the lobe of my ear, to catch it lustfully between his teeth. "And please, my darling, innocent bride, when you're naked and writhing on my bed, call me Javier."

Eleven

As daylight peeked through the blinds, Kiki opened her eyes and took inventory of her surroundings. She was next to Ethan in his big, four-poster bed, wearing a baby doll nightgown and no panties.

Last night, after the hot-wax play, Ethan had given her Nicole's wedding reception letter as a reward. Then, with her Nicole-Javier fix sated, they'd eaten dinner and gone to bed to fuck each other's brains out. For the fun of it, she'd put on a cotton candy–colored nightie, wondering if her innocent look would excite Ethan.

He'd loved every lash-batting minute of it. He'd restrained her with lace-wrapped chains and asked her if she wanted to call him "Daddy." They'd both burst out laughing, but in the end, the sex had been hell-burning hot and lollipop sweet. They never failed to miss their hungry-for-each-other mark.

Kiki turned to watch Ethan sleep, wondering how long those feelings would last. Did chemistry that strong fizzle out? Or did the fires keep burning? All she knew was that the next two weeks belonged to their affair, to their chemistry, to their heat. What happened beyond that was anybody's guess.

Should she wake him with a kiss or let him sleep? She opted to let him sleep, simply because she enjoyed looking at him. He was naked, but the sheet was draped across his hips, so she couldn't see his nether regions. As for his chest, it was lusciously smooth, and the chain he always wore with the dungeon master key was looped to one side of his neck. She was temped to right it, but she left it alone.

His expression wasn't particularly peaceful, but it wasn't fitful, either. He appeared strong and solid, with his angular features and with his edgy black hair spiked against a fluffy white pillow.

Maybe she *should* kiss him. Maybe she should wake her prince—

Her thought stalled, but not because she wasn't thoroughly captivated by her sleeping lover. Kiki sensed someone leaning over her—someone soft and gentle.

Nicole.

She turned, hoping to see a misty form, but the ghost wasn't visible. Still, she was there. Kiki could feel her.

"Were you watching him, too?" she asked the other woman.

Nicole didn't respond, but Kiki knew that was what she'd been doing.

"He's handsome, isn't he?"

Once again, there was no verbal response. But there was a slight touch, a physical warming. Nicole had put her hand on Kiki's shoulder.

Oh, God, she thought. Javier's wife was in bed with her and Ethan, cuddling up to them, feeding off Kiki's emotions. How bizarre was this? How tragic?

"I was right about you. You do have romantic notions about us. But it's okay. I don't mind." She spoke softly. "I can't wait to read your next letter. Ethan won't tell me what happened on your wedding night, whether Javier restrained you. If he was gentle, if he was rough."

The hand on her shoulder tightened, and a tingling sensation tripped through Kiki's blood. She didn't know what it meant, other than that Nicole had reacted to her words.

"I wish I could see you. Are you wearing your wedding dress? Do you look like your picture?" Kiki angled her head toward the framed photograph on the nightstand. "You were an incredibly beautiful bride."

The tingling sensation got deeper.

Then Ethan's gravelly voice shot out of the silence, making Kiki nearly jump out of her skin.

"Who are you talking to?"

She spun around to face him. He squinted at her, then pulled himself up to a sitting position. The sheet around his waist pooled lower, but not low enough to expose his full nakedness. Kiki wasn't exposed, either. Her lower half was draped with the same sheet.

"Nicole is here." She expelled a shaky breath and pointed

to the blank space behind her. Nicole was still resting a hand on her shoulder.

Ethan frowned, drawing his brows together, creating deep, hard lines in his forehead. "I thought she wasn't supposed to intrude." He made a tight gesture, indicating the state he was in. The outline of his penis, his morning woody, was somewhat apparent, making a slight tent in the sheet. "This is pretty damn invasive."

"Don't get mad. You'll scare her off. Besides, you're covered."

He quit scowling. He wasn't a modest man, at least not around living, breathing women. So apparently he'd decided that a dead woman wasn't much different. "Should I uncover myself? Does she want to check me out for real?"

"I think she just wanted to watch you sleep."

That perplexed him. "Why?"

"Because that's what I was doing, and she . . ."

"She what?" He looked beyond her to the empty space.

Without thinking, Kiki spoke for Nicole. "She likes the way it feels when I get moonstruck over you."

Ethan snared her gaze, dragging her into the brilliance of his eyes. Blue boom. Blue bam. She tried to look away, but she couldn't.

"You were getting moony over me?" he asked. "While I was asleep?"

She shrugged, wishing she'd kept her mouth shut. Silence chopped the air. Even Nicole reacted to the obvious discomfort. Kiki could feel the ghost's bodyless form go still.

"It's no big deal," Ethan finally said, stirring the air again.

Or that was how it seemed. Kiki was able to breathe again. Nonetheless, her heart pummeled her chest.

Especially when he said, "Sometimes I get moonstruck over you, too."

"Really?" Instant warmth bathed her skin. Or was it the sun shining through the blinds, heating the temperature of the room? "You do?"

"Yeah, but like I said, it's no big deal."

Nicole cuddled closer to Kiki, as if to say that it *was* a big deal. But it wasn't, was it? She and Ethan were new lovers. They were bound to have some enthralled-with-each-other moments. Like now, she thought. She wanted to kiss him senseless.

"Mostly it's when your hair blows across your face," he told her. "Or when you twitch your nose and your freckles do this fairy dust kind of thing." His voice turned raspier, more rugged. "Or when you're all sweet and slippery and rubbing against me."

Kiki could almost hear Nicole sigh, and she wanted to nudge the ghost in the ribs, if the ghost had ribs. She didn't need encouragement from the peanut gallery. She was enraptured all on her own.

"Come closer," Ethan said. "So I can feel you."

She knew he meant the bareness between her legs. "Nicole is still here."

"Then tell her to go away."

"I can't do that."

But she didn't need to. Nicole squeezed her shoulder one last time and vanished.

Kiki experienced an immediate sense of loss, of sadness, of frazzled emptiness. "She's gone."

"Then come here."

She wanted to. Lord, how she did. But she held back. "Not until you let me read the next letter. I want to know what Nicole's wedding night was like. I want to know what Javier did to her."

"It was just sex, Kitten."

"Maybe it seems that way to you. But I'll bet it will seem like more to me." Because she was connected to Nicole. Because she could feel Nicole's emotions.

Ethan didn't argue her point. He simply gave Kiki what she craved.

Someone else's wedding night.

My Dearest Thinking Woman,
Mr. Curtis lived on the top floor of the hotel, where the view was even more magnificent. Everything reeked of his money, of his power. The furniture was richly textured, and to me, the brass canopy bed was a testimony of fear.

I stood like an ice sculpture, wearing my gown and trembling beneath it. I was terribly nervous. I kept glancing away, and my eye-contact avoidance annoyed him.

"Look at me," he demanded.

I lifted my gaze to his, and he assessed me in heart-bumping silence. His stare was hot upon my own, and the darkness in his eyes made my trembling worsen.

He barked out another order. "Say my name."

Now? Before I was naked and writhing on his bed?

I wanted to blurt out, "Mr. Curtis." But no matter how I sliced the situation, I'd pledged my troth to thee, and I was bound to obey him. Defiance would get me nowhere.

"Javier," I said quietly.

"Good. Now think of me that way. Use my name in your mind."

Once again, I behaved accordingly, planting his name in my thoughts.

Javier took what appeared to be a pleased step in my direction. Apparently he could see by my expression that I was being a loyal bride. But what would happen later, when I feigned passion? When I pretended to enjoy his depraved acts?

He skimmed my cheek. "Are you afraid of me, Nicole?"

I was not strong enough to lie. "Yes."

"Because Lenore told you about the type of sex that excites me?"

"Yes."

"I cannot help what I am."

"I understand," I said, even though I didn't. I couldn't fathom being aroused by such things. "Ropes and blindfolds and hot wax."

He ran a finger across the seam of my tightly drawn lips. "Sometimes I gag my lovers, too. And paddle their bottoms when they're bad."

Heaven help me, I thought. "I won't be bad."

"Won't you?" He smiled as if my response was part of a game, as if I were a sweet, little toy who'd sold herself to him for rough play.

Which was exactly what I was.

He walked away to turn off the electrical lamps on either side of the bed, replacing them with groupings of lit candles. Under normal honeymoon circumstances, I would have found the ambience romantic.

When he returned to me, I was twisting the lace that cuffed my sleeves.

"Quit fidgeting and undress me," he said.

He wanted me to remove his clothing? I'd expected him to tear into mine first, to rip my dress from the top of the bodice to the bottom of the bell-shaped hem.

I inched closer to him.

"Have you ever seen a naked man?"

"Of course I have."

"In person or in paintings?"

"In paintings, but I know what's what."

"Do you?" Again, he seemed amused. Then he gestured for me to do his bidding, to strip him where he stood.

I started with his tie, loosening the ends and unfurling the elegantly knotted bow. Once the tie was free and clutched in my hand, I didn't know what to do with it.

He noticed my dilemma. "Just drop it, Nicole. Toss it to the floor."

"Yes, Javier." I used his name of my own accord, showing him that I was being good, that he wouldn't need to paddle my bottom.

The tie fluttered to the ground, and I battled with his vest and jacket, then tentatively slid the formal braces that were attached to his trousers off of his shoulders. As I lifted the tails of his starched white shirt, as I tugged the fabric loose from his waistband, his chest rose and fell.

In reaction to me? To my shaky ministrations?

I continued at an inexperienced pace. Finally, I discarded his shirt, and although I didn't touch him purposely, his flesh accidentally preyed upon my fingers. His chest was splendidly formed, and his nipples peaked with small, brown nubs. I skipped past his navel and focused on the front of his trousers, preparing to open them.

Then suddenly I remembered his shoes and socks and got on my knees to remove them, buying myself more time. I could only imagine how I looked in an elaborate silk gown with a delicate veil covering my upswept hair, tending to my husband's feet.

He glanced down at me. I could tell that he was aroused. Not just from the hunger in his eyes, but from the mighty bulge in his trousers. My face was erotically close to his fly.

"Stay there on your knees," he said. "Stay there to undo my pants."

Oh, goodness. My cheeks turned hot.

"Look at you." He continued to watch me, to analyze me. "Blushing like a new bride."

"I am a new bride." Who'd claimed that she knew what was what. Forcing myself to stay strong, I popped the buttons on his trousers, opening them one by one.

I encountered his summer drawers and tried to make haste with them, but pulling them down his hips wasn't an easy task, not when his erect penis sprang free. Proud and thick *and jutting out from a patch of dark hair, it protruded against his stomach.*

While he stepped out of the legs of his drawers, I stared at his arousal. With the foreskin drawn back, the head was big and plumlike. I wondered if it would taste as sweet. Somehow I didn't think so. Sooner or later, I was sure to find out.

Maybe even now, I thought. He very well might push it into my mouth.

"Do you like my cock?" he asked.

"Yes," I responded truthfully. His erection fascinated me. So did his testes. The sacs were drawn tight.

"Then tell me you like it."

I noticed how heavily veined it was. I noticed everything about it. "I just did."

"Say it again. But use cock. I want to hear you talk dirty."

I stalled. I wasn't accustomed to reciting vulgarities.

"Say it, Nicole."

"I like your . . . cock." As soon as the word slipped out, I wanted to swallow it back up. Or was it the body part in question I wanted to swallow? On the day Javier had agreed to marry me, I'd fantasized about sucking him, and now I was on my knees, just inches from his penis.

His cock.

Sake's alive. What kind of woman was I? Excited by naughty words? I couldn't seem to stop the moisture that tingled between my thighs.

He reached out and removed my veil, and I shivered.

Determined to destroy my coiffure, he ran his hands through my hair, dislodging pins and tangling the loosened curls around his fingers.

He kept mussing my hair, making it as wild as a lion's mane. Then he said, "Undo the front of your dress."

I managed a jerky nod and released the pearled buttons, opening my gown until the top of my corset cover was visible. From there, I exposed my corset. The delicately contoured, ruffle-edged, ribbon-trimmed garment hugged my bosom, pushing my breasts forward.

"Now undo that. I want to see your nipples."

My corset laced in front, so I was able to undo the ties while he watched. My ministrations were far from deft, far from seductive. I was as clumsy as a schoolgirl. Javier's penis was still positioned near my face.

Finally, I got my corset open far enough to show him my nipples, and my heart pounded beneath my exposed breasts.

"Very nice. Now stand up."

Fearing that my knees would buckle, I didn't want to rise. But I wasn't brave enough to disobey him. I got to my unsteady feet.

"Remove your petticoat," he told me. "Then take off your drawers. And when you're done with that, get in bed and spread your legs."

"With my dress on?"

He nodded. "I want to admire my bride. I want to see how naughty she looks with her tits spilling out of her corset and her dress bunched around her hips."

What he asked of me seemed embarrassingly lewd. Not at

all what I imagined a lady should do. But none of this was ladylike.

"Are you going to deflower me that way?" I asked.

"When I take you, you'll be naked."

So this was just for fun? A game he was playing?

"Get on with it," he said, wicked as ever.

I wanted to please him, so help me, I did. Yet it was foolish of me to care. He was a sexually depraved man, a scoundrel who'd claimed that he wouldn't be gentle.

So why did I have warm feelings toward him? And what happened to feigning passion? The heat between my thighs was real, and so was the honey-slick moisture.

I removed my flounced petticoat, then got rid of my silk drawers, both of which had been designed as bridal lingerie. As instructed, I climbed in bed and opened my legs. But I didn't hike up my dress.

He approached the footboard. "Are you challenging me?"

I shook my head. The top of my dress remained open, but the skirt was gathered around me like tablecloth. Beneath it my knees were bent. "I'm summoning the courage."

"To show me your cunt?"

My cheeks flamed. "That's a vile word."

"Not to me. I like how it sounds. Show me, Nicole. Show me what I want to see."

I battled for oxygen, for as much air as my lungs could hold. His eyes were pitched with desire, luring me into their sinful depths. Struggling to stay strong, I gazed at his un-abashed nakedness, admiring his body as I bared mine.

Up went my skirt. Just a fraction.

"More," he demanded.

Another bashful lift.

"More," he repeated.

I slid the hem to my thighs.

"Higher," he ordered.

I went all the way, scrunching the fabric to my hips and exposing myself.

He reacted like a man who'd been struck by lightning. He all but jerked forward. "You're more beautiful than I could have dreamed."

"Am I?" I asked, feeling strangely coquettish. "Am I really?"

"Truly you are." He got into bed with me, and the air I'd tried so hard to breathe whooshed out.

In the next instant he was kissing me down there, swirling his tongue over a taut little nub at the top of my vagina as if it were a treat and he was in desperate need of something soft and sweet.

I lifted my dress even higher, mostly so I could watch. I'd fantasized about sucking him, but I hadn't considered him performing the same act on me.

While he licked, he slid his fingers into my center, first one, then two, moving in a warm, copulating motion. Sensation built upon sensation, and I squirmed deliciously against his tongue.

I glanced at the nightstands beside the bed. The candles he'd lit earlier burned softly, but the shadows they created were dark and mesmerizing. The scent of wax filled the air, making me excited, making me afraid.

"Will it always be this way?" I asked.

"What way?"

"Will I always panic about the way you make me feel?"

He looked up and saw me gazing at the candles. "I could use them on you now." He rubbed the taut nub. "Right here. All over your clitoris."

I tugged my bottom lip between my teeth, imagining hot wax dripping between my thighs. Would it burn? Would it scorch my flesh? Would it feel horribly, painfully good? Would it make me as perverse as my husband? "I've never heard that word before."

"It's the part that makes women climax."

"Don't do it."

"Make you climax?"

"Drip candles on me. Not now. Not ever." I didn't want to become depraved.

He whipped a harsh look upon me. "When you proposed this marriage, you promised to succumb to my every desire, to be beholden to me."

"I know, but . . ."

The look turned sharper, slashing the wax-scented air. "Don't you understand? I couldn't stop myself if I tried. It's what I do. This kind of sex sates the monster in me."

To hear him call himself a monster intensified my fear. Yet I longed for more. He kept rubbing my clitoris, making my ache deeper, hungrier, bending me to his will.

His confused wife, I thought, wearing a skewed corset and dislodged wedding dress, with her hard, little nipples exposed and her vulva spread slick and wide.

Javier lowered his head to lave me again, flicking his tongue in butterfly strokes. He'd lied about not being gentle. He treated me with the utmost care, pushing my confusion to gripping heights. Clutching the hem of my gown, I lifted my bottom in the air, presenting my husband with a naughtier view of my nakedness.

He paused to stare up at me.

My breath caught. "Why did you stop?" I needed him to keep going.

"I want you to have what I'm having. To know how sweet and juicy you are."

A sudden rush of embarrassment flowed through my brain, my blood, my lick-me loins. "I couldn't possibly—"

"Yes, you can."

He dipped a finger inside and brought it to my lips, making me taste my own cream. He watched me through erotic eyes, pleased with my reaction. I sucked diligently on his finger, not because I liked the flavor, but because I was aroused by the act itself.

"It's tangy," I said. "Not sweet."

"It's sweet to me. When I eat you, I can taste your innocence."

I reached for him, and we kissed, our mouths fusing. He was on top of me, and the weight of his body pinned me to the bed. Nervously excited, I squirmed beneath him. His cock created friction between my legs.

On and on the kiss went. He behaved like a marauder, pillaging his captive bride. As he took my mouth, he stroked my clitoris, making me burn from the want of him.

Just when I thought I couldn't bear any more, when I was sure that I was going to orgasm, he stopped and flashed a demonic smile, denying me my pleasure.

"Javier," I begged. "Please."

"Not yet."

He tugged on my dress, pulling the wrinkled garment from my body and tossing it carelessly aside. Next, he undid the remaining laces on my corset, divesting me of it, too.

Completely bare, I gazed up at him, my pulse galloping like hoofbeats.

He lifted a long, tapered candle from its holder, and my pulse screeched to a stop.

"Hold still," he ordered, when I flinched. "Or I'll drop this damn thing and burn us both to death."

I didn't move a muscle. I didn't twitch in the least. I was so scared, I refrained from blinking. I even tried not to breathe.

"That's right," he said, praising me. "Stay like that."

In my mind, I made the sign of the cross, asking the saints I'd learned about in his church to protect me.

Was he going to coat my clitoris in virgin white wax? Was that his intension? To brand his innocent wife?

He was a monster, I thought. A carnal beast—a man with a sickness that couldn't be cured. The fact that he was so handsome only made his sickness all the more frightening. Monsters were supposed to be grotesque.

"I'm afraid," I admitted.

"It doesn't matter, as long as you hold still."

He tipped the candle over my stomach. Was he going to

start there and work his way to the intimate area between my legs?

Drip.

A dollop of wax fell, and the heat it produced shocked my skin. Why didn't he just plug an electric lamp into my navel and fray the wire? To me, the sensation would have been the same.

Two more drops fell. Double heat. Double fire.

To keep myself from lunging off the bed, from expressing my discomfort, I watched the flame on the candle. I watched the wax pool around the wick, too. Then I looked at Javier. His expression was wildly intense. He seemed captivated by how desperately I was trying to behave.

"You're sensitive," he said. "Some women feel it deeper than others do."

Lucky me, I thought, grappling the sheet below me, using it as an anchor.

"It will get easier with each drop."

Would it? I wasn't sure if I believed him.

The torture continued. But soon I realized that the pain was in my mind. I was getting used to the heat. My skin was welcoming the fiery sensation. My body was beginning to crave it. But I was still afraid of him doing it to my clitoris.

Thankfully, he didn't.

What he did do was write his name on my stomach. That was how he branded me—with "Javier" in clumpy white letters.

It was a deeply possessive gesture, a statement only a husband could make. Instinctively I knew that he'd never branded another woman in quite the same way. I was oddly touched, emotionally wrought. I wanted the wax to stay there forever.

He returned the candle to the nightstand, fitting it back into its holder. "Now you're truly mine. To do as I want, as I will."

"Yes," I responded dutifully, giving myself over to him.

What came next were four pieces of twisted rope. As soon as I saw them, I warned my fear-struck heart to be still. This was who I'd married. This was part of my vow.

"Put your arms behind you," he told me. "And hold on to the headboard."

I gripped the brass railing, folding my fingers around it. The air in my lungs chopped out. I was trying to relax, but I couldn't. This was how my husband was going to deflower me, bound to his bed like a slave.

He secured my wrists and proceeded to tie my ankles, as well. My legs were open wide enough for him to slip between them. I glanced at his cock and saw how wickedly aroused he was. By now he was leaking ejaculate.

But he didn't take his pleasure. He put his face between my thighs and finished what he'd started earlier. He licked me until I climaxed, until I shook and shivered and gasped in wild spasms.

As I thrashed back and forth, I pulled helplessly at my restraints, and the tension caused the ropes to make marks on my skin.

Another branding, I thought.

He came forward to kiss my lips, to whisper "You're mine" against them, telling me what I already knew.

Then he said, "When I fuck you, it's going to hurt."

I already knew that, too.

He settled between my legs, and when I felt him nudge my entrance, I tensed. He stroked my tousled hair, as if to calm me.

"I'm not going to make it hurt purposely, Nicole. It's something that can't be helped."

Because I was a virgin. Because I'd never had a man inside me. I nodded in understanding, and he pushed forward, slowly, ever so slowly. My inner folds stretched to make room for him, but he seemed too big for my tight channel.

He gazed upon my face, watching me wince, watching me contort my features.

Then . . .

Pow!

He thrust all the way, nearly shredding my chaste body to bits. It hurt so badly, so fiercely that I cried out.

He swallowed my cry with an open-mouthed kiss, and I clawed my own palms. He tried to be gentle, to make it good for me, but the pain continued. Finally, he gave up the fight and used me for his pleasure, pumping hard and fast, taking what he needed.

I lost my maidenhead in a flurry of primal sensations, in rough groans and raging heat. But somewhere near the end, I stopped hurting and looked into his eyes.

He kissed me once again, telling me how perfect I was.

And when he spilled into me, when he bathed me with his seed, I was grateful that he was the man—the monster—I'd married.

Twelve

After Kiki finished reading the letter, Ethan felt compelled to say, "I used to feel like a monster."

She put the correspondence next to Nicole and Javier's portrait on the nightstand and turned to face him, giving him her undivided attention. She seemed surprised by his admission. Obviously she'd expected him to pick up where he'd left off earlier and slide his hand between her legs. But he started a conversation instead.

"Because of your lifestyle?"

"This was before I got into the lifestyle. But it was based on me having those types of fantasies." He blew out the breath he was holding. He rarely talked about his feelings. Expressing himself through his art was easier. "It started when I was about fourteen. I was with a friend, and we were hanging out with his older brother and his buddies. Then someone passed around some S and M magazines. It was more of a dirty joke than anything. Everyone, including my friend, started cutting up and making gross remarks, saying how sick it was. But I got turned on. *Really* turned on. Of course I behaved as if I thought it was disgusting, too."

"And that made you feel bad about yourself?"

"Lord, yes. But I couldn't seem to stop my 'sick' urges. When I went home that night, I masturbated like crazy, imagining that I was doing the things I saw in those pictures. I even wrapped an old bicycle chain around my pillow and pretended that I was restraining a hot redhead. There was a model in one of the magazines who had long, wavy red hair. A lot like yours." He reached out to touch one of Kiki's gypsy curls. "She fueled my first fantasy."

She looked into his troubled eyes. "So that's where your redhead obsession comes from?"

He nodded and released her hair. He'd never told any of his other lovers this story before, least of all any of the redheads. "When I wasn't fantasizing about bondage and domination, when I wasn't jerking off, I was drawing pictures of my fantasies."

"So you were a fetish artist way back then?"

"Yes, but I tore them up after I drew them. I shredded them into little pieces."

She was still looking into his eyes; she was still riveted to him. "I can only imagine how confused you were."

"I did everything I could to cure myself. I prayed. I said extra rosaries. I begged God to make me well." Ethan paused.

"I was too ashamed to tell a priest, though. I couldn't bring myself to say it during confession. I guess because I knew that I'd only repeat the sin, and then I'd have to confess it again and again."

"When did you learn more about BDSM? When did you begin to understand what you were feeling?"

"I did some research when I was an older teen. I wasn't brave enough to look it up at the library, and the Internet was new then, so it wasn't a wealth of information, not the way it is now. But I found a few online articles. I learned that there was a whole community out there, living the way I wanted to live."

"Did that help?"

"In some ways it did, and in some ways it didn't make a difference. I was still afraid that my friends would think I was sick. That I'd be ostracized if anyone found out."

"So you lived a lie?"

"There was no way I was going to ask the girls I dated if I could try it out on them. When I was lucky enough to get laid, I'd have vanilla sex and imagine that I was a Dom. I was always playing scenes in my mind."

Beneath the blanket, Kiki's foot touched his. They were still in bed, curled up together, with the room illuminated in a warm, sunny glow. "When did you have your first BDSM experience?"

"When I was in college, and it was the most amazing, most freeing feeling. That's when I started focusing on fetish art, too. When I quit tearing up my drawings and went public with my work. Of course my parents freaked out. They hadn't sent me to a private art institute so I could become a crazed painter. I was supposed to get my degree and join the family business as a fabric designer." He waited a beat, reliving the turmoil. "Mom automatically assumed that I'd fallen in with the wrong crowd, and Dad wanted me to see a psychiatrist. They were appalled by who I'd become."

"Little did they know that's who you'd always been."

"My saving grace was my grandmother. She convinced them to leave me be. To let me express myself however I chose. But they changed their tune after she died."

Kiki frowned. "Did they disown you, Ethan?"

He struggled to bank the pain, but he knew it wasn't working. He was wearing his emotions on his sleeve. Or his shirtless shoulder, he supposed, considering he was bare. "Yeah, they did."

"I'm sorry."

"I've learned to deal with it."

"By painting yourself as a fallen angel?"

The look in her eyes made him uncomfortable. But it gave him comfort, too. Kiki was more than a sub. She was fast becoming his friend.

"Are you still interested in seeing the parlor?" he asked. "And my family photos?"

Her frown deepened. "You don't keep pictures of your parents around, do you?"

"Yes. But only to remind myself of who they are and why they can't accept me."

"Not because you miss them?"

He copped a half-shouldered shrug. "I suppose that's part of it. But I miss my grandmother more."

Kiki skimmed his jaw, but he felt as if she were grazing his spirit. He took a moment to breathe in the feeling, to put his arms around her.

Then he asked, "So, do you want to see the parlor?"

She nodded and got out of bed, removing her pink night-gown and climbing into basic white undergarments, a gauzy blouse and denim shorts. He got dressed, too, putting on a pair of old jeans.

After a bout of silence, they went into the bathroom to wash their faces and brush their teeth. Later he would shower, shave, and tame his hair.

Together, they left his suite and headed downstairs. He unlocked the parlor door, and they entered a room decorated with cane seat settles, leather cushioned chairs, and sconce lighting. Elegant curtains with double-tassel tiebacks dressed the windows, and a dark oak table held a collection of framed photographs.

Kiki zeroed in on a picture of his parents when they were young and newly married. Ethan leaned over her shoulder and gazed at the familiar image. His mom was a poised and proper brunette, and his dad was tall and trim with jet black hair and powerful blue eyes.

"You look like your dad," she said. "But you resemble your mom, too. They were both really attractive."

"They still are." He showed her a more recent photograph. Or the most recent one he had. "Older, but just as church-and-charity perfect."

She nodded in agreement. "So when did they disown you? How long ago was it?"

"It's been about three years. They sprung it on me right after Granny died. They sat me down and said that I was no longer welcome at their home, particularly during religious holidays. Christmas was coming up, and they wanted to be sure that I knew that I wasn't invited. Not unless I changed the style of my art and denounced my lifestyle."

"That's a heavy cross to bear."

"It was. It still is," he amended. "Especially after all those years I prayed for my 'sickness' to go away. I might not live a conventional life, but I'm still a religious man. My faith still matters to me." He dragged a hand through his sleep-spiked hair. "I needed my parents to love me after Granny died, not make me feel badly about myself again."

"Maybe they'll come around someday."

"Maybe, but I doubt it."

"Is this you?" She pointed to a picture of him when he was about five, a happy little boy on a shiny red bike. "Look how sweet you were."

"All kids are sweet at that age."

"Are you an only child?"

He nodded, wishing he had siblings, wishing there was someone left in his family who cared.

She turned to another photograph, an image of a white-haired woman in gold jewelry and a Chanel suit. "Your grandma, I presume?"

"That was taken the year before she died." His heart warmed. "She was a classy lady. She was an artist, too. But her specialty was fiber art. She's the one who founded Tierney Textiles."

"And now it belongs to your dad?"

"Yes, but she left me her other investments. My net worth actually exceeds my dad's."

Kiki graced him with a grin. "That's a bit of vindication, isn't it?"

He managed a light laugh. He knew she was only trying to make him feel better. "I suppose it is."

She moved forward and into his arms. "I'm glad I'm with you, Ethan. I'm glad you're mine."

He inhaled the fragrance of her hair. Normally he wouldn't allow a woman to claim him, but he knew she wasn't referring to forever. Whatever they felt for each other would eventually end. "I'm yours, huh?"

"You are for now." She kissed him, and he latched on to her hand and took her to the nearest playroom.

To make the rest of their morning shine.

⌒

Kiki marveled at all of the mirrors. They covered the walls and shimmered from the ceiling. Some were simple and others were magnificently ornate.

She looked around for the angel and found him, tortured as ever. In this depiction, he stood naked in front of a tall, beveled mirror. Although he was in fine form, with undamaged wings, the image inside the glass was horribly shattered, distorting his perfection.

She glanced at her lover. Now she understood where his pain came from. Now she understood his self-portraits. And that made her feel closer to him.

Too close?

"Is this the Mirror Room?" she asked, warning herself to relax. When the time came, she would let him go. She wasn't Nicole, and he wasn't Javier, no matter how emotionally similar they seemed.

"It's the Glass Room," he responded.

"That works, too." She noticed glass shelves with hundreds of glass dildos, each with its own unique shape and translucent color. The display was wickedly beautiful. "Are those useable?"

"Absolutely. But we're not going to use any." He butted up against her, nuzzling the entire length of her body, warming her from neck to navel and beyond. "We're going to have vanilla sex."

Her pulse fluttered. "Oh, sure." Regular, traditional sex? In a room cluttered with mirrors and Pyrex phalluses, in a room with a satin-draped bed and the usual array of dungeon furniture?

"You don't believe me?" He stepped back to look at her. "Why don't you take off your clothes and I'll show you."

He made it sound like a challenge. Kiki never could resist a challenge. She removed her top and peeled off her shorts. Sans underwear, she got in bed, waiting for Ethan to follow.

But he didn't. He left the room, promising, of course, that he would be back. So she waited, wondering what he had in store for her. Propping a pillow behind her back, she caught sight of herself. She was flanked by mirrors. Her reflection was visible from every angle.

Feeling self-conscious, she tugged at the sheet, pulling the satin up and covering her nakedness. The last thing she wanted was to sit there and focus on her flaws. She figured most women would have reacted the same way.

Then again, most women weren't having torrid affairs. What was the point of covering up? Ethan would only tear the sheet from her body. No way would he allow her to hide from the mirrors.

Summoning her inner diva, she fluffed her hair and tossed the satin aside, determined to feel pretty.

Ethan returned carrying a glass tray. But before he set it down, he stood at the foot of the bed and stared at her. She could tell that he was pleased with the way she presented herself. Feeling even prettier, she opened her legs a smidgen and made him smile.

Then he moved closer and put the tray beside the bed. It contained bottles of Mexican, Indonesian, and Tahitian vanilla extracts.

"Vanilla sex," he said.

"Are you sure we're not making cookies?" she said, teasing him.

He lifted his brows at her silly joke, but she couldn't tell if he was amused, especially when he said, "I'm going to pour it all over you."

"Me?" Her heart picked up speed. "What about you?"

"I'm the Dom, Kitten. No one pours anything on me."

He was staring at her again, only more roughly this time, making sure, it seemed, that she didn't forget who was in charge.

As if she could . . .

He was reminding her more and more of Javier, and she was as nervous as Nicole.

"Are you going to restrain me?" she asked, trying to shed her vulnerability. Vanilla extract wasn't supposed to be scary.

"No," he responded. "No restraints."

"Why not?"

"Because I want your hands free so you can push your tits together. So I can fuck you there."

"Oh, okay." Was that a dumb response? Kiki was still nervous. Only she didn't know why.

Was it because she was getting closer to him? Because they'd begun to form more than a sexual bond?

Ethan lifted the Tahitian extract from the tray and uncapped the bottle. "This is the sweetest and fruitiest of the vanillas."

"It is?" Was that another dumb response?

"It has sort of a cherrylike, licorice taste." He got in bed and held the bottle over her, then poured it over her breasts, where it stimulated her nipples.

"And this one," he uncapped the Mexican extract, "is smooth and creamy."

He doused her stomach with it, and the liquid trailed down her body in rivulets, pooling inside her navel and dripping between her legs.

"What about the Indonesian vanilla?" she asked.

"It has a woodsy flavor. But I'll save it for later. I've coated you enough for now."

She thought so, too. She was warm and wet, and in spite of her silly joke earlier, she smelled like cookies.

"Push your tits together, Kitten."

She did as she was told, lifting her boobs and squeezing tight.

Ethan unzipped his jeans and dragged them down his hips. His erection sprang free, and Kiki caught her breath. She loved seeing him like that, big and hard just for her.

Between his beautifully formed cock, and the clear, glass shapes of hundreds of artfully designed dildos, she was in phallus heaven.

"I like this room," she said.

"I like you," he responded in a gruff voice.

He got into position, and she waited for him to make contact. He looked incredibly sexy with his stomach muscles rippling and his pelvis jutting forward.

When he slid between her breasts and moved in a sleek, sensual motion, she wanted to eat him alive.

Now he smelled like cookies, too.

He thrust higher, and the tip of his penis bumped her mouth. She darted out her tongue, tasting vanilla on his flesh.

He continued fucking her that way, invading her cleavage and making her lick his cock.

Kiki kept her breasts plumped, shoving them up as far as she could. She went mirror crazy, too. It was like being a voyeur at your own private orgy.

Ethan's rock-hard reflection excited her beyond reason, but so did her own. Her legs were desperately spread, and her nipples were as ripe as cherries.

She wanted to frig her clit, but she couldn't because her hands were plastered to her boobs. She squirmed and moaned, struggling for relief.

"Turn over," he said suddenly.

Lost in the moment, she merely blinked at him.

"Get on your hands and knees."

She snapped out of her confusion and obeyed his order. He got behind her, and she heard him open a drawer beside the bed, then tear into a condom.

He was going to do her doggie style.

Once again, Kiki relied on the mirrors. In this position, her breasts hung down, and her hair was a fiery mane of curls that framed her face. Ethan kissed the back of her neck, making her sigh.

In the next instant, he entered her with a pounding thrust, and she shook and shivered.

In a blast of sensation, he poured a stream of the Indonesian extract down her back.

While dark, amber chills vibrated her body, she pushed back against his thrusts, making the friction deeper, hotter, and wetter.

He moved in and out, his strokes deep, then shallow, then insanely deep again.

When he started licking the extract from her skin, she arched and moaned and lifted her ass in the air. She felt like a dog in heat.

Now all she needed was for him to collar her.

Would he? she wondered. Or would he keep fighting it? And what about her? Would she keep fighting her fantasies about switching?

Everything seemed so uncertain, so crazy and mixed up. He reached around to rub her clit, giving her more of the pleasure she craved. His fingers were damp from the extract, and the sensation made her creamier.

"After we're done here, I'm going to finish your painting," he said. "I'm going to immerse myself in you. In every way I can."

Although his declaration seemed romantic, it also proved possessive. He tugged on her hair, encouraging her to twist her body and crane her neck so they could kiss.

Rough and carnal, he whispered between tongue thrusts. "I want you to watch yourself come."

God, yes, she thought, her breath hitching. She wanted to lose herself in own convulsing reflection. But she wanted to watch him, too.

So, apparently, did he.

When they quit kissing, they both looked up, their gazes meeting in the same mirror.

Together, they watched. While he fucked her, while he stroked her clit, she came first, shuddering in a slick, sugary mist.

Dizzy and replete, she pitched forward, but he didn't let her fall beyond his grasp. He held her so tight and pumped her so hard he nearly knocked the wind from her lungs, forcing her to feel the brunt of his passion.

And right before he came, he poured the rest of the extract down her back, reminding her that he was still her Dom in every hot, hammering, vanilla-soaked way.

Thirteen

Ethan worked most of the day and part of the evening to complete Kiki's painting, and now she stood in his studio, gazing at a stunning image of herself.

Too stunning, she thought. Way too beautiful.

"You made me look better than I do," she said.

"No, I didn't." He studied the portrait with an artist's intensity. "That's how you looked that day. In person and in your photographs."

"I remember looking hot, but not *that* hot." The woman in the painting took her breath away. Her passionately tousled hair was the color of richly textured merlot, and her bare-breasted, chastity-belted body was long, lean, and catlike. With her arms chained to a metal grid and her legs roughly parted with a spreader bar, she was as bewitching as a bondage-bound female could be, especially with a portion of her face hidden mysteriously behind a mask.

He turned his intense stare on her. "You are *that* hot, Kitten."

She wasn't going to argue the point, not with the way he was looking at her. Instead she eked out a shy "Thank you." Kiki couldn't seem to get ahold of her emotions, and she hated feeling this way.

Ethan didn't give her a chance to collect herself. He pounced like the aggressor he was, pulling her into his arms and kissing her.

After all of the sex they'd had, after all of the kinky things they'd done, his kisses still managed to make her weak, especially when he gentled his hold.

Kiki felt as if she were floating, as if her feet were hovering above the floor. She clutched Ethan's shoulders, curling her fingers around his T-shirt.

He softened the kiss even more, and she nipped at his lips, trying to make it rougher, trying to abolish that damned floating feeling. Her eyes were squeezed tight.

"Easy," he whispered, running his hands along her spine.

By now she was digging her nails into his shirt and probably leaving marks on his skin. "I'm trying to stay grounded."

"Grounded?"

"Never mind."

He implemented his magic again, his mouth warm and man-hungry sweet. He tasted as fresh as frosted mint. There was no way she could stay grounded. The length of his body grazed hers, his muscles taut. He cupped her rear and brought her closer, but the gesture didn't strike her as sexual. It seemed loving.

Not Dom loving. Just *loving.*

Surely her brain was frazzled.

Or was it Nicole's brain? Was it Nicole's thoughts mingling with her own? Suddenly she realized that the ghost was behind her, touching the back of her hair, drawing strength from the way Ethan was kissing her.

Panicked, Kiki opened her eyes and pushed him away.

He stumbled to catch his footing. "What the hell was that for?"

Grateful that she'd killed the moment, she felt her panic subside, not completely, but enough for her to catch her breath. "Nicole is here."

"No shit?" He looked around. "Where?"

"She's behind me." She swatted at the back of her hair. Nicole was tugging on one her corkscrew curls. Clearly the ghost was flustered; clearly she hadn't wanted the kiss to end.

Ethan seemed flustered, too. "Why can't I feel her? Why is it only happening to you?"

"Maybe it's easier for her to feed off my energy." Maybe he was too much like Javier. Too strong. Too intimidating. Either way, Nicole was still tugging on Kiki's hair, making her pesky presence known.

"But I want to get to know her." Ethan walked in a purposeful circle, attempting to make contact. He even reached out, trying to touch Nicole.

Surprisingly, it almost worked.

Kiki felt Nicole reach out to him, too. But they never quite connected.

"She's trying," Kiki said.

"Really?" As he angled his head, the skylight showered him in a lapis glow. The halo effect made him look like one of the angels in his paintings.

Moonlight suited him.

"Is she still hanging around for the romance?" he asked. "Is that what she wants from us?"

"Yes."

"What's going to happen when we stop seeing each other?"

Something inside Kiki twisted, creating a knot in the vicinity of her heart. "I don't know. Maybe she'll stop haunting your house."

"Yeah, maybe she will."

Kiki expelled a heavy breath, trying to cleanse her lungs. The knot was getting tighter.

Why? she asked herself. Because she didn't want to think about losing Ethan? Or because Nicole's emotions were still tangled with her own?

Whatever the case, the ghost's energy was fading, as if the tightness in Kiki's chest was too much for her to bear.

"She misses Javier," Kiki said.

Ethan's halo continued to shine. "Then maybe she should float on up to heaven to see him."

"What if he's in hell?" Kiki heard herself say.

He frowned. "For what? Being a Dom?"

"No. Of course not. I didn't mean it like that."

Silence fractured the air, making the walls of the massive studio seem narrower, making Kiki feel as if she and Ethan were standing too close.

"You know what would be romantic?" he said suddenly. "Finding a way to get them back together."

God, she thought. Now her chest really hurt. She gazed in the direction of where Nicole had been, but the ghost was gone. Her energy had faded completely. "I don't see how that's possible."

"I suppose not. Considering they're dead and all that." He shrugged away the idea. "It was a crazy notion. Let's just concentrate on us instead."

"Us?"

"Yeah, you know. You and me."

She got a tender urge to kiss him. But that would only put her back where she'd started, so she refrained.

"When do you want to go to L.A.?" he asked.

"Anytime," she responded.

"Then we'll go this Friday."

Nighttime clouds shifted across the sky, darkening the room and taking away Ethan's halo. That relaxed her a bit.

Then he asked, "Do you think Nicole will be all right while we're gone?"

"I'm sure she'll be fine." Lonely, but fine, she thought. Somehow that made no sense. "Do you think I could read another letter?"

"Right now?"

"Yes."

He agreed without asking for anything in return, proving just how deeply Nicole was affecting him, too.

My Dearest Thinking Woman,
The morning after my deflowering, I awakened alone in Javier's bed. Or should I say our *bed? I lived at Curtis House now, too.*

Naked and slightly sore, I walked to the dresser to retrieve a princess slip to cover myself. It was a long, gossamer white garment that had been made as part of my bridal trousseau. Prior to the wedding, all of my belongings had been brought to Javier's room—our room?—and unpacked by a maid.

I checked my appearance in a dressing-table mirror and wondered where my husband was. Surely he hadn't returned to work during what was considered our honeymoon, leaving me to fend for myself. Surely he was somewhere nearby. Surely he desired me again.

I hoped so. I wanted him to desire me so badly that he would ache with masculine fury.

To calm my morning-after jitters, I brushed my hair, allowing the golden locks to fall over my shoulders and down my back.

My reflection looked positively wanton. My eyes were seductively sleepy, and I had bee-stung lips. Of course the bee who'd stung them was Javier. I could still taste his nectar-flavored kisses.

Completing my toilet, I washed my face with cleansing cream and tissues. Once I made my way to the bathroom, I would freshen my mouth with peppermint tooth powder.

Venturing into the hallway, I peered this way and that. The entire third floor belonged to Javier, with rooms that made up his luxurious quarters, but I didn't want to run across a housekeeping maid or worse yet a male employee. My slip was shamefully sheer, and I was bare underneath.

I dashed across the Spanish-tiled floor and darted into the bathroom.

Then lost my breath.

There was Javier, bathing in the tub, with his knees bent to accommodate the length of his legs and his shiny black hair damp and messy. Rather than being combed straight back as it normally was, portions of it were falling onto his forehead. A cigarette burned in a crystal ashtray on the side of the tub.

"Morning, Nicole." He smiled like the handsome rake he was. "Did you sleep well?"

"Yes, thank you." I stood there in my see-through slip, unsure of what to do. Seeing him like that—wet and naked—made my heart jump. "I came in here to brush my teeth, but—"

"Go ahead," he interrupted. "Brush away. Then you can join me."

My heart jumped again. I wanted him to desire me, and he did. He was assessing me through my flimsy garment, his expression dark and hungry.

Although I was self-conscious about brushing my teeth in front of him, I wanted my mouth to be clean. So I could kiss him, I thought.

I used the tooth powder, tasting the mint when I was done.

"Take off your clothes," he ordered, refusing to let me dawdle.

I lifted the slip over my head, knowing he was watching. When I was naked, with my skin tingling and my nipples erect, he snuffed out his cigarette.

I climbed into the tub, but before I got the opportunity to sit, he gave me another order.

"Move closer. Stand over my face."

Was I blushing? My cheeks felt hot. But I did as I was told.

He parted my curls and put his tongue against my clitoris. While he licked me, I played with his hair. I got wetter and wetter, my juices warm and sticky.

"My sweet Nicole," he whispered against my private place.

I swayed on my feet.

His tongue, the flutter of his breath, his endearing words—all of it made me climax. Steeped in sensuality, I nearly melted into the water.

By the time I recovered, he was easing me down to sit across from him.

"Do you like the ring I gave you?" he asked, catching me off guard.

I glanced at the sparkling diamond on my finger. Like everything else Javier purchased, it was exquisite. "Yes, very much."

"I like owning you," he said.

I didn't protest. We both knew that I was his property. That I'd sold myself into human bondage.

He spoke again. "I pleasured you, now it's your turn to pleasure me."

I knew he meant orally. I glanced at his penis beneath the surface of the water. He was already partially aroused.

"I want to pleasure you that way," I admitted. "I've even fantasized about it."

"You have? Oh, Christ."

Was he cursing or praying? I couldn't tell. But I knew he was thoroughly captivated by me, as I was by him.

"When Candace did it to me," he said, "I used to imagine that she was you. Sweet Nicole and her sweet mouth."

I didn't want him elaborating about Candace, so I ignored his mention of her. "Tell me what to do. Show me the way you like it."

He sat on the side of the tub and opened his legs, inviting me to kneel between them. "Do whatever feels natural."

My nerves skittered. "But I—"

"Seduce me with your innocence, Nicole. Give me what I need."

His words should have empowered me, but they didn't. My innocence was genuine, not something I could purposely use to seduce him.

I pulled my bottom lip between my teeth. Should I start with the tip? Maybe kiss it? Or lick it?

Javier watched every inexperienced move I made.

I lowered my head and darted out my tongue. He tasted like human salt and fancy-milled soap. I ended up licking his stomach, too, because his cock was pressed against it.

He didn't give me direction. Silent, he continued to watch.

I hoped that I wouldn't disappoint him. I wanted to be

better at this than Candace, than any other woman who'd ever used her mouth on him.

For easier access, I gripped the base of his shaft and brought his penis closer.

"What's this called?" I asked.

His voice went rough. "What's what called?"

"Sucking a man."

"You're not sucking me yet."

"I will be." I wrapped my lips around the tip, testing the circumference.

"Oh, fuck," he said.

I nursed the head, prodding the hole gently with my tongue. His cock was long and hard and thick, but it was silky, too.

He tunneled his hands in my hair. "It's called fellatio."

I released him from my mouth, and the suction made a popping sound. "How would you say it in Spanish?"

"Sexo oral."

"Oral sex," I mused. "That's a simple translation."

He still had his hands in my hair. "Yes. Now quit talking and do it."

"But you told me to seduce you." And I could tell that my slow persuasion was seducing him. My innocence, it seemed, was working in my favor.

I rubbed my cheek against his hardened length, teasing him with the softness of my skin. The hands in my hair tightened, pressing my scalp.

"Be careful or I'll spend in your face."

He wouldn't dare. Would he? I glanced up at him. He would, I realized, if I continued to stimulate him that way.

Now my innocence was working in his favor. I was nervous again. But I was wickedly aroused, too.

Was I as depraved as my husband? I feared that I was.

Still, I behaved wantonly and licked his entire cock. I even laved his testes. I wanted to show him how willing I was to please him.

His response was gruff and excited. "Look at you. Naughty Nicole."

Yes. Naughty me. I gave him what he wanted and took him deeply into my mouth.

I thought about the sword swallowers I'd seen at the circus years before. One of them had been a woman and her skills had fascinated me. I did my best to emulate her. I relaxed my throat so his cock was able to go all the way in and all the way out.

I used my hands, too. I did everything I could think of to make it good for him.

I bobbed up and down and he thrust forward and gripped the back of my head. Our combined motions allowed him to fornicate with my mouth.

To fuck it hard and fast.

He pumped until my lips turned gloriously sore. He pumped until I moaned and squirmed in the water, barely aware that it had gone cold.

I loved being at his mercy. I loved being beholden to him.

While I sucked, he got into a standing position, and it made him seem even more powerful. I looked up at him to get the full effect, knowing he was looking down at me.

His loins tensed, the head of penis flaring. I could taste the onset of his climax.

Warm. Wet. Salty.

A raw sound emitted from his throat, and he spilled, full force, into my mouth, holding me there, watching me swallow his ejaculate. I relished every milky drop, certain I'd lost my mind.

Once his labored breathing subsided, he withdrew, and I licked him one last time, bathing him luxuriously with my tongue, enjoying the erotic feeling.

He toyed with my hair, twining the strands gently. "If you weren't already my wife, I'd ask you to marry me."

I sighed like a smitten bride, and he lifted me up and kissed me, making me fully aware of the vows we'd taken.

Of promising to spend the rest of our lives together.

Fourteen

Ethan stood at the edge of the pool and watched his lover. Eyes closed, she drifted on a lounge float with a plastic cup of lemonade in the drink holder, while he debated a dilemma in his mind.

To collar or not to collar. That was the question.

In a few days he and Kiki were leaving for L.A. In a few days, he would be taking her to his favorite club, where he'd taken lots of other subs.

But Kiki was different, and he wanted everyone at the club to know that she was special to him. Still, he was uneasy that he'd put himself in this predicament. He was supposed to know better. Subs weren't supposed to matter so damned much, at least not to him.

She opened her eyes and squinted at him, the sun beating down between them.

"Are you sure you should be out here?" he asked. "You and your fair skin?"

"I'm not that fair."

"You're a natural redhead. Redheads tend to burn."

"I'm being careful." She indicated the sunscreen she was using. "SPF thirty." She shielded her eyes with her hand, making it easier to gaze across the pool at him. "I'm just trying to get a little color."

"I like your complexion."

"I'm not going to California looking like a ghost. Not with all of those bikini bunnies running around."

"Most of them get spray tans now. And what's wrong with looking like a ghost? It works for Nicole."

She splashed some water in his direction, missing him by a mile. "As if we've actually seen her."

"Someday we might." Ethan still hadn't even *felt* Nicole, but he had hope that it would happen. He stepped into the shade. "Just be careful out here, okay?"

"I will. Where are you going?"

"In the house where it's air-conditioned." He wanted to make a phone call that she couldn't overhear.

"Says the man with the natural tan."

"I'm not a redhead."

"Lucky you." She wrinkled her cute little nose at him.

He watched her for a moment longer. Why did she have to make him so emotional? So frustratingly affectionate?

He pushed open the sliding glass doors, went inside, and speed dialed a number on his cell phone.

Derrick Roberts answered on the fourth ring. He was a

jeweler who specialized in custom-made collars. He was also a close friend.

"Hey, Derrick. It's Ethan."

"I know. I saw your name on my caller ID. What's up?"

"I need a collar by Friday."

"*You?* What is this, an April Fools' joke?"

"The last time I checked it wasn't April."

"Okay, so you're serious. She must be some sub."

Ethan glanced out the glass doors. Kiki was still floating in the pool. "She is. But she's only going to wear it for one night." That, he decided, would solve his dilemma. A temporary collaring.

"So you want something simple?"

"Hell, no. I want diamonds and rubies. And I want them as close to flawless as possible." Ethan knew that nearly all gemstones contained tiny fractures and inclusions, but he still wanted the best. "The highest quality you can find."

"Jesus," Derrick muttered. "By Friday? And for her to only wear for one night? What are you, Howard Hughes? Oh, no, wait. You kind of are."

Ethan ignored the other man's goofy sarcasm. "Can you accommodate me or not?"

"Absolutely. Whatever you say. Whatever you want. You're the crazy billionaire."

Yeah, he thought, I am. *I totally am.*

⌒

Kiki and Ethan flew into LAX, where Ethan arranged for a limo to take them to his house in Malibu.

And what a house, Kiki thought. It wasn't a mansion, not by Southern California standards, but it was big and trendy and perfect for a rich bachelor.

Surrounded by flowering shrubs and perched on a small embankment, the stucco-and-glass structure offered a stone stairwell that led to a private beach.

Inside, the pristine décor was ivory and blue, a color scheme that complemented the foaming ocean and the modern architecture. Ethan's second-story bedroom, which doubled as a playroom, faced the sea.

"This is gorgeous," Kiki said. No wonder Malibu was a celebrity-studded town.

"I'm glad you like it. It's my main residence. Or it used to be until I bought Curtis House. I'm addicted to Santa Fe now."

"Because of Nicole and Javier?"

"And you." Ethan hooked his thumbs in the front pockets of his jeans, and his body language made him seem boyish.

Kiki studied him in the bright white light, touched by his sentiment and captivated by his demeanor. He rarely behaved in a boyish manner. It made her want to skim his whisker-scruffy jaw and smooth his jagged hair.

Struggling to temper the affectionate feeling, she glanced at a collection of whips on the wall. He'd yet to incorporate whips in their scenes, even though she'd agreed that he could. Of course there were lots of devices he hadn't used yet. Their relationship was still new, and there was still time.

Wasn't there?

Focusing on the wall once again, she pointed to a bullwhip. "What's it like to crack one of those?"

He no longer seemed boyish. His posture went tense. "Are you still having fantasies about switching?"

Was she? Yes, she thought. Along with every other crazy emotion swirling around in her brain, she still wanted to be a dominatrix. Just once. Or maybe twice. Or possibly three times because that would be a charm.

"Are you?" he pressed.

"No," she lied.

"Then why are you asking about bullwhips?"

"I'm just curious."

"You know what they say about curiosity."

"That it killed the cat?" Nervous, she backed herself against the wall, wedged between a riding crop and a cat-o'-nine.

The cat-o'-nine was a multi-tailed whip that had been originally designed for severe physical punishment. These days they were used for sexual pleasure.

"I'm not switching," Ethan said.

"I know."

"Not ever," he reiterated.

"I know," she said again.

"Just so we're clear." He leaned in to kiss her. Harshly. But it felt good. Painfully good.

She tried to close off her mind, to not think about switching. But it poisoned her libido, making her desperate to do something hard and rough to him, too.

She moaned and slid her hand between their bodies, cupping his fly. He made an equally aroused sound. Then he ended the kiss and stared at her, as if he were attempting to read her thoughts.

She masked her expression. His hips were still locked against hers, and his belt buckle pressed into her. The silver edges were cool and sharp.

She wanted to switch so badly, she could've screamed.

"Don't ruin our affair, Kitten."

"I won't. I'm not."

He touched her cheek, going gentle, going gentlemanly. "You're my favorite playmate. You're special to me."

Her knees turned rubbery, so she stayed against the wall for balance. "Likewise."

After a moment of tender silence, he changed the subject. "What do you say we get dinner? We can have something delivered. Is Chinese okay? I've got some take-out menus."

"That sounds good." Anything to free her mind.

After the food arrived, he opened a bottle of wine and they spread a blanket on the beach, eating off paper plates and sharing the entrees while the sun went down.

"This is nice." Romantic, she thought. "I guess I didn't need that tan after all."

"Why? Because it's a private beach?"

She nodded. "No bikini bunnies." She paused. "But there's always tonight for me to show off my itty bitty glow." Her tan wasn't much of a tan. "Should I wear something provocative to the sex club?" She'd brought a few racy outfits along, nothing too revealing, of course, because she wasn't an exhibitionist. But she still wanted to look enticing.

"You can wear whatever you want, Kitten."

She made a joke. "So a high-neck blouse, a long, plaid dress, and Mary Jane shoes would be okay?"

He laughed and gave her a quick kiss. "Funny girl."

They finished their meals, and later that night, they got ready to go out. She chose a silk camisole with carnal cleavage and no bra. She also went for a black leather miniskirt, thigh-high stockings with crisscross lacing, and a pair of shiny red heels.

Ethan dressed a bit more retro, and the slim black trousers and button-down shirt seemed like something Javier might have worn in his day.

"I have something for you." He presented her with a gift box. "It's for you to wear tonight. But only tonight."

She couldn't imagine what it was. Anxious, she removed the top and leafed through tissue paper, finding a glamorous choker.

A BDSM collar.

For one night? She wasn't sure what that meant or how she was expected to feel, so she focused on the design.

"Oh, my goodness. Please tell me the jewels aren't real." The sparkling stones looked like diamonds and rubies, and in the center was delicate bondage ring.

"Of course they are. I had it especially made."

She gaped at him. "Why would you do this?"

"Because I want everyone at the club to know you're mine."

Still confused about how to feel, she said, "Possession is nine tenths of the law."

"In this case it is."

Meaning that someone couldn't take from him what he already had. "Is it white gold or platinum?" she asked.

"Platinum. Like I said, I'm only collaring you for tonight. But you can keep the choker itself as a memento or whatever. I won't have any use for it later."

She struggled to breathe. "Are you sure?"

"Positive. Here. Let me put it on you."

He fastened the jewelry around her neck and it seemed oddly ceremonial, as if he'd just made a commitment to her. But he hadn't, she reminded herself. Not beyond tonight.

He stepped back to gaze upon her, and she reached up to touch the faceted stones. "How does it look?"

"See for yourself." He led her to a mirror.

She stared at her reflection, and Ethan attached a slim leather leash to the ring, giving her the full effect. She looked frighteningly sexy, but so did he.

"It's beautiful." And she was having trouble breathing again. "The most beautiful thing anyone has ever given me."

Instead of reacting to her compliment, he said, "Take off your panties."

She started. "What?"

"No panties tonight, Kitten. You're going commando."

"Is that an order?"

"Yes," he responded a bit gruffly, a bit softly.

He continued to hold the leash while she bent down to remove her underwear. "Good girl." He tugged her back up. "Now kiss me."

Emotionally attached and wildly aroused, she did as she was told, her tongue slipping past his lips.

"You better be a loyal sub tonight," he whispered in the midst of their kiss.

"I will." She kept her arms around him, blocking images of switching from her mind. "I promise I will."

⌣⃨

The Scarlet Scandal was an upscale, members-only, adult nightclub located in West Los Angeles that catered to a variety of lifestyles, including BDSM, group sex, and voyeurism. Straight, gay, bi, and bi-curious were welcome.

The moment Kiki and Ethan entered the double-front doors, music pounded and lights flashed. The first floor of the trilevel establishment offered a decadent dance-club setting where well-toned bodies gyrated and champagne flowed from fountains.

Large flat-screen monitors projected highly erotic images, some of which Kiki recognized as Ethan's art. He was a Scarlet Scandal celeb. He was greeted with respect and groupie-type affection. So was Kiki, since she was the collared sub by his side.

But Ethan wasn't the only celebrity. There were quite a few rich and spoiled members. She'd never seen so many beautiful people in one place. She recognized a busty blond starlet, a notorious rocker, and a famous lingerie model.

But what did she expect? For Ethan to frequent a club with cheesy, middle-aged swingers? Women with sagging bosoms and cellulite butts? Men with beer bellies and receding hairlines?

"I'll give you the grand tour," he said above the music.

"Okay." She was anxious to see some flesh. Everyone on the first floor was clothed. Dancing wildly and rubbing up against each other, but dressed just the same. Some were in fetish gear and others sported designer fashions.

He led her to the second floor and into the Foreplay Room, where Doms, subs, and potential lovers cozied up on decorative sofas, kissing and petting.

Incense swirled in the air, the sweetened smoke clinging to tapestry-draped walls. Colored-glass lanterns provided filmy light.

Kiki caught sight of a female Dom, a sultry brunette, with a hunky male sub kneeling at her feet and stroking her shapely calves. Like Kiki, he was wearing a pricey collar.

Of course there were lots of male Doms, both gay and straight, but the domineering woman fascinated her. Instantly, she imagined acting like her.

Becoming her.

When Kiki's nipples tightened, she glanced away. She'd promised to be good.

Forcing herself to speak, she gestured to a connecting hallway. "What's in there?"

"Bedrooms and playrooms, but they're private."

"So we can't watch any of these people later?"

Ethan shook his head. "Not in this area. The foreplay couches are as public as it gets."

It was just as well. Better for her not to see what transpired between the brunette and her sub, even if, heaven help her, she wanted to.

"Where can we watch?"

"On the third floor. There's an Orgy Station up there, as well as an observation deck with VIP showrooms."

"That sounds sexy."

"It is. I already reserved my usual showroom."

They ascended the stairs, at the top of which they immediately came to a hotel-type desk. Ethan presented his membership card, and they were escorted to a large, finely furnished room. One entire wall, which Kiki assumed was a floor-to-ceiling window that overlooked the Orgy Station, was draped with a heavy curtain. At the moment, it was closed.

Once the employee left with a generous tip, Ethan locked the door and asked Kiki if she wanted a drink. Their showroom had a wet bar.

"I'll take a blue lady." Oh, God, she thought. The female Dom had been wearing blue. She fidgeted with her collar. "Do you know how to make one?"

Ethan nodded, but he frowned, too. "Vodka, vermouth, and schnapps."

He mixed her cocktail and grabbed a beer for himself, twisting the cap and guzzling half of it.

"When are you going to open the curtain?" she asked.

"When you stop fantasizing about switching."

Oh, shit. Her breath rushed out her lungs. "I'm not. I wasn't."

"A blue lady. Come on, Kitten. I saw you checking out the girl Dom and her boy toy."

She defended herself. "I turned away as soon as I could."

"Drink your damned lady, then forget about her."

"I don't want it anymore. I don't want to put her in my bloodstream." She refused to take the still-full glass.

"No more switching fantasies?"

"No."

He squinted at her. "If there're any female Doms in the Orgy Station, you'd better not focus on their activities."

"I won't misbehave."

He poured her cocktail down the sink. "Like I haven't heard that before."

"I'm going to keep my promise. I swear, I am."

"Then go stand in front of the curtain. And don't turn around until I give you permission."

She did as she was told, facing him, until he instructed her otherwise.

He moved past her, and she could hear him opening the curtain. Her heart pounded in sensual anticipation. She didn't know what to expect, except that safe sex was mandatory. The exchange of body fluids wasn't permitted at sex clubs.

"Are you ready, Kitten?"

"Yes."

"Then take a look."

She turned and staggered on her feet. The window showcased a huge dungeon that was obviously the BDSM section of the Orgy Station, where a variety of hot scenes were happening.

Young, gorgeous people were everywhere, using built-in restraints on beds, getting flogged and spanked, being suspended from swings and nets.

Kiki felt like a kid in a nasty candy store.

One long-limbed brunette, chained to a sex machine, was getting fucked by a dildo that rotated as it penetrated her. In the process, a real, live man straddled her face.

In another scene, two bisexual guys pleasured each other while they played with two artfully roped girls.

In yet another scene, a tuxedoed man, bound to a cross, was being roughed up by two women dressed as maids. They tugged at his suit, yanking buttons from his crisp, white shirt. They even broke his zipper to free his cock.

Kiki got warm and weak-kneed. Immediately she looked away. The maids were female Doms.

"Can they see us watching them?" she asked.

"No." Ethan came up behind her and slipped his arms around her waist. "The window is one-way glass, like in police interrogation rooms." He nuzzled her neck, nipping at her collar. "Of course they know they're being watched, and they enjoy it."

"So it seems." She cheated and glanced at the tuxedoed man and the maids. As the women fitted him with a leather cock ring that harnessed his penis and separated his balls, Kiki imagined doing it to Ethan.

"You're shivering," he said.

"I'm fine. I'm just . . ."

"Getting turned on?"

"Yes."

Before he could follow her line of sight, she glanced quickly in another direction, where three virile men were dominating one voluptuous woman.

It was sexy, too. Very sexy. The male Doms teased their sub with sensation toys, like ticklers and silk roses, bending her every which way and preparing her for group sex.

As Kiki watched, Ethan hiked up her skirt and stroked her

clit. She leaned back against him. Now she knew why he'd made her remove her panties.

The naughty foursome continued their feather-and-flowers orgy. By now, the willing girl was being penetrated by all three men in different orifices of her body.

As much as Kiki loved it, as wildly voyeuristic as it was, she wanted to watch Tuxedo Guy.

But she didn't. She kept her promise and avoided the forbidden zone.

Only it didn't help.

Even as she came, as Ethan stroked her into a submissive frenzy, she fought for sanity, praying her dominatrix desires would truly end.

Fifteen

Kiki was back in Santa Fe and struggling with her feelings.
What was she going to do about her switching fantasies? How
was she going to curb the wannabe dominatrix in her?

She glanced over at her friends. She was with Amber and
Mandy at the Spanish Colonial Revival mansion Amber's family owned. It wasn't nearly as big as Curtis House, as it had
never been a hotel, but it was just as impressive, with a clay
roof, domed archways, and imposing pillars.

They sat in a gazebo in the garden, sipping sweet tea like
Southwestern belles. All three wore jeans, colorful T-shirts,
and cowboy boots. They hadn't consulted one another about
their wardrobes. It just sort of happened that way.

"Maybe you should have watched Tuxedo Guy," Mandy

said, commenting on Kiki's dilemma. "Maybe that would have helped you get over this."

"Maybe. But I was trying to be good."

"Good smood." This from Amber. "Ethan should give in to your needs. He should let you beat the crap out of him."

Kiki blew out a sigh. "I don't want to beat him. I just want to hold a whip in my hand and make him behave for me." To experience the thrill of a switch.

Amber smoothed her sleek bob. "I'd beat him if it were me."

Kiki and Mandy exchanged a look of amused disbelief, and they all laughed. Amber certainly had a way about her—spunky, sultry, and sometimes just a little bitchy. But that was part of her charm, her Euro-American appeal.

A moment later, the trio fell silent. Kiki's problem still hadn't been solved.

"What about those people from the party?" Mandy asked.

Kiki responded, "What party? Oh, you mean the one I first attended at Ethan's house? Brad, Fiona, and Lynn? What about them?"

"Maybe you can ask Ethan to invite them over and perform for you again. But to switch this time with the girls dominating Brad. Watching them might help you get past this, especially since you were deprived of Tuxedo Guy."

It seemed worth a try. If Kiki didn't do something, she was going to lose her frigging mind. "I'll have to tell Ethan that my fantasies aren't going away. I'll have to admit how deeply this is affecting me, and I don't think he's going to like it."

"Screw him," Amber said with her trademark snippiness.

"You've been available for him and his fantasies. He owes you." She sipped the last of her tea. "By the way, how are those ménage lovers? Are they still happily living together?"

"As far as I know they are." Kiki angled her head. She wasn't surprised that Amber was interested in Brad, Fiona, and Lynn, considering that Amber had gotten locked into her own hot threesome. "Are you thinking about visiting Jay and Luke? About seeing them again?"

"I don't know. Maybe." The brunette waved a manicured hand, as if to dismiss her feelings. "Or maybe not. I haven't decided. But it doesn't matter because this conversation is supposed to be about you and Ethan."

"Yes, but we just came up with a solution to my problem." Or so she hoped. "I'm going to insist that he arrange a switch for me to watch."

And pray that it worked in her favor. That it cured her of her dominatrix ills.

⌒

Ethan scowled at Kiki from across his dining room table.

Fuck, he thought. *Fuck*.

He didn't appreciate Kiki's admission. He didn't want to hear that her switching fantasies were escalating.

And on top of that, her timing sucked.

Here they were, eating roasted lobster, parmesan scalloped potatoes, mushrooms with garlic butter, and almond-seasoned green beans. A meal he'd slaved over.

He'd actually cooked the whole goddamn thing by himself,

which wasn't a typical part of his DNA. Not that he was a helpless male who didn't know his way around the kitchen. He could throw a simple meal together when he had to, but he relied on his chef for fancy dishes.

Not tonight. Ethan had spent hours preparing dinner.

And now it made him feel henpecked.

Or maybe he only felt that way because Kiki had just foisted her dominatrix desires on him. He'd thought they'd gotten past that. He'd thought that she was going to let it go. Forget about it.

But no. Not her. She was too damned stubborn.

"Say something, Ethan."

"Say what? That I'm okay with this?"

"I can't help how I feel."

"And neither can I." He wanted to dump the table until it the hit the floor, until crystal goblets broke and china shattered, until the food went flying. But he didn't do it, because he would only end up looking like a spoiled kid who'd upset a game table because he wasn't winning.

"Don't you want to help me through this?"

"What if it doesn't help?" he countered. "What if it makes you want to dominate me even more?"

She took the avoidance route, stuffing a forkful of potatoes into her mouth. That pissed him off even more. They both knew it was a possibility. There was no telling how a switched ménage would affect her.

"It will help," she finally said. "It has to."

Now she sounded desperate, making him wonder if he

should break up with her. But even as the thought crossed his mind, he knew he couldn't do it. He wasn't ready to let his kitten go.

His feisty, fire-haired sub. Her spirit was part of what had drawn him to her.

Fuck, he thought again. She was doing a dangerous number on him.

"It better work," he ground out.

Her eyes went wide. "Is that your way of saying that you'll arrange the ménage?"

"Yes. But I'm going to watch it with you." To make sure that she didn't get more aroused than was necessary. To remind her that she was still the sub, and he was still the Dom.

"I'd like that. Very much. Oh, God, Ethan." She made a breathy sound. "I'm so excited for this to happen. How soon do you think you can arrange it?"

"I don't know. I'll have to call Brad and see what their schedule is like." And he would have to fly the trio in from L.A. His hometown, he thought, with a grimace. He should have never brought Kiki there. Taking her to the Scarlet Scandal had only added fuel to her forbidden fantasies. The blue lady. The domineering maids and the man in the tuxedo. Even the whips on his wall at the Malibu house had played a part in it.

Ethan had messed up. Big-time.

"Thank you," she said.

He shrugged and resumed eating. He didn't want to talk about it anymore.

"Thank you for the fabulous food, too," she added, even

though she'd already praised him for dinner earlier. "No man has ever cooked for me before. My husband couldn't boil an egg."

"Your *ex*-husband. You're not married to the guy anymore."

"You knew what I meant." She made a wounded face. "Don't be mad at me. Please. I hate fighting with you."

He reacted to the sincerity in her voice and reached across the table. "Sparks are always going to fly between us, Kitten. That's who we are."

She reached for him, too, and their fingertips connected. "If we get too romantic, Nicole might show up."

He'd meant for their meal to be romantic, but he scoffed at it now. "I'm never doing this again."

"That's okay. Next time I'll cook for you."

Fighting his feelings, he took his hand away. "Next time you'll dip yourself in gravy and lie across my bed."

"With whipped potatoes on the side?"

"Not if you're actually going to whip them with a whip."

She lifted her eyebrows at him, and they both ended up laughing. But the underlying tension was still there.

Nicole didn't show up, but she stayed on Ethan's mind. He excused himself and went upstairs to get a letter for Kiki to read. Not as a reward. She had done nothing to earn his favor. But the next letter seemed fitting somehow.

Because it involved a ménage disagreement, too.

My Dearest Thinking Woman,
Two months after I'd been married, I strolled along the Curtis House grounds, thinking how grand life was. Although Javier

worked quite a bit, he spent all of his free time with me. For the most part, we were inseparable.

When we weren't making thrilling love, we were dining on fine food or curling up together, reading our favorite books. We danced, too. Javier was teaching me to tango. Oh, and he'd promised to teach me to drive, as well. He owned several custom-built automobiles, but he'd purchased an assembly-line Ford Model T, too. Javier was fascinated by the automobile industry.

And me? I was fascinated by him. My husband consumed my every thought.

"Nicole!"

I turned to the sound of Lenore's voice. She remained at the hotel as Javier's guest, and I was glad to have her nearby. She was fast becoming my dearest friend. Only today she looked troubled.

She rushed toward me. I moved swiftly toward her, too. We met in the middle of a stone walkway.

"Candace is back," she sputtered. "I haven't seen her yet, but I heard that she was parading around the lobby like she's some sort of queen."

"She's here?" My heart hit my stomach, falling like a rock. "No," I murmured. "No."

"Yes, and that little bitch finagled the best room in the hotel. Better than my accommodations."

"Does Javier know?"

"I'm afraid so, dear girl. From what I was told, he greeted her when she arrived."

Greeted her how? I lifted my chin, struggling to maintain

my dignity. But my limbs were shaking. If my husband car-
ried on with his former mistress, I would kill both of them.

"I'm so sorry," Lenore said.

"He's the one who's going to be sorry. Do you know where
he is now?"

"In his office, I think." She reached for my hand. "Do you
want me to go with you?"

"Thank you, but no. I'd rather speak to him alone."

"He deserves your ire."

Yes, he did. But that did nothing to settle my nerves. I
squeezed her hand. "I'll check with you later."

She watched me walk away, and I made haste, taking the
shortest route back to the hotel building.

I entered through the lobby with determined strides. I
feared that if I didn't keep moving, I would falter. I was still
trembling like a leaf.

I pushed open Javier's office door. Normally I would have
knocked or simply left him alone altogether. My husband
didn't like to be disturbed while he was working, not unless I
was soliciting him for sex. Then he was happy to accommo-
date me.

"Nicole?" He glanced up from his desk and glowered at
the intrusion.

Apparently he could tell by my expression that I wasn't of-
fering myself to him.

"You heard about Candace," he said.

I crossed my arms over my chest. Just that morning, he'd
bound my breasts with rope and sucked my rosebud nipples
until they ached. "How could you?"

"How could I what? Allow her to stay? I invited her."

"You bastard. You—"

He held up his hand. "Before you curse me into hell, I didn't bring her here to tryst with me. The rest of her party will be here soon."

"The rest of what party?"

"She's going to be joined by two men."

I maintained my staunch posture. "So?"

"So they're coming here to fuck her." He smiled wickedly. "An orgy for us to watch." He shrugged a little. "Of course I offered to pay Candace. Otherwise she would have refused."

Appalled, I glared at him. "I'm not watching your old lover have sex, and I'm certainly not going to allow you to give her money."

"She's an actress, Nicole. She gets paid to perform. And you aren't in the position to allow or disallow anything."

"I'm your wife."

"And I'm your husband." He got up from his desk and came toward me. Once we were face-to-face, he said, "You'll do as I say."

"No, I won't."

"Yes, my sweet. You will." His black eyes bored into mine. "You agreed to see to my needs, and I have a carnal need for this. Besides, I don't actually intend to watch. The show is for you."

Now I was thoroughly confused. "Me? By myself? I couldn't possibly—"

"You won't be by yourself. I'll be there, but I just won't be

*watching." He explained further: "I'm going to cut a peep-
hole in the wall of the room next to Candace's. Then you can
peer through it and tell me everything you see. And while
you're telling me about the orgy, I'll be doing things to you."
He whispered in my ear. "Wild things."*

I went dizzy on my feet. "You can't be serious."

"You know full well I am."

"Why her, Javier? Why Candace?"

*"Because she knows where she stands. She knows this is
strictly business. Would you rather I hire a whore off the streets?
Or bring in a woman who might set her sights on me?"*

"I'd rather you not do this at all."

*"It's too late. It's already done. I already gave Candace an
advance on her pay. I suspect that she's readying herself for
her lovers as we speak."*

"Does she even know these men?"

*"No, but they're local admirers of hers, so she's excited to
meet them."*

"You chose the men?"

*"I made certain they were attractive. I want this to be pleas-
urable for Candace." He touched my cheek. "And for you."*

*"It's not right," I said. "You shouldn't make me watch
something like that." But deep inside, I was aroused.*

Horribly, shamefully aroused.

Kiki handed the letter back to Ethan. They were still seated
at the dining room table, and he was still steeped in frustration.

He tucked the envelope in his pocket, and she said, "Now I'm anxious to read the next letter. To know what happened at the ménage."

"Then I'm going to make you wait."

"For how long?"

"Until our ménage is over." Until that damned switch took place. "I wish you were more like Nicole."

"Because she did everything Javier expected of her? That was 1913. Women don't behave that way today."

He gave her a hard look across the table. He was feeling ornery. "Then I wish I'd lived in their era."

In spite of her scowl, she looked soft and pretty, her hair twining around her shoulders, her blouse gold and glittery. She'd dressed for dinner. They both had. He'd suggested it, but that was before she'd sprung the switching topic on him.

"Don't be a chauvinist, Ethan."

He would be whatever the hell he wanted to be. It was his fucking house, and he was the fucking Dom. For all the good it did. Kiki had gotten the best of him tonight.

Before things turned too quiet, she said, "I'll help you do the dishes."

He sat back in his chair. "What made you think that I was going to do them?"

"You were going to leave them for me?"

"I was going to leave them for my housekeeping staff. They'll be here tomorrow."

She shook her head. "You cooked, but you won't clean?"

"That's right. And I'm not cooking anymore, remember? I'm done with trying to impress you."

"You did impress me." She got out of her seat to come over to him.

Shit, he thought. He could smell the enticement of her perfume. She always wore the same fragrance, and it always affected him in the same way. He loved the rose-soft scent.

Bold as could be, she climbed onto his lap, wedging herself between him and the table. He itched to touch her, but he kept his hands at his sides. He wasn't going to give her the satisfaction of knowing how seductive she was.

"Tell me what you want, Ethan, and I'll do it. I'll be a good, good sub."

His cock went hard, and he cursed her for it. "I want you to forget about switching."

"I'll forget about it after I watch the ménage. After I get it out of my system."

And in the meantime, she was going to drive him erotically mad?

"Tell me what you want," she all but purred.

The smart thing would be to dump her on her pretty little ass, but his libido wouldn't let him. His cock was burning a hole in his trousers. "Undo my pants."

She worked his zipper and waited for another order.

"Put your hand inside."

Once again, she obeyed. She stroked him hard and deep, but her touch was soft and silky. While she made him more erect, he kissed her, tasting the gourmet flavors that lingered on both of their lips.

When the kiss ended, he could barely breathe. She was so willing, so able, so beautifully sensuous, he wanted to collar her again. But once was enough, he reminded himself. Their relationship was already on shaky ground.

Besides, collaring her a second time would be too much of a commitment. He knew better than to put himself in that kind of mess.

He looked into her eyes. Once again, she was waiting for an order. Aroused by her subservience, he took his dominance to the limit.

"Get on your knees," he said, commanding her to perform the most erotic of acts. And under the table, no less.

Kiki's eyelashes fluttered, just once, making her seem coy. But nonetheless, she did his bidding, and he pushed back his chair and spread his thighs, preparing to watch.

She gave him head exactly the way he craved it, laving the tip in a sweet, little circle. She played with the opening, too, licking him until pre-cum leaked out and dissolved on her tongue.

He lifted his ass off the chair and shoved his pants down even farther, making sure the fabric didn't obstruct his view. He wanted to see every detail.

Murmuring a soft sound, she nursed the head, then moved lower, taking more of him. Slowly, seductively, she teased him with the warmth of her mouth.

He admired her erotic beauty and pushed deeper, staking his masculine claim. Her lips were wide open and wrapped fully around his cock.

Needing to dominate her even more, he tunneled his hands in her hair and set a powerful rhythm. Giving him what he wanted, she sucked him as deeply as she could.

Her soft, pretty mouth. His big, pulsing penis. It was a thrilling sight, and he couldn't tear his gaze away.

Transfixed, Ethan gripped the edges of the table. While she sucked him raw, he battled the raging beats of his heart.

He tried to hold back, to make it last, to exercise more control. But he couldn't. She made him desperate to come.

Lost in the throes of a climax, he ejaculated hard and fast, watching her swallow.

In the aftermath, he caught what was left of his choppy breath, and she blotted her mouth and smiled up at him. Willing, it seemed, to do it all over again.

Confused, he blinked through a post-orgasmic haze, wondering just who was dominating whom.

Sixteen

The day of the ménage came quickly. Brad, Fiona, and Lynn were readily available and more than happy to oblige Kiki's fantasy.

The Blue Room, the same playroom as before, had been chosen as the location, and Kiki helped the women pick their outfits. Fiona, the butterfly girl, was attired in a see-through jumpsuit unzipped to her navel, and Lynn, the flower girl, sported a latex minidress with a garter belt, fishnet stockings, and a silk rose in her hair. Both wore stiletto heels and no underwear.

Brad, with his leanly muscled body, kohl-lined eyes, and dyed black hair, waited in the center of the room, kneeling in the slave position. His wardrobe consisted of a pair of cock-hugging jeans. Brad already had an evident bulge. He was always ready to play.

Kiki and Ethan waited, too. Seated on a velvet sofa, they remained quiet. Kiki's heart pounded so fast, she feared everyone in the room would hear her excitement. Ethan was a bit sullen, but she'd expected as much. Still, he sat extremely close to her, with his hand on her knee. His touch was possessive, and the fact that he was threatened by her fantasies created even more sexual tension.

Kiki took an anxious breath. She could feel Ethan staring at her profile, and she struggled not to turn toward him. What if he was right? What if this didn't curb her hunger to be a Dom? What if it made her crave it with greater intensity?

Lynn walked over to Brad with a slim and agile flogger, a small, multi-stranded whipping device, in her hand.

Behaving like a loyal sub, Brad kept his head bowed, but Kiki could see that his breathing had accelerated. Was he aroused by the flogger? By the way Lynn was wielding her feminine power over him?

"Look up at me," she said.

He lifted his head, and Fiona joined the party. She came up behind Lynn and raised the hem of the other woman's dress, flashing Brad with Lynn's waxed pussy.

"Lick her," Fiona said.

Oh, God, Kiki thought. They weren't wasting time. They were getting right to it, making Brad provide pleasure.

"Yes, mistress," he said, putting his mouth against Lynn and laving her slit.

"More," Fiona ordered, still holding Lynn's hem and leaning over to watch.

Kiki was watching, too. So was Ethan. But he seemed more

interested in Kiki's reaction than in the actual threesome. She glanced at him, and his gaze was hot upon her own.

Lynn teased Brad with the flogger, rubbing it in his hair while he gave her oral sex. He stayed there on his knees, taking direction from Fiona and licking Lynn until she made naughty sounds and climaxed in his face.

"Good boy," Fiona purred. "Now stand up."

Brad got to his feet, and the female Doms assessed him as if he were a piece of mouthwatering meat. He was unusually attractive, Kiki thought, sensuous in an androgynous kind of way. He was perfect for Lynn and Fiona. The three of them were beautiful together.

"Get over there," Lynn told him, pointing to a metal bar with shackles attached.

"And wait until we're ready for you," Fiona added.

Brad obeyed his mistresses and stood patiently with a look of submissive arousal in his eyes. The ridge in his pants was getting bigger. Kiki couldn't stop herself from staring at his fly.

The women took a quiet moment to kiss each other, to put on a pretty show for everyone, including Brad. As their tongues swirled, his Adam's apple bobbed. Clearly, he wanted to be part of the kiss, too.

Ethan's hand was still on Kiki's knee. Unable to help herself, she slid her hand to his zipper and pressed against his jeans, giving him a hard-on. He cursed beneath his breath and leaned into her. Like Fiona and Lynn, they kissed, only it was rougher, much more aggressive.

Kiki wished that he was standing in Brad's place and that

she was Fiona or Lynn. That she was his Dom. That she had a collection of whips and chains at her disposal.

Ethan's fingers crept upward and clamped her thigh like a torture device. She moaned and bit his lip. They were still kissing.

She had no idea what Lynn and Fiona were doing. She heard their high-heeled footsteps clicking across the floor, but she couldn't tear herself away from Ethan.

Finally she pulled back and noticed that his lips were bleeding. He wiped away the ruby drops with back of his hand and stared at her in a battle of wills. She wanted to punish him for looking so insolent, but he wanted to punish her, too. Mutual domination, she thought.

Damn it, why couldn't they switch?

Fiona cracked a bullwhip, and Kiki snapped to attention. Brad reacted in a loyally submissive, wildly sexy way, his breath catching loudly. As for Ethan, he scowled like the rebellious Dom he was, but he stayed erotically close to Kiki, making her want to kiss him again.

"Take off your pants," Fiona said to Brad.

"Yes, mistress," he responded.

He unzipped his jeans and pulled them down, freeing his erection. Kiki went warm all over. She couldn't wait for the women to play naughty games with him.

"Put your arms above your head." This from Lynn.

Brad did exactly as he was told, and the Doms chained him to the metal rod. They used a spreader bar on his ankles, keeping his legs wide apart. Kiki knew what that felt like.

When Lynn produced a stainless-steel cock trap, Kiki

scooted to the edge of her seat. The device had been designed to capture, confine, and tease the penis.

Fiona lubricated Brad's cock, and Fiona put the trap in place. It fit like a mini-cage. But the wildest part was when they attached the trap to a metal chain and suspended it from the same rod where Brad's arms were bound. The pressure pulled his penis up, making his erection stand at full attention.

Kiki doubted that they'd pulled it far enough to create unbearable pain, but it still looked torturous, and he grimaced accordingly. Even so, excitement shined in his eyes. Apparently he enjoyed being harnessed to a pole. Kiki wondered if he was going to come inside the trap.

The women stripped off their own clothes, leaving nothing on but their shoes. Then, going soft and pretty again, they climbed on a bondage table and used sex toys on each other, ordering Brad to watch.

Oh, yes, Kiki thought. Sooner or later, he was going to come.

"Damn," Ethan said. He was checking out the girls, too.

So was Kiki. She was watching everyone. Fiona. Lynn. Brad. Ethan. She even glanced at the Blue Room angel and his broken wings.

Then something changed in the air. A shift. A sad and lonely emotion.

Nicole was here.

Kiki gasped, and at the same time, Ethan turned toward her and grabbed her hand, as if Nicole had finally connected with him, too.

"Do you feel her?" she whispered.

"Yes." His voice was gruff, shaky. "But—"

"But what?"

"There's someone else here. Someone stronger, someone . . ."

Javier, Kiki thought.

Suddenly she sensed a rush of wildly dominant energy, surrounding her like a raging sea. She felt as if she were being tossed from side to side, yet she was sitting completely still.

"Fuck," Ethan said. Apparently he was trapped in the storm, too.

Only that wasn't the worst of it. Kiki could tell that Nicole and Javier weren't able to connect with each other. The ghosts were in the same room, yet they weren't together. Javier's energy was spinning in all sorts of frustrated directions, and Nicole's genteel vibration floated aimlessly.

The threesome continued, the games getting hotter, naughtier. Kiki wanted to enjoy it, but she couldn't concentrate.

She was too wrapped up in Javier and Nicole.

Right up to the moment they faded into nothingness, leaving Kiki staring hopelessly at Ethan.

⌒

After the ménage, Brad, Lynn, and Fiona went out for the night, but Kiki and Ethan stayed home to discuss the other couple.

The ghosts.

Damn, Ethan thought. He'd actually felt them. He was still blown away by the experience.

"It's a crazy feeling, isn't it?" she asked.

Crazy. Amazing. Scary. "It almost seemed as if Javier was trying to possess us." But Ethan recognized that it was just the other man's energy. If Ethan were dead, he would probably put out the same tumultuous vibe.

Kiki nodded and sipped her chai tea. She was seated across from him at a glass-topped table on a lantern-lit patio, with moonlight shimmering through the trees. A soft breeze blew, stirring scents from flower beds.

Ethan reached for his beer. He wasn't a chai kind of guy. But the floral aroma was nice. "They used to do stuff like this."

"Javier and Nicole?"

"They would sit outside and talk. He'd have a brandy and a cigarette and she'd . . ." Ethan glanced at the cup in Kiki's hand. "Drink hot tea."

"So we're behaving like them?"

"A little, I guess."

She didn't respond. Instead she looked up at the stars or the heavens or whatever. She seemed out of sorts. But he understood. His emotions were wrought, too.

In the silence, her hair fluttered across her shoulders. The wind loved her unruly curls. But so did Ethan. She looked as beautiful as ever.

As he swigged his beer and watched steam rise from her cup, he wondered if the ménage had been successful, if her switching fantasy had been sated. God, he hoped so. But with the inclusion of the ghosts, it was difficult to tell.

She made a pensive face, drawing him back to their conversation. "It's weird that the very first time Nicole showed up was during a threesome," she said. "And now Javier shows up during one, too. Do you think it's significant? Do you think it has anything to do with the orgy that involved Candace?"

He blinked at her. Because her question made perfect sense. Because he should have considered it himself. But his thoughts had been too scattered.

"You need to read the next letter, Kitten."

She scooted closer to the table. "I do?"

"Yes." Still feeling a bit scattered, he reached out, almost as if to capture one of her curls, but he dropped his hand and stood up, preparing to get the letter. "You do."

My Dearest Thinking Woman,

I was so nervous, I feared that I wouldn't survive what I was about to do, but Javier insisted that I go through with it. Not that I didn't want to. I did. But I think that was what frightened me most of all.

Who had I become? What kind of woman was I?

"Breathe, Nicole."

I glanced up at my husband. We were in the room next to Candace's and a peephole had already been cut to accommodate my height. All it needed was my eye pressed against it.

"I am breathing." If I wasn't, I'd be dead.

"You're not breathing very well." He made an exaggerated gesture, encouraging me to inhale, to exhale.

I cleansed my lungs, but I only felt marginally better. "Do the men know that they're going to be watched?"

"Yes, but they don't know by whom. I would never allow

them to know that my beautiful young wife was on the other side."

"Why?" I queried. "Would that make you jealous?"

"Hell, yes." He took my hand, then pressed his thumb into my wedding ring so hard, the diamond left a mark on his skin. "You're mine. You belong to me."

I kissed him, and he pulled me closer. We rubbed against each other, and when we separated, he said, "I'm still a monster."

"You are," I agreed. But we were both smiling.

"I can tell this excites you, Nicole."

"It's nervous excitement," I explained.

"It's erotic excitement," he countered.

Someone rapped lightly on the wall, and I nearly jumped out of my clothes. I'd chosen to wear a delicately embroidered dress with lace trim and matching undergarments. Not that my attire mattered, but I wanted to look pretty for my husband.

"That was Candace," he said, referring to the knock. "She's letting us know that she's almost ready. She'll signal us again when it's time."

Oh, goodness. The waiting was killing me.

Javier walked away to get a candle. He'd lit a grouping of them when we'd first entered the room, and now they were melting and dripping.

He brought the candle near my face. "Blow it out."

"Shall I make a wish, too?"

"That's your prerogative."

I wished for my nerves to steady.

After I extinguished the flame, Javier began to rub the tip of the long, thick candle, molding the wax that had melted. Perplexed, I watched him. Soon a shape began to appear. He'd made it look like a penis.

I gasped like the innocent I still was. "Javier," I scolded.

He grinned, wicked as could be. "I'm going to tease you with it. I'm going to slide it between your legs while you're peeking in on the orgy."

"You'll do no such thing." But of course I knew that he would. He always did as he pleased. Besides, hadn't Lenore warned me that Javier used candles in all sorts of naughty ways? I should have been prepared for this.

He unhooked the back of my dress and removed it, along with my underskirt, leaving me in a chemise and modesty-free drawers.

"I love how you look in your undergarments," he said.

I turned and touched his cheek. "My garter has your name embroidered on it."

"Does it? Truly?"

I smiled at the pleasure in his dark eyes. "It's all the rage."

"For a woman to wear her beloved's name on her garter? That's a fashion rage a man can appreciate."

I nearly melted, as warm and waxy as the candle he was going to use on me. He'd just referred to himself as my be-loved.

Candace tapped on the wall, signaling her readiness.

"It's time to watch, Nicole," my husband said. "To enjoy the show."

I put my eye against the peephole, and there was Candace,

wearing nothing but her *undergarments. Besieged by two men, she began to strip for them.*

And for me.

It was strange to spy upon another woman, but Candace was quite beautiful, and I found myself captivated by her curvaceous body. Off came her chemise and corset, then went her drawers and garters and stockings.

The men were broad-shouldered and fair-haired, like Vikings. They looked like brothers, or possibly cousins, and I realized that they probably were related in some way. One was as handsome as the other. They didn't hesitate to join in. They sandwiched Candace between them.

The slightly taller Viking stood behind her, while the blonder one stood in front. The men rubbed their clothed bodies against her bared flesh, and I would've fanned my face if I hadn't been pressed against the wall.

"Tell me what's happening," Javier said.

I relayed the scene, my voice vibrating. "The man in front is kissing her now, and the one in back is nibbling on her neck."

"Like this?" Javier came up behind me, teasing me with sweet little bites.

I shivered and moaned.

Soon, the men led Candace to the bed and she lay upon it, exposing her full nakedness. I could see her cherry-ripe nipples and darkly nested mound. She touched herself, and my cheeks flamed. Javier was still biting my neck.

"The men are taking off their clothes," I said, watching them toss their garments aside.

"*Are their cocks big?*"

"*Yes.*" Oh, my, oh yes.

"*Look at them, Nicole.*"

"*I am.*" How could I not? It was like being in a forbidden nickelodeon. "*They're rolling around with Candace. All over the bed, passing her back and forth for more kisses.*"

"*She prefers more than one partner.*"

"*I can tell.*" Candace was blatantly aroused. "*She just climbed onto one of their faces. The blonder one. She's making him . . .*"

"*Eat her?*"

"*Yes. She's spreading herself with her fingers.*"

"*And what about the other man?*"

"*He just stood up on the bed. I can't see all of him, but I can see his lower half.*" It was a highly powerful image. "*He's bringing his cock to Candace's mouth.*"

"*Tell me when she sucks him.*"

I watched, then said, "*She's doing it.*" And she looked darned good at it. But I was just as good, I thought. I pleasured Javier just as well.

"*Is she still sitting on the blonder one's face?*"

"*Yes.*"

"*Maybe I should give you oral sex,*" my husband said.

I nearly bumped my head on the wall.

"*Would you like that, Nicole?*"

"*Yes,*" I blurted shamefully, prompting Javier to get on his knees and taste me through the opening in my drawers.

I sighed. I shivered. I watched the orgy. But mostly I got wet and slick. Javier drove me mad. He used his tongue in *carnivorous ways. He laved me so deeply, I rocked back and forth against his face, much in the way Candace was doing to the blonder Viking. Of course her mouth was still filled with the taller Viking. He pumped his hips, making her take every inch of him.*

Candace planted her hands on his buttocks and squeezed tight. I could tell that she was having an orgasm. I had one, too. Right then and there, at the very same time.

Javier sipped the last of my juices, and after I recovered, he stood up and whispered in my ear, "You're a naughty girl, Nicole."

I merely nodded. I couldn't deny his claim. The taller man pulled back, and Candace opened her mouth so I could watch him spill into her.

I told Javier, and he held me while I trembled. I was embarrassed and aroused and strangely confused.

While the blonder man had intercourse with Candace, Javier used the candle, stimulating me in a wildly decadent way.

He didn't put the candle inside. Instead, he teased me with it, sliding it along my slit, then to my clitoris, where he rubbed in a circular motion.

It felt so illicit, so improper, I climaxed again and again.

So did Candace. The orgy went on and on. I watched things I'd never dreamed possible.

Finally when the trio was spent, I turned away and fell into my husband's arms.

He kissed me softly on the lips and asked, "What would I do without you, sweet Nicole?"

The same thing I would do without him, I thought. Live in sheer and utter loneliness. I put my head on his shoulder, breathing in the spicy scent of his aftershave.

I loved Javier Curtis. I loved him with all of my heart.

And I believed that he loved me, too.

Seventeen

Ethan waited to see what Kiki would say, to see if she got the significance of the ménage.

She did. She looked up at him and said, "So that explains it. It was the first time she'd realized that she loved him."

"And chose to believe that he loved her."

She wrapped both hands around her teacup, holding it as if she were seeking warmth, as if thinking about Nicole not being with Javier had made her chilled. "We really should try to get them back together."

"Yes, but how?"

"I don't know. Maybe we should involve a medium."

"I'd rather not bring a stranger into this. Nicole and Javier appeared to us. It's us they need." Ethan couldn't help feeling possessive. His house. His ghosts. He wanted to control the situation.

Kiki met his gaze. "How many more letters are there?"

"Just one. It was written on the night they died."

Her eyes remained locked on his. "Then maybe I should read it."

"Maybe you should." There was no reason to hold on to the letters, to use them as rewards. It had gone beyond that. "Come with me. Let's go upstairs."

"To get the letter?"

"To mess around. I want to touch you first."

She tilted her head. "You want sex? Now?"

"Why not?" He was feeling oddly romantic. Was it because Kiki looked so vulnerable, sitting there clutching her chai tea? Or was it because he was caught up in Nicole and Javier's tragedy and he needed physical contact to stay grounded?

Grounded?

Kiki had used the same term when he'd been kissing her last week.

He stood up and reached for her. "Come with me," he said again.

She put her hand in his, and they went upstairs to his bedroom. He turned down the lights and lit a long, thick candle, similar to the type Javier had used on the day of the ménage.

"Have you ever done what he did?" Kiki asked.

"Shaped a candle into a penis? No. They sell them like that now."

"It seems more interesting to make your own."

He sat on the edge of the bed and removed his shoes, getting more comfortable. "Do you want to try it?"

"Could we?" She seemed fascinated by what Javier had done to Nicole with the homemade candle.

Ethan wasn't about to deny her. "Of course we can. But the candle needs to melt before we can shape it." He watched her through appreciative eyes. "We might have to kiss while we're waiting."

"I think that can be arranged." She sat next to him on the bed, and they moved into each other's arms.

Their mouths came together, and as their tongues mated, warmth spread through his body, making him deepen the kiss.

Mesmerized, he stripped her down to her underwear, to a jade green bra and matching lace panties.

"I should get you a garter with my name embroidered on it," he said.

"And an old-fashioned chemise and lacy drawers?"

"You're already wearing lacy drawers." He traced the skimpy lines of her panties.

"I'll bet Javier would have loved the changes in women's lingerie." Kiki flashed a TV commercial smile. "We've come a long way, baby."

"So you have." He smiled, too. "But your gender has always had the power to drive my gender crazy."

"Your gender is easy." She bumped his fly. He was already half-hard.

He toyed with her bra straps. "Did you know that the brassiere was invented the year Nicole and Javier died? By a socialite named Mary Phelps?"

"Really?" Kiki seemed amused that he knew the history of the bra.

"Mary was getting ready to go out one night and the new dress she'd purchased was too sheer for a whalebone corset. The whalebones stuck out. So she used two silk handkerchiefs and some pink ribbon and made herself a bra."

"Thank goodness for Mary."

"Yeah, or you'd be sitting here in a corset." He spouted more of his knowledge. "Which, by the way, was invented by Catherine de Médicis in the mid 1500s. She was the wife of King Henry II of France."

She cuddled up to him. "And here I thought I was the historian."

"I know a few facts." He kissed her again. He liked flirting with her.

When they separated, they both glanced in the direction of the candle. "Is it ready?" she asked.

"I think so. We might as well give it a try." He brought it over to the bed and let her blow it out, telling her to make a wish the way Nicole had.

He suspected that she wished for Javier and Nicole to reunite, to be together for all eternity. Ethan probably would have made the same wish.

"You should shape it," she said. "You're the artist."

"I'd be glad to." But he was going to make his candle much more detailed than the one Javier had used on Nicole.

Ethan went to work, molding the melted wax and using sculpting tools. By the time he was finished, the candle was a lifelike replica of an erect penis with veins and ridges and a big, bulging head. As for the wick, it was sticking out of the hole at the tip.

"Now that's impressive." Captivated, Kiki stared at it.

"I'm glad you think so." He stroked her cheek with it, and within no time, they were rolling around on the bed, laughing and playing.

He removed her bra and peeled off her panties, spreading her legs and causing her to quiver. Then, completely turned on by what he was about to do, he teased Kiki with the candle, lubricating the wax and rubbing it softly against her clit.

She looked into his eyes, and he could see that she was lost in the moment, caught in the sensuality between them.

But so was he.

He made her come, just like Javier had done to Nicole. Kiki panted and purred, yet it wasn't enough. Ethan needed to be inside of her, too. So he put the candle in its holder and lit the wick, and while it burned, while its flame flickered, he made mind-spinning love to her.

And gave her the final letter when he was done.

My Dearest Thinking Woman,

Javier entered our bedroom, sporting cuffed pants and a wool sweater. He also wore a gray and white checkered cap.

"Are you finished?" he asked. He'd been waiting for me to complete my toilet. "Almost," I responded, wrapping a scarf around my hair.

On this early winter day, we were going for a drive, with me behind the wheel. Javier had kept his promise and taught me to operate his Model T. Sometimes I made mistakes, like shifting into high gear when I was supposed to be in neutral. Also, I wasn't very good at turning the crank, so Javier always started the vehicle for me. If it wasn't done right, a person could twist a wrist or break his or her thumb. But regardless, I enjoyed driving and Javier indulged me.

By now, I'd been married for six months, with barely any time to keep up with these letters. I was a busy young woman, and my life was filled with splendor. With each day that passed, I was convinced that my husband was the most compelling man in the world.

Would our happiness progress? Would we have a family someday? Would I raise his sons and daughters? I surely hoped so.

I wanted everything with him, everything life had to offer. Of course, our sexual escapades were still quite forbidden. Nothing had changed in that regard, and I doubted that it ever would. In our hearts, we would always be wild and wicked. But I'd convinced myself that in spite of our deviations we were decent people. Javier was no more a monster than I was.

"You look sporty," he said.

I, too, was attired in a wool sweater, only mine was trimmed with a collar, belted at the waist, and paired with a skirt. My scarf-draped hair was twined into an intricate bun.

Javier moved forward to kiss me, and our lips touched softly.

Oh, how I loved him. But I'd yet to say the words out loud. I wasn't sure why I'd been holding back. Maybe because I wanted him to declare his love for me first.

But that was foolish, I knew. So long as one of us broke the ice, what did it matter who said it first?

He stepped back to analyze me. "What's going on in that pretty head of yours, Nicole?"

Did he know what I'd been thinking? Had he sensed it? "Why do you ask?"

"I can always tell when your mind is engaged."

"You make it sound as if I were scheming."

His lips tilted a fraction. "Women always are."

I smiled, too. "Are we now?"

"Yes, you are." Still teasing, he pinched me.

"You're right," I admitted, summoning the courage to speak out. "My mind was engaged. But I wasn't scheming. I was thinking about how much I love you." I paused, took a deep breath. "And about how much you love me."

He went dreadfully quiet.

As I struggled to ease the tension, an unyielding frown carved grooves into his forehead and bracketed his mouth.

"Honestly, Nicole," he mocked. "What could you possibly know of love?"

My heart grew heavy in my chest. I blinked to keep from crying. But that didn't stop me from lifting my chin, from exhibiting a well-meaning spark of defiance. "I know what we have together."

"A marriage based on sex? You sold yourself to me. That's not love."

"But I love you now, and you love me. I know you do. I can feel it when you hold me close, when we sit outside and talk, when you drink your brandy and smoke your cigarettes, when

you watch the steam rise from my tea, when we dance, when we laugh, when you crank up the auto for me to drive."

"So I'm fond of your company. So you amuse me. That does not mean that I love you."

The old Javier was back. The hard, cold man who'd scandalized me on the very first day I'd met him. The hard, cold man who'd married me to sate his carnal desires. But it seemed like a front, a ruse to protect himself.

"You love me," I insisted. "You do! You even referred to yourself as my beloved."

"That was a figure of speech."

Desperate to convince him otherwise, I protested. "It was not. You meant it."

"Stop behaving like a child," he scolded. "It's unbecoming."

I wanted to show him how childish I could be. To throw a full-fledged tantrum, to scream, to call him a bastard, to tell him that I hated him. But I didn't. I still loved him.

"You're afraid," I said. "You're afraid of how I make you feel."

He raised his brows at me. "I fear nothing, least of all you. Now drop this nonsense before I change my mind about having you as my wife."

"You'd divorce me over love?" Tears, threatening to fall, burned the back of my eyes. "You'd send me away rather than admit that I live in your heart?"

"Oh, Christ," he cursed. "Keep it in perspective, will you? You're a delicious piece of tail, and you suck cock like nobody's business, but I'm not pining for you."

I swallowed the lump in my throat. He'd reduced me to his

whore. Nothing could have hurt me more. "Maybe you really are a monster."

"I told you I was." His tone was matter-of-fact, but it was icy, too. "Now go cry or blow your nose or whatever it is that women do in these types of situations, then compose yourself and meet me in the garage for that damned drive."

That was it? That was how he expected to end the argument?

He left the room and shut the door smartly behind him.

I sat on the edge of the bed and burst into tears. Not because he'd told me to cry, but because the pain ran so deep, I couldn't stop myself.

I cried until there was nothing left, until every part of me shattered. But even so, I knew that Javier was lying—to himself, to me.

I didn't meet him in the garage. We didn't go for a drive. We didn't speak at all for most of the afternoon. But later in the day, I asked him if he would dine with me. I decided that I would dismiss the kitchen staff and prepare the meal myself. Javier loved it when I cooked for him. Another proof, I thought, that he loved me.

His Nicole. His wife. The woman determined to make him see the truth.

That his tortured heart belonged to me.

Kiki looked up at Ethan. She could tell that he was waiting for her reaction to the letter. Instead of starting their conversation with the love issue, she asked, "Did they die while she was fixing dinner?"

He gave her a solemn nod. "According to witness reports, they were arguing before the fire broke out. A couple members of the staff heard them snapping at each other. Then the staff walked away, and a short time later, the kitchen nearly exploded. It was a grease fire, accelerated by some chemicals that were in there."

She didn't want to think too deeply about Javier and Nicole burning to death. But worse yet was knowing that they were fighting when it happened. No wonder their ghosts weren't able to rest.

Now she broached the love angle. How could she not? It was the catalyst that drove Nicole. "I think she was right. I think he loved her."

"So do I. I didn't think so before, but I changed my mind when Javier's ghost showed up. So what do we do about getting them back together?"

An idea came to mind. A crazy idea. A certifiably insane idea. But since it was there, knocking around in her brain, she said, "Come outside with me, and I'll tell you."

"Why can't you say it in here?"

"I don't want them to hear us. You know, in case they show up." And she needed a breath of fresh air. No, she needed more than a breath. She needed lots of oxygen.

"They could show up outside, too."

"Nicole never has. She's always appeared in the house. I imagine it will be the same with Javier."

Ethan accepted her reasoning and escorted her onto the balcony.

"Okay," he said, moving to stand very close to her. "We're alone."

His proximity made her uneasy. She wanted to tell him to back away from her, but she knew that would sound foolish.

"We could pretend that we're in love," she blurted.

He went motionless. He simply stood there, dumbfounded, staring at her.

"Is this your idea of a joke?" he finally asked.

She wished to God it were. But she was serious. *Dead* serious. "Nicole has been feeding off my energy, especially when I'm in a romantic situation with you. I suspect Javier will be feeding off of us, too. If the energy they feel is love, it might break down the barrier between them. It might give them the positive force they need to reunite."

Ethan pulled a hand through his sex-tousled hair. "Our acting isn't that good."

"We can try." For the sake of the ghosts, she wanted to add. But somewhere deep down, she knew that this wasn't just for Javier and Nicole.

It was for herself, too.

Because she was falling in love.

With Ethan.

To keep from hyperventilating, she gulped the air she needed, fighting for steady breaths.

"I wouldn't know how to pretend," he went on to say. "I've never been in love. I've never even been close."

She should quit before she got hurt, admit that it was a stupid idea and drop it. Instead she said, "I could teach you." Because she knew how it felt. It was happening to her now, this very instant.

A rapid heartbeat. A dry mouth. Emotional chaos.

"I got the impression that you've never been in love, either," he said. "That you only thought you were in love with your ex."

"Yes, but it's the same feeling." That was a lie. Her attachment to Ethan was something altogether different from what she'd felt for her ex.

Deeper. More frighteningly intense.

He quit tugging at his hair. "What if we blow it? What if it doesn't work?"

"Then we'll try something else. We've got nothing to lose."

Nothing to lose? Who was she trying to kid? She'd already gone and lost her heart.

"Would we have to say it?" he asked. "Out loud?"

Kiki gave a jerky nod. "We'd need for the ghosts to hear us."

"This sucks," he said, making her feel worse.

She tightened the belt on her robe. She was uncomfortably naked underneath. "Are you willing to try it?"

He stalled, and she thought he was going to refuse. But then he responded, "Yes. But I can't guarantee that I'll be any good at it."

"I'll be good enough for both of us."

"You only need to be good enough to convince Javier and Nicole. You don't need to do a number on me, Kitten."

"I wasn't planning on it." Another lie, she thought. She wanted Ethan to fall in love with her.

"When should we start?"

She had a ready answer. "Right now. Tonight."

He made a pained face. "So soon?"

"You already made sweet love to me. The energy is already there."

"It wasn't *that* sweet."

"Yes it was." Everything he'd done had seemed romantic, even his use of the candle. "You didn't even restrain me."

"Okay. Fine. Whatever." There was anxiety in his voice. "Let's just go inside and get the 'faking it' stuff done."

She reached for his hand and felt her own tremble. Kiki was panicked, too.

Far more than he could possibly know.

Eighteen

Ethan and Kiki returned to the house, and Ethan hoped he'd made the right decision. As it was, he had butterflies in his stomach, making him even more uncomfortable. Men weren't supposed to have winged creatures fluttering around. He'd always considered that to be a girl thing.

Kiki pulled him closer. They were standing in the middle of his bedroom.

"Tell me you're falling in love with me," she whispered, guiding him into the charade.

Shit, he thought. He looked into her eyes, and the butterflies got worse. "I'm falling in love with you," he whispered back, sounding like a boy whose voice was still changing.

"Say it louder," she coaxed.

A deep breath. Another jerky motion in his stomach. He raised his cracking voice. "I'm falling in love with you, Kiki. I don't know when it happened or how, but I am."

Her gaze never wavered. She stared right at him. "I'm in love with you, too." She caressed his jaw, her touch light and fluid. "And it just happened for me. Or I just realized it happened. And it made me scared."

Damn, she was good. She sounded totally sincere. "I guess we're both scared." He would be shaking in his boots if were wearing any. "Who would have thought? You and me?"

"It was only supposed to be sex, but it's more." She put her head on his shoulder and held him tight. "Life is crazy that way."

Beyond crazy, he thought. They were putting themselves on the line to bring a couple of dead people back together. Regardless, he stroked Kiki's unruly hair and breathed in the luscious scent of her.

"What are we going to do about it?" she asked, playing her part to perfection.

"We're already doing it. We're already admitting how we feel."

"You're right." She looked up at him. "It's all we can do at this point."

He couldn't help himself: he leaned down to kiss her, to put his mouth gently against hers. She reacted like a woman in love, absorbing his princely kiss with an emotional sigh.

Then Ethan felt a chill run up his back. A soft chill. A ghostly chill.

Nicole.

Oh, Christ. She was there, watching them, listening to them, feeding off them. Now he was really nervous.

He squeezed his eyes shut a bit tighter and deepened the kiss. Kiki shivered, but he wasn't sure why. Had she felt the ghost, too? Or had she lost herself in their faked romance? It did seem kind of real, even to him.

But not to Javier, he realized. The male ghost was nowhere to be found. He didn't whip into the room with his testosterone-generated energy. He wasn't drawn to the charade.

Ethan released Kiki from his kiss, and they gazed longingly at each other, staying in character. Nicole was swirling delicately around them. Ethan couldn't see her, but he felt her invisible mist. She'd fallen for their charade, but she was desperate. She needed to believe in love.

"Do you know that she's here?" Ethan asked.

"Yes," Kiki responded.

"Do you also know that he isn't?"

"Yes," she said again. "Maybe he needs more time."

And maybe he would never fall for a lie, Ethan thought. Maybe all of this was going to be for nothing.

⌣

Kiki and Ethan worked on their romance for nearly a week, but Javier was an impossible sell. On occasion, they felt snippets of his energy, but not enough to draw him to Nicole, to break the barrier between him and his wife.

Kiki had no idea how she and Ethan were going to solve the problem. But even more stressful was the turmoil it caused.

Sometimes Ethan's acting seemed authentic, as if he were actually falling for her. But then he would pull away and threaten to quit, cursing their charade.

He was an even harder sell than Javier. Or an equal match, she supposed.

As always, Kiki had gone to her girlfriends for help. But they'd come up empty on this one, too. Amber had scolded her for falling in love. She'd been warned not to let it happen.

Easier said than done.

So now Kiki was sitting beneath a big, shady tree in Ethan's grassy yard, with a daytime view of Santa Fe spread out before her.

The City Different, she thought. Santa Fe had earned that title in Javier and Nicole's day. If only she could go back in time and knock some sense into Javier. The way she wanted to knock some sense into Ethan.

But time was running out either way. Kiki's vacation was almost up. Soon she would be back at her own apartment, far, far away from Curtis House. Or far enough away to leave her in a state of loneliness.

Damn Ethan, she thought. Damn him all to hell.

He came outside with two glasses of iced tea and handed her one. She mumbled an annoyed "Thanks" and took a sip.

He joined her on the grass. He was shirtless and shoeless, and his hair shined beautifully in the sun. So did his eyes. He was more handsome than he'd ever been.

"You're in an off mood," he said.

"I'm trying to figure out what to do about Javier."

"I told you we should just let it go. He probably didn't love her anyway. We were probably wrong about him."

"No we weren't." She couldn't stand to think that the horrible things Javier had said to Nicole on the night they'd died were true. Nor could she stand to leave Nicole all alone, missing her husband, longing for him. "It was fear that kept him from admitting it."

"So what does that mean? That he's still panicked? We can't do anything about that."

"I don't think fear is holding him back, not now. I think it's you."

"Me? What the fuck is that supposed to mean?"

Already an argument was brewing, and Kiki was going to make it worse. She was going to tell her lover the god-awful truth. "It happened to me, Ethan. I—" She stalled, her nerves jarring.

"You what?" he asked impatiently.

"I fell in love with you."

He flinched, reacting as if she'd slapped him, as if she'd just left a stinging imprint of her hand on his cheek.

But he composed himself soon enough. Ethan never faltered for long. "You don't know what you're saying, Kitten. Nicole is getting to you. She's making you—"

"It isn't Nicole. It isn't her fault. It's me."

"Then you need to undo it. You need to fall out of love with me."

Kiki gaped at him. "I can't undo how I feel. I can't just make it go away."

"You made your switching fantasy go away."

"Is that what you think? That it disappeared because I haven't mentioned it? The ménage didn't work, Ethan. I'd chain you up in a New York minute, if you'd let me."

"Chain my body? Chain my heart?" He spilled his tea onto the grass and cursed. "Commitment. Love. Submission. Damn it, Kiki. None of that is me."

"I know. But I kept hoping, praying . . ."

He shook his head. "Don't hope. Don't pray. Just make it end."

"I can't," she snapped. Did he think she was a robot? A windup toy? A Stepford sub?

"And I can't handle being smothered like this. It makes me fight to breathe. It makes my chest hurt. It makes everything go tight inside."

Did he think that she wasn't smothering, too? That the tightness wasn't inside of her? "I should go home. Now. To-day."

He didn't say anything. He went morosely mute, making the moment more awkward.

Kiki stood up and waited for him to stop her from walking away, but he didn't. He just sat there with his tea spilled into the grass.

She went inside, took the stairs to the third floor, and entered Ethan's room, preparing to pack.

Nicole showed up, her energy swirling softy, wrapping itself around Kiki. The ghost was trying to comfort her.

Kiki struggled not to cry, for herself and for the other woman.

"I'm sorry," she said to Nicole. "I'm so sorry we couldn't help you."

For a moment, Kiki thought she heard a whispery voice inside her head say, "I'm sorry, too," but then footsteps sounded in the hallway, and Nicole's energy vanished into thin air.

Ethan walked into the room, looking tall and dark and troubled. "I'm sorry, Kitten. But it wasn't supposed to be this way."

Too many I'm sorrys, Kiki thought. Too many painful apologies. "It's okay, I understand. I just need to go home."

"And never see me again?"

She tried to pack as quickly as she could, but her focus was scattered. "Seeing you again isn't an option."

"Maybe if your feelings change . . ."

And she fell out of love? "That isn't going to happen." The best she could hope for was the old adage that time healed all wounds.

Not that time had worked for Nicole.

"I'll bet she's going to hate me for this," he said.

Apparently he was thinking about Nicole, too. "Why would she hate you when she doesn't hate Javier?"

He shrugged in response. Then he pinned her in place with those stunning blue eyes and asked, "Do *you* hate me?"

Tortured by the impact of his gaze, she fussed with a blouse in her hand, dropping it, picking it up again. She was experiencing a myriad of emotions, but hate wasn't one of them. "No."

They both fell silent, and when she came across the jeweled collar he'd given her, she offered it back to him.

He refused to take it. "I gave that to you as a gift."

"I know, but . . ."

"But nothing. It's yours. Lock it away in a drawer. Sell it. Whatever."

She might lock it away for safekeeping. But sell it? She would never do that. The collar meant more to her than money.

He snared her gaze again. "I wish I could touch you. Just one more time."

The tightness came back, tampering with her lungs, with her breathing, with the unsteady beats of her heart.

"Touch me or fuck me?" she asked without malice. She wanted to put her hands all over him, too. Any way she could—gently, roughly—it didn't matter.

"I don't know." He seemed as confused as she was. He pointed to her partially packed bags. "I'll help you with your luggage when you're ready."

She nodded and turned her back on him, moving at a jittery pace. Finally, she crammed the rest of her belongings into her suitcases, and he carried them downstairs and walked her to her car.

They rushed through an uneasy good-bye, barely saying the parting words, and keeping a deliberate distance. They didn't dare get close enough to touch.

Misty-eyed, Kiki drove away from Curtis House.

Leaving Ethan and two unsettled ghosts behind.

Ethan spent the next two days locked in his house and acting out his feelings.

His *feelings?*

His rage was more like it.

He'd done all sorts of angry things. He'd splashed paint all over his studio, staining the walls with a morbid color; he'd roamed the hallways at night, spewing profanities at himself; he'd gotten drunk and thrown beer bottles at the fireplace in the parlor, behaving like a clichéd hero in a bad B movie.

But none of it helped.

Nor did the ghosts. Neither of them connected with him. He didn't blame Nicole. She'd been through enough. But Javier, that selfish prick, could have showed up for some demented male bonding.

"Screw you," he said to the other man, blaming the ghost instead of himself. "Nicole should have known better than to love you."

And Kiki should have known better than to love Ethan.

He considered drinking himself into oblivion again, but getting wasted was useless, so he tackled the mess in the parlor. The bottles hadn't just smashed inside the fireplace, they'd bounced onto the floor and shattered there, too.

Why was he was so angry? Because Kiki left or because he was too damned scared to admit that he loved her, too?

"You and me," he said to Javier. "We're quite a pair."

Suddenly Ethan smelled smoke. In a panic, he whipped around and thought about the fire that killed Javier and Nicole.

Oh, Christ. Was his house burning now?

No. No. No. It wasn't fire smoke he smelled. It was cigarette smoke.

Not only could he smell the tobacco, he could see it curling into a mist, into the shape of a tall, trim man.

Javier, he thought.

The smoke created a hazy outline, but he recognized Nicole's husband. Ethan just stood and stared.

Finally, he got a grip on himself. "So you decided to show up after all," he said.

Javier didn't respond, but his image got a bit sharper. The smoke kept moving, almost like a pencil sketching details. Ethan could have been drawing him.

Once the smoke settled, a cigarette appeared in Javier's hand.

Ethan made a stupid joke. "Those things will kill you, you know."

The ghost smiled.

Ethan smiled, too. At least Javier had a sense of humor.

The lighthearted moment didn't last.

Javier drifted over the table where Ethan's family portraits were displayed. The wedding picture of Javier and Nicole was there, too. Ethan had removed it from his bedroom and put it back in the parlor.

The ghost traced the image of his wife, touching her in a loving, gentle way.

"I know," Ethan said. "You miss her. I miss Kiki, too." And it had only been a few days. Javier had been missing Nicole since the last century. "We tried to get you and your wife back together. But it didn't work."

Javier raised his sketched eyebrows, and the mocking expression made Ethan scowl.

"Okay, so we were trying to fake you out. At least we gave a damn enough to try."

Javier winged his eyebrows even more.

"What are you doing here anyway? Trying to make me see the error of my ways? I already know I screwed up."

The ghost drew on his cigarette and blew smoke in Ethan's direction. The smoke curled in the shape of a broken heart.

Great, Ethan thought. Parlor tricks. "What's that supposed to mean? That I broke Kiki's heart, like you did to Nicole?" Flustered, he defended himself. "If I go to Kiki, if I tell her that I love her, I'll have to submit to her fantasy, too. I'll have to go all the way." Fear balled up inside of him. "I'll have to switch."

Javier blew another stream of smoke. Another heart appeared, only this one had a chain around it.

"Now what are you trying to say? That I'm already enslaved by love?"

The chain got tighter around the heart.

"Okay, so you've got a point. But you don't know what it feels like. Nicole didn't have switching fantasies. You didn't have to submit. You got to play the Dom, right up to the day you died."

Javier's eyebrows shot up again.

"All right. Fine," Ethan said, continuing the one-sided conversation. "Being a Dom at the end didn't get you anywhere. But my situation is different from yours."

The heart bloomed in a bouquet of flowers. Love was love.

And pain was pain, Ethan thought.

The flowers drifted away, leaving nothing but emptiness. Javier began to drift away, too.

When he was completely gone, when Ethan was alone with

the same ache that had been killing him for the past two days, he knew Javier was right.

He needed to go to Kiki.

And admit that he loved her.

Oh, God, he thought. Could he do it? Could he submit that deeply? That fully? Could he sacrifice his body and his spirit? Could he give to Kiki what she'd been giving to him?

He had to, he told himself. If he didn't, he would have to live this way for the rest of his life.

Needing her. Missing her.

Determined to stay focused, he went upstairs and took a shower, scrubbing the fireplace grime from his skin.

With his hair freshly washed, he rubbed some gel into it and styled it in its usual way. For his wardrobe, he chose a simple white shirt, a notched-collar vest from Javier's era, and a pair of jeans.

"I'm representing both of us," he said to Javier, even though the ghost hadn't reappeared. A modern man, a vintage man.

A scared-shitless man.

He climbed into his favorite Jaguar, a classic car he thought Javier would appreciate.

Of course the ghost wasn't riding shotgun. Ethan was on his own.

He arrived at Kiki's apartment complex and parked in a spot marked for guests. She lived in a nice neighborhood, but it wasn't anything fancy. The suburban-style normalcy made Ethan miss what he'd never had. All he'd known were mansions and maids and personal chefs.

Yeah, right. Boo hoo, he thought. Who wouldn't envy him? A rich and spoiled artist who got whatever he wanted.

Except for now. He was going to give Kiki what she wanted. He was going to submit.

He took the stairs to her apartment. His heart was banging so hard, he could barely hear his knuckles rapping on the door. But he was knocking. He was summoning her. It was late enough in the day that she would be home from work.

Amber Pontiero answered, throwing him for a confusing loop.

"What are you doing here?" he asked.

"I should be asking you the same thing." She looked him over with a bitchy vibe. She was one of the most gorgeous women on the planet, but he'd never been interested in her. Nor had she ever been attracted to him. They understood each other's money, though, the sense of entitlement that came with the silver spoons that had been shoved into their mouths.

"I'm here to see Kiki," he said, stating the obvious.

"She's at the store. She's having a little get-together tonight, and she forgot the chips and salsa."

"A get-together?"

"For girls only."

"I'd like to wait for her."

"Suit yourself." She pointed to the porch stoop. She wasn't going to invite him inside.

He wanted to tell Amber to go to hell, but he said instead, "I came here to tell her that I love her."

"That's just peachy, Ethan. But it better come with a

guarantee. Because if you hurt her again, I'll use one of my great-great-granddaddy's pistols on you."

Her great-great-grandfather had been an American gunsmith who'd had an illicit affair with a European princess or duchess or some damn thing, getting himself killed over it.

"I'm offering a guarantee," he assured her. The switching, he thought.

"Fine," she said in her usual snippy way and shut the door. She still wasn't inviting him inside.

Once again, he was on his own.

Nineteen

Kiki walked up the steps, saw Ethan, and nearly stumbled. He got to his feet and met her halfway to take the bags from her hands.

"I love you, Kitten," he said right away, almost making her stumble again.

Oh, dear God. She tried to respond, but she couldn't seem to find her voice. She sat next to him on the stoop and reached up to smooth a piece of hair that fell across his eye. Not touching him was impossible.

"Do you still love me?" he asked.

"Yes." The word came out in a nervous rush. She loved him beyond belief.

He told her about his visit from Javier, and she listened

with awe, envisioning the ghost and the smoky conversation they'd had.

"I'm willing to switch." Ethan extended his hands, as if he were offering to let her bind him here and now. "I'll do anything. No limits. Whatever you want, I'm yours."

"You really mean that, don't you?" She saw the sincerity in his eyes.

"I absolutely do. But it isn't going to be easy for me."

Kiki nodded. It was probably the most difficult thing he'd ever agreed to do, and she loved him even more for it. She was insanely aroused, too. Knowing that he was giving himself to her was a powerful aphrodisiac.

"Let's go back to your house. Right now. Let's play, Ethan."

He blew out an audible breath. "So soon?"

"Why wait?" She was almost as nervous as he was. But in a good way. Her heart pounded in rapid excitement. Her dominatrix dreams were about to come true.

With the man she loved. With the man who loved her.

"What about your get-together?" he asked.

She'd forgotten about the female friends she'd invited to her place. Women who were coming over to cheer her up. "They can party without me. Amber can be their hostess."

"Yeah, she's good at being a party girl. And she can tell them why you skipped out."

"Because I went to my lover's house to chain him up?" She smiled. "They're going to want all the erotic details later."

"I don't mind if you tell them."

"Good." Kiki intended to make it a night to remember, a

night to boast about. She leaned over to kiss him, drawing him closer, tasting the heat of his lips.

He was going to be an incredible sub.

Thirty minutes later, they arrived at Curtis House and entered the Red Room, where Kiki's portrait hung on the wall.

She went into Dom mode right away, leading him to a suspension bar that faced her painting and removing his shirt. Then she bound his wrists to the top of the bar, making him stand with his arms raised above his head.

"This feels strange," he said.

Because no one had ever restrained him before, she thought. And it made him look wildly sexy. Animalistic.

"You'd better get used to it."

"How often are we going to switch?"

"As often as I want." She kicked off her sandals, preparing to change into something a bit more dominatrix. For now she was wearing a gypsy-cotton dress. "Do you have a problem with that?"

"I guess not."

"You guess not? Is that any way to talk to your mistress?"

A smile tilted one corner of his lips. Suddenly he seemed amused. "No."

"No what?"

"No, mistress." He quit smiling. He was steeped in his situation now, caught in the throes of the sacrifice he was making.

Kiki couldn't help but notice the heavy emotion in his eyes.

She approached him and unzipped his jeans and pushed his boxers down a bit, exposing a hint of pubic hair. It made him look even more gorgeous.

Anxious, she ran her fingers along his abs and made his stomach muscles jump. "I'll be back in a few minutes."

She searched the fetish closet for something to wear, and came up with a red bustier, matching panties, a ladylike garter, black stockings with seams down the backs, and a pair of slinky black heels.

She styled her hair in a messy chignon and darkened her eye makeup. For the final touch, she put on the collar Ethan had given her. She'd brought the jeweled necklace with her.

She returned to him, and he took in her appearance, eyeing every seductive inch of her.

"Do you like what you see?" she asked.

"Yes," he responded. "Very much." He zeroed in on her collar. "But I didn't expect that."

"It's my way of saying that I still belong to you, even when I'm the Dom."

"We belong to each other," he said.

"Completely." She scraped her nails down his stomach again. "We're each other's plaything. Only tonight, you're *it*." She emphasized "it," saying it the way a kid would say it during a game of tag.

"I'm starting to feel like a boy toy."

"Good. Because you are. Now tell me where the cock and ball torture items are."

"There aren't any in this playroom."

Of course not, she thought. The Red Room was his private

dungeon, and, up until now, he hadn't had any personal use for CBT toys. "Then I'll need the master key to the other playrooms." She removed the chain he always wore from around his neck.

Kiki left and returned with a slew of items, including a thick leather collar. "Look what I found for you to wear."

He eyed it warily. Clearly he'd never envisioned himself in a collar. "I keep stuff like that here for my guests."

"And now it's yours." She buckled it around his neck. It looked dangerously sexy on him. Rough and masculine.

He glanced at the other items she'd brought into the room. The CBT toys. Was he nervous? His chest was rising and falling. He was breathing heavily.

She rifled through the toys. The collection included penis whips, penis leashes, ball dividers, ball stretchers, ball vises and crushers, cock cages, and cock harnesses.

"Which ones should I use?" she asked.

Ethan didn't respond.

She picked up a whip. "This is fashionable."

He frowned. "Fashionable?"

"It's red. It matches my outfit. I like this, too." She dangled a harness. "It reminds me of the device the maids used on Tuxedo Guy. Only this one looks a little more brutal."

"It's a deluxe model."

"So I see." The harness had a cock ring made of leather, a steel ring to go around the base the shaft, a ball stretcher with a divider, and D ring equipped for weights or a leash.

"Hurry up and decide," he said, then he caught himself and winced. "Sorry. It isn't my place to give orders."

"No, it most certainly isn't. You just earned yourself a lash." She twirled the red whip. "With this."

"Fuck," he mumbled.

"That's another lash. Subs aren't supposed to curse."

"Since when?"

"Since I said so. But before I use the whip, I'm going to lock you in this." She dangled the deluxe model again. "And you're going to like it."

Kiki approached him, got on her knees to remove his shoes and took off his pants and boxers. She rubbed her cheek against his cock and made him hard, taunting him into submission.

She knew he was struggling not to curse, especially when she strapped him into the harness, causing his penis to become engorged even more.

Kiki licked him, intensifying the ache. The harder he got, the tighter the device would get and the more tension he would feel.

Good pain, she thought.

When she sucked him, he groaned. She couldn't give him a deep-throated blow job, not with the harness on. But she was able to nurse the tip, and she knew he liked what she was doing. She used her tongue to massage the slit because she knew he liked that, too.

He looked down at her, and she looked up at him. The exchange was incredibly intimate. But she didn't let it continue for too long.

She got up off of her knees and aroused him with the whip,

running the tails along the sensitive head. She gave him a few naughty lashes, too, and his breathing turned even rougher.

He was torn between enjoying the whipping sensation and disliking it. She could tell that he was erotically confused. Still, he remained rock hard. He couldn't seem to control his big, blasting erection.

"Did you like the way Lynn and Fiona teased Brad?" she asked. "The way they touched each other and made him watch?"

"Why?" He blew out the air in his lungs. "Are you going to make me watch something?"

"I think I just might." Playing the ultimate Dom, she retrieved a bullwhip and carried it over to Ethan.

"Be careful," he warned. "Those are dangerous when you don't know how to use them."

She reprimanded him for interrupting her fantasy, reminding him of who was in charge. "I'm not going to crack it. I'm just going to hold it." At some point, she intended to learn how to make it snap. But for now . . .

She sat on the edge of a bondage table and faced Ethan. Then she spread her legs and used the whip to push her panties to one side and expose her nether lips.

"Fuck," he said. "Oh, fuck."

"No cursing," she scolded. But she knew he'd said it because he was turned on. Kiki went right ahead and masturbated with the whip, rubbing the braided leather against her slit.

She made sexy sounds. She arched her back. She opened her legs nice and wide. She did everything she could to tease Ethan.

To make him throb and burn.

She gazed at his harnessed cock while she pleasured herself. But she made eye contact, too. And that drove him crazy.

"I need you," he said, his voice raspy, his chains rattling.

"Not yet. But you can have this." She brought the whip to his mouth.

He tasted it willingly. He even sucked on the portion that had been pressed against her.

Deciding to reward him, she discarded the whip and released him from the suspension bar. But she locked him up again.

This time she chained him to a recliner chair that was designed for oral sex, took off her panties, and straddled his face.

While his cock was still harnessed, while he was still steeped in good pain, he gave her cunnilingus.

He kissed her vulva, then slid his tongue inside, arousing her with long, luscious strokes.

She adjusted her position, sitting farther upright so she could watch, and he circled her clit, pleasuring her until she came.

She convulsed in shivery waves, and afterward he whispered, "I love you, Kitten. I love you so much."

Kiki skimmed his cheek, thinking how beautiful he looked, professing his feelings with her juices on his lips.

Finally she removed his restraints and unbuckled his harness, giving him mobility. She ordered him to carry her to bed to play some more.

Dom to sub, she thought. Sub to Dom. Lovers sharing fantasies.

All night long.

⌐⌐

Kiki awakened to the aroma of eggs, potatoes, onions, tomatoes, peppery spices . . .

She opened her eyes and, sat up in bed, and there was Ethan, setting a tray of food on the nightstand.

She gave him a sleepy smile. "Is your chef back?"

"No. I made breakfast."

"You? I thought you were never cooking for me again."

He shrugged, smiled a little. "I was never going to switch, either. But I was a damn good sub last night."

"Yes, you were." And this morning, he looked as dominant as ever with his messy black hair, slight beard stubble, and powerful blue eyes.

He sat beside her and gave her a committed kiss, the kind that comfortable couples shared on snuggly days. Thank goodness it was Saturday and she didn't have to work.

She reached for a plate. He'd made Spanish omelets for both of them. Coffee and orange juice, too. "This looks yummy."

"It was easy to make."

"I still owe you a home-cooked meal."

He stole another kiss. "You still owe me your body smothered in gravy."

She balanced her plate to keep from spilling the contents. God, how she loved him. He made her heart rejoice in wild and tender ways.

Ethan settled in with his food, and they ate in companionable silence.

Until Nicole showed up.

Not only could Kiki feel her energy, she could see her. Nicole was a white mist, a flowing entity in a filmy dress with a ruffled apron draped over it, the outfit she must have been wearing on the night she'd been cooking up a storm in the kitchen and died.

"Do you see her?" Kiki asked.

"Yes," Ethan responded, then shivered. "Javier is here, too."

"He is? Oh, God, you're right." His presence hit her like a ton of broken bricks. She glanced up and saw his smoky image in the opposite corner to where Nicole was. He was wearing a suit, and his hair was slicked straight back. He was wickedly handsome, even as a ghost.

But his image was flickering, as was Nicole's.

"Damn," Ethan muttered. "They're still not able to connect."

"I know. I can tell." She could feel the blocked energy. She turned back to Ethan. Why hadn't their love reunited the other couple? Why were Nicole and Javier still struggling to be together? "What happened? What went wrong?"

"I have no idea."

Silence befell them once again, only it wasn't companionable. This time, the quiet was troubling.

The ghosts were still flickering.

"Maybe they need more from us," he said suddenly.

"What do you mean?"

"Maybe they need to feed off of our sexual vibrations. Maybe they need a combination of love *and* sex."

"We messed around for hours last night. Shouldn't that have brought them together?"

"Not with me as a sub. That wasn't the right energy for Javier."

"But he helped push you in that direction."

"Because he knew it was right for us." Ethan looked from one ghost to the other, and so did Kiki. Both entities were starting to fade. "He encouraged me to do it for us, not for himself and Nicole."

"So we need to make love, with you as the Dom?"

He moved closer to her. "Yes, but I don't think it's going to be quite that simple. I think we're going to have to give ourselves to them."

Her pulse hopped, skipped, and jumped. "You mean loan them our bodies so *they* can make love? So they can become physical again?" She paused, tried to envision it. "An erotic séance? With us as the mediums?"

He reached for her hand and held it. "I can set the scene. I can get the house ready. I can bring it back to its Edwardian roots. We should dress from the era, too, so it feels more natural to them. So they can strip each other the way they did in real life. I'll call my stylist and have her send over some vintage clothes for you. For me, too. I've already got a few things from that time period, but not everything I'll need."

"Oh, my goodness, Ethan. Do you know how serious this is? Giving ourselves to ghosts? Letting them possess us?"

"You want them to be together, don't you?"

"Yes, of course." But she was nervous, scared beyond sensual belief. "I wonder how it's going to feel. Having them take over our bodies? Having them inside us?"

"I don't know. But I hope it works. Because if it doesn't, they might be lost to each other forever."

Twenty

Getting ready for a sexual séance wasn't easy. After several days of preparation, the transformation was still under way. But Ethan wanted everything to be perfect. He wanted to give Javier and Nicole the most incredible night of their lives.

Or their deaths, or whatever.

He'd decided that the séance should take place in their old bedroom, which was his room now. But since it was too modern, and Javier hadn't been exposed to dungeon equipment in his day, Ethan closed off the connecting Red Room and focused on the bedroom itself.

Determined to re-create an environment that was straight out of 1913, he'd arranged for his room to be redecorated to match the original décor by using Nicole's letters and old Curtis House photos as guides.

Naturally he'd paid a ridiculously high price to have it done as quickly as possible.

The same went for Kiki's clothes. Ethan's stylist brought a large selection of vintage dresses to choose from, but if they weren't horribly frayed or moth-eaten, they simply weren't right for Kiki. Or for Nicole.

Finally, a dress was delivered that suited both women, but it needed major alterations to fit Kiki. As for undergarments, they needed alternations, too. A skilled seamstress was hard at work.

For himself, Ethan chose an assortment of antique accessories, including two-tone shoes, a pair of lightweight drawers, and onyx and diamond cuff links to go with an Edwardian suit he already had.

The time was getting closer. Things were getting done. But he was impatient.

He'd offered to bring a hairstylist in to give Kiki an old-fashion coiffure, but she insisted that she could do it herself, using pictures from historical magazines. Apparently she'd done a friend's hair once for a costume ball and nailed the vintage look that had been required.

For now, the house was a zoo. Ethan had brought his chef back to keep people well fed. His cleaning crew was around, too. But as soon as Kiki's clothes were altered and the final touches on the bedroom had been implemented, Ethan was getting rid of everyone again.

So he could be alone with the woman he loved.

And share her and himself with two beautiful ghosts.

⌣⟶

Everything was ready, including Kiki. She gazed at her re-flection in the dressing table mirror. She didn't look like Nicole, but she embodied Nicole's ladylike style and grace. Her gold-toned dress was silk charmeuse, trimmed in lace and accented with pearl beads. A wide band of netting cinched the waist, and the skirt gathered in back and draped delicately in front.

"You look amazing," Ethan said from behind her.

"Thank you." She turned to face him. "So do you." He was attired in a three-piece suit, with his hair slicked straight back and his expression dark and serious. He fit naturally into their surroundings.

"Before we lose ourselves in the séance," he said, "I have something to ask you. Will you move in with me? Here? At Curtis House?"

Her eyes welled with tears. "I'd be honored to live with you." She couldn't imagine *not* spending every waking mo-ment with him.

He took her in his arms and kissed her, and they pressed their bodies close. Lovers, she thought, preparing to reunite the dead.

They'd already agreed to forgo condoms. They were both clean and safe, and they wanted Nicole and Javier to have the familiarity of flesh-to-flesh sex. Javier never used rubbers, which was the opposite of Ethan. He'd admitted that this would be his very first time without protection.

Kiki nuzzled his chin. It almost made him seem like a virgin. *Almost.*

"I'm going to use twisted rope tonight," he said. "And long, tapered candles."

The candles were a given. They were already burning beside the bed. "Javier's favorite toys?"

He nodded. "I'm going to use a silk scarf, too."

"A blindfold?"

"No." He removed the scarf in question from his pocket. The material matched her dress. "To put around your lips."

"A gag?" Kiki wasn't afraid of being gagged, yet she got chilled all over.

Then she realized why. Javier was in the room. His power-wielding presence had burst onto the scene. But he always made a gripping entrance.

Her heart struck her chest. "He's here."

"I know," Ethan responded, catching his breath.

Together they turned to see the ghost, hovering in a dark, smoky haze.

Javier seemed to know exactly what all of this was about, and he wasn't shy about the invitation. Instantly, he moved toward Ethan.

Oh, God, Kiki thought. *Oh, God.* Just like that. Javier was going to merge with Ethan.

Take over his body. Possess him.

The ghost created a filmy aura around her lover, giving him

a gunmetal glow. She watched Javier meld into Ethan, using him as a flesh-and-blood vessel.

In the process, Ethan's eyes turned darker, more midnight instead of blue, and he held his head at a regal angle. Even his posture changed, becoming more matador-like.

When he turned to look at Kiki, sliding his gaze over the length of her finely clothed figure, her mouth went dry. To keep herself from trembling, she crossed her arms, shielding herself from a man who suddenly seemed like a stranger. Or a partial stranger. Mostly he still looked like Ethan.

To be sure, she moistened her lips and asked, "Ethan? Is that you?"

"Yes." His voice sounded the same, except for a slight inflection, a roguish arrogance that belonged to the other man. "But he's inside me, too. He wants to know where his wife is."

"I don't know." Kiki looked around for Nicole. "I don't feel her. I don't see her."

"Maybe I should undress you. Maybe she'll appear if I touch you. If the sexual energy increases."

Kiki shivered just thinking about it. What if Nicole didn't show up? What if Kiki was left alone with Ethan *and* Javier? With their hands on her body? With ropes, candles, and a silk gag?

She looked into Ethan's eyes. By now they were pitch black. There was no mistaking the ghost's influence. The transformation was getting stronger.

Fear dripped like IV fluid into her arms, into her blood, into every part of her. Could she do this? Could she allow it to happen?

Yes, she thought. She could. But only with a warning. "You have to stop if Nicole doesn't appear," she told Ethan. "You can't keep undressing me."

"We'll stop. He only wants his wife. He isn't trying to seduce you."

Lord, she hoped so. Ethan was sounding more like Javier with each minute that passed.

She smoothed her gown. "My dress fastens in back."

"Then turn around."

Pulse pounding, she did as she was told.

"I'm not used to such tiny buttons," Ethan said. "But he is."

Her pulse pounded faster. Ethan even smelled like Javier, like cigarettes and spicy aftershave.

The unfastening was handled with ease, and Kiki was instructed to step out of her dress and underskirt, then turn back around.

Once again, she did as she was told, standing before both men in a chemise and corset and open-crotch drawers.

"Javier thinks you're beautiful," Ethan said. "He thinks I'm a lucky man."

"Tell him thank you," she responded.

"He can hear you, *Gatito*."

"*Gatito?*"

"It means kitten."

In Spanish, a language Ethan had never used until now. Self-conscious, Kiki closed her eyes.

That was when Ethan brought the gag up to her mouth.

Her eyes flew open.

He tied it gently in place. "This will keep us from kissing you until Nicole gets here."

Us? Him and Javier? Nicole better show up soon, Kiki thought.

"Maybe I should tie you up, too," he said.

He led her to a straight-back chair, and she sat down. He secured her wrists and ankles, and she caught a hint of erotic enjoyment in Javier's black eyes. He liked what Ethan was doing to her. But it wasn't enough to mask his impatience. His hunger. His need.

Javier wanted his wife.

As sexual silence sucked oxygen from the air, something soft touched the back of Kiki's head.

Nicole!

Ethan looked up, and Kiki could tell that Javier had just connected with his wife for the first time since they'd died.

Boom!

Nicole was no longer gentle. She entered Kiki's body in a mad rush, nearly drowning Kiki in desperation. The female ghost wanted her husband as badly as he wanted her.

Ethan removed the gag and leaned over to kiss Kiki, and it was the most powerful kiss she'd ever experienced.

Because it was Javier kissing Nicole.

Their lips met in a heart-thrilling, pulse-palpitating frenzy, a century of passion sizzling between them.

Ethan untied the rope and freed Kiki's wrists and ankles, and she jumped up and threw her arms around him. But in actuality, it was Nicole tossing her arms around Javier. Kiki was reacting to Nicole's needs, to her wants, to an ache so deep, she could barely breathe.

"I love you," Ethan said, speaking for Javier and sounding eerily like him. "And you were right. I was afraid to admit it." He stroked her cheek, tracing the angles of her face. "I feared that I wasn't good enough for you."

"You're not a monster," Kiki said in a voice that belonged to Nicole. "You're my beloved."

"And you're mine." His black eyes latched on to hers. "But sometimes I can be terribly wicked."

She ran her hands through his hair. "I like it when you're wicked."

Kiki liked it, too. She liked when Ethan did the same sorts of things to her that Javier had done to Nicole.

And now they were going to indulge in a tryst that involved two people and two ghosts.

A foursome like no other.

Kiki went after Ethan's clothes because Nicole craved the feel of male flesh beneath her fingers. Kiki hungered for it, too. She removed his jacket and divested him of a pin-striped vest and crisp white shirt, but that was as far as she got.

He backed her against the wall and tugged at her undergarments, stripping her bare, putting his hands all over her.

Lord Almighty.

He put his mouth all over her, too. He sucked on her nipples so hard, he made them devastatingly sore.

She dug her nails into his shoulders, and he got on his knees and scraped his teeth along her stomach, biting her skin and licking her navel. When he kissed her mound, when he put his tongue inside of her, she widened her stance.

Kiki had never felt so decadent. Javier was feasting on Nicole while Ethan devoured her.

Both men were sexy as hell.

Nicole thought so, too. The ghost moaned through Kiki, rocking against Ethan's mouth. Javier was using Ethan to pleasure his wife as thoroughly as he could.

Colors swirled before Kiki's eyes, and she put her hands flat against the wall to keep from falling over.

The orgasm that blasted through her body was twice as powerful, twice as hedonistic as anything she'd ever felt. She convulsed in a kaleidoscope of body and soul, of time and energy, of need and primal desire.

Nicole hadn't come in a century, and Kiki could feel every nerve ending ignite, sweeping her into a carnal abyss.

Before she melted into a pool of bubbling liquid, Ethan scooped her up. He laid her down on a luxurious antique quilt and tied her, spread-eagle, to the bed.

When he reached for a candle, she felt Nicole's restless heart beating inside her.

Javier wanted to drip wax on Nicole's clitoris.

No, Kiki thought. *It's my clit. My body.*

And Ethan wasn't using any of his usual safety precautions.

Silent, she questioned him with her gaze.

"I'm playing the way he plays," Ethan explained.

And that didn't include safety gear. Kiki remained as still

as she could, afraid that the slightest movement would upset the candle. No way would she fight her bonds.

With his left hand, he exposed her clit, and with his right hand, he tipped the candle.

Nicole caused Kiki to moan. The ghost was wildly aroused.

Drip. Drip. Drip.

The wax fell on Kiki's most intimate body part, creating hot and erotic sensations.

Ethan blew out the candle, waited a beat, and rubbed it between her legs, intensifying the feeling and making her come all over herself.

"Did you like that?" he asked, even though he knew damn well she had.

"Yes," she panted.

"Did Nicole like it?"

"She loved it." The ghost was looking right at her husband.

Dark and sexy, he undid his pants, climbed over her face, and freed his cock, putting it against her lips.

Javier longed for his wife to pleasure him. Ethan craved a blow job, too. Both men were eager to dominate their women.

Kiki opened her mouth, and Nicole encouraged her to take as much as he could. Nicole wanted to suck Javier all the way to the back of her throat.

The act was hot and hungry, and Ethan tugged on Kiki's coiffure, dislodging pins. Javier and Nicole were having naughty fun, and so were Kiki and Ethan.

She wanted him to come, to fill her with the taste of his semen.

And he did. Oh, how he did. He spilled enough of it for both men, thrusting one last time before she swallowed.

In the minutes that followed, Ethan smiled at her, but it was Javier's wicked smile Kiki saw. He was one powerful ghost. Or maybe it was Ethan emitting all that power. None of this could have happened if it weren't for him. The séance had been his idea.

Still tied to the bed, Kiki asked, "What are you going to do about the wax between my legs?" It was tight against her clit.

"I'm going to leave it until we're done playing."

Then he would have to remove it with a knife, she thought. He had better choose a dull blade. A butter knife, she hoped.

Ethan analyzed her expression. "Don't worry. I'd never hurt you."

And Javier would never hurt Nicole, she thought. Not ever again.

"Nicole wants Javier to hold her," Kiki said, relaying the other woman's thoughts.

"He wants that, too. But he wants to look at her for just a little longer. He can see some of her features in you."

"I resemble Nicole?"

"You have her eyes now, and her smile."

"You have his, too."

"He loved her so much. The way I love you, Kitten."

"*Gatito,*" she said, finding herself—or was it Nicole?—attached to the Spanish translation.

"Yes." He looked longingly at her. "*Gatito.*"

Time passed softly, with Ethan and Kiki staring at each other, connecting through ghostly gazes.

Finally, he removed her bonds and held her. She reached down to skim his open fly. He was raging hard all over again.

She finished undressing him, and they pressed their naked bodies close, kissing, touching, and rolling over the satin-draped bed.

He entered her, and she wrapped her legs around him.

"Damn," he said. "Oh, damn, you feel good."

Her heart pounded against his. She never wanted the intimacy to end. "So do you."

She wasn't sure if it was her and Ethan or Nicole or Javier who'd just spoken. Maybe it had been both couples. Maybe the flesh-to-flesh sensation was driving them all a bit mad.

They went missionary, looking deeply into each other's eyes. But that wasn't enough. They wanted more.

He flipped her over, and she gripped the bedposts. He did her doggie style, pounding her hard and deep. Getting hotter and wilder, he reached around and bound her breasts. He had lots of rope.

"Is this pleasantly unpleasant?" he asked.

Now that, she thought, was Javier. Ethan would have used the term "good pain."

Nicole answered her husband. "Yes, it's pleasantly unpleasant. Tighten it some more."

He added another knot, and Kiki moaned from the pressure.

"You okay, Kitten?" That was Ethan. He was still fucking her from behind.

She nodded. It was dangerously romantic. Perilously sexy. Even the wax on her clit made it more erotic.

"That's my girl," he said.

Yes, she was his. She belonged to him. But he belonged to her, too.

He turned her over again, and she could only imagine how she looked, with her legs wide open and her breasts tightly bound.

Ethan reentered her, thrusting roughly, and Kiki had two successive orgasms, one for herself and another for Nicole. Her body shook; her heart drummed in thunderous beats.

Ethan kissed her, and she clawed his back. Nicole scratched Javier just as deeply.

The men were close to climaxing.

When it happened, their eyes changed colors, going from ebony to blue to ebony again.

Afterward, Javier whispered endearingly to Nicole.

To his wife. To his beloved.

She reacted to her husband, telling him that she would be with him always.

In the next heart-skipping moment, Kiki felt Nicole leave her body, just as Javier left Ethan's. The ghosts drifted upward and disappeared in a soft mist.

Leaving Kiki and Ethan alone.

So they could be together always, too.

Epilogue

Kiki and Ethan were having a party. Not a black sheet party. This gathering wasn't about sex. It was simply a way to merge their lives a bit more, to bring their friends together.

Earlier in the evening, Kiki had introduced Ethan to Mandy and her lover, Jared. The men had liked each other instantly, bonding over beer and billiards.

As for Kiki, she was enjoying her role as the Curtis House hostess. But more importantly, she thrived on being Ethan's significant other. She continued working at the museum, of course. She had no intention of giving up her job because her boyfriend was a billionaire. But she did let him spoil her, in and out of bed.

"This is a great party," Mandy said. She was standing beside Kiki in the living room, snacking on appetizers. "The food is heavenly."

"Ethan has an amazing chef."

"He has an amazing girlfriend, too. You two are wonderful together."

"Thank you." She glanced over and saw Amber sitting on the wooden settle by herself. "What's with her?"

"I don't know. Maybe we better find out."

Concerned, they approached the sullen brunette. "Are you all right?" Kiki asked.

Amber shrugged. "I was hoping Brad, Fiona, and Lynn were going to be here. I wanted to meet them."

"Oh, I'm sorry. They couldn't make it. But that's not what's wrong. Something else is on your mind."

"It's Jay and Luke. I can't stop thinking about them."

"Does that mean you're going to go to L.A. to see them?"

Amber scowled. "Yes."

Kiki couldn't imagine being attached to two men. One was usually trouble enough. She glanced at Mandy, and they exchanged a worried look.

"You're probably going to be next," Kiki said.

"For what?"

"To fall in love."

"Oh, right." Amber pointed indulgently to herself. "*Moi?* I just want to get laid again. I had fun with them."

"Yes, and it was only one night. But you can't seem to get it out of your head."

"What can I say? It was a romantic ménage."

"That's why I think you're next."

Mandy, who'd been quiet up until now, said, "I agree. You've been thinking about them for months."

"Oh, please." Amber rolled her eyes, making her false lashes flutter. As always, she embodied a sixties mod. "I'm not going to fall in love with two men."

"Then be careful," Kiki warned. "Because choosing between them could cause a lot of hurt."

"I just told you. I'm only in it for the sex."

"That's what I thought about me and Ethan." She glanced his way. He and Jared were still shooting pool. "But I was wrong. I found everything I needed in him."

"The way I did with Jared," Mandy added.

The brunette scoffed. "Cut the girly crap and let me brood in peace."

She was scared, Kiki thought. Amber, of all people. The rich, spoiled heiress was fretting over two men she barely knew.

Men who'd already begun to change her life.